GOLDEN RUIN

Emma Kennedy

Published by *of the page press*

Copyright © 2024 by Emma Kennedy

ISBN 979-8-9913258-6-8

Cover Art by Charles Utting

Title Page Art by Theresa Chiechi

Map Art by Emma Kennedy

GOLDEN RUIN

EMMA KENNEDY

CONTENTS

CONTENT INFO

Potential spoilers ahead:

This story contains the following topics and situations that might be difficult for some readers. If you have any questions, or would like specific passages to avoid, please reach out to me at emmakennedywrites@gmail.com.

Animal death – graphic, on page

Drug use – mentioned and on page

Chronic illness – core theme of the story

*Gun use – graphic, on page

Human death – graphic, on page

Sexual content – PG-13

Vomiting – on page

*This story depicts an alternate California to the one we know today, and as such, the people react to situations differently. While I chose to arm most characters with guns, I am strongly opposed to gun violence and the immense lack of gun control in America. Please do not take the narrative choices within this story to reflect my views on the matter; they are simply a factor of this harsher California I have created for *Golden Ruin*.

The Waterfall
The Ranch
The Church
Finn's
To Resort
The Clinic
Sam's

N
W
E
S
To Mariposa
The Saloon
Grocer
To Train Station

CHAPTER I

A BOLT OF LIGHTNING soared through the sky before making landfall, narrowly missing the train. It had been sunny mere moments ago, but the clouds were now so thick that Cassidy couldn't see where the storm ended or began. What she'd heard about California was correct; it was as unpredictable as it was wild. The thought was less than comforting as she headed farther through the wastelands on the hypertrain.

"Ticket?" intoned the android sweeping down the aisle of the train car. Cassidy leaned on the window, the coolness of the glass seeping into the skin of her cheek. She was alone, save for one other passenger. He was sitting across three seats with his hat hung over his face, his all-white outfit stark against the dark leather. He would have been considered impolite if there were anyone else on board. It was not surprising, since they were almost to the last stop on the entire line.

Cassidy held out the palm of her left hand so the android could scan her data for the ticket. The small, circular pad on her palm held data for a chip, a small device that connected to the user's brain. The neural device stored information—bank accounts, medical records, news, everything was transmitted via chip. You couldn't earn a living under the Corporation or in the outer states without one, or even do so much as open an automatic door.

Her head throbbed. She hadn't gotten any sleep since the train had left two days before. Cassidy popped a vita pill in hopes of making up for it, but the effects were minimal. The silence—which should have been a reprieve—made the pain echo around her skull, amplifying it.

Cassidy traveled with just one backpack stuffed under her seat. It was lightly packed with a few outfits and some of her grandmother's old things. She considered breaking out the small pouch stashed in a secret compartment, full of little emerald crystals. They were the kind of thing that, if discovered, would get her kicked off the train and taken straight to the police. They had also cost her enough that she had to be sparing with them, and she wasn't desperate, yet. But they were so tempting, and normally she'd give in.

The other passengers had disembarked earlier in Nevada, where the bulk of Corporation mines were established. Since the gold rush, and the war that followed, the Corporation had seized a monopoly on the natural resources found in mining, and the technology they produced. Any tech with gold was Corporation-made, and all Cassidy ever saw was gold.

She continued west, to some tiny little town in California,

the last populated northern town before the rest of the coast became uninhabitable from radiation. It had been abandoned by the Corporation during the war, and the rumors about it were substantial. It was plagued by electrical storms, dust bowls, bandits, and worse. California was not the place for an easy life.

Her life in Chicago had been comfortable, and she was unwilling to leave it behind. She already missed her friends, her favorite bars, the way it was impossible to get bored with all the shops and museums. Most of all, she loved how busy and anonymous the city had felt. The Corporation was an assurance of order and safety. Where she was headed was the antithesis of that. But she wouldn't have gone so far if she'd had any other options.

Her comm buzzed with several pings from her friends, but she wasn't ready to talk yet. She hadn't told them why she'd left Chicago so suddenly, and it was her hope that she wouldn't be gone long enough for them to care. She needed to find one specific person, get what she needed, and get gone. California was not the place for her, and she would count down the days until she could be back on this very train, returning to civilization.

An announcement rang out; they'd be approaching the last stop in two minutes. Cassidy straightened up, stretching her hands above her head. The sleek metal of the cybernetic implant on her left hand glistened in the reflection in the window. Gold coated each of her fingers and dripped across her palm, stopping just shy of her wrist. It was a newer model—she had barely made a dent in the payments—but it was agile, strong, and unbelievably useful. She couldn't even remember life before her tech.

The train pulled into the station, although calling it a "station" would have been generous. A long, wooden platform rested on the flat of a small hill. A tiny booth stood at the end for purchasing tickets, offering a single bench to wait on. Cassidy exited the train car, the air thick with the approaching storm, so damp that it was already clinging to her skin. The train departed in the direction it had come from, disappearing into the angry clouds. But the sky above the station was clear for the time being. She hoped it was a good omen.

Cassidy slung her bag over her shoulder and walked towards the booth on the lonely hill. Cobwebs had formed across the flickering timetable screen, and a layer of dust settled over everything. The Corporation logos had been ripped off, leaving faint traces like ghosts. Through the murky glass, it was apparent that no one had worked here in a very long time.

The station was about three miles outside where she needed to be, as the line had never been completed after the war and lacked stops at either of the two remaining California towns. There had been efforts in the past, but relentless bandit attacks halted the whole project. So, she walked north for what felt like hours, and by the time she reached any sign of civilization, her feet and knees were screaming in protest. Cassidy continued down the dirt path stretching towards a row of buildings. The sun reached high overhead and blanketed her shoulders in a soft heat. A thin layer of dust had already settled on her damp skin and clothing, the grime making her itch.

As Cassidy continued, she was unnerved by the silence. The road was absent of cars, hovers, or horses, and none of the shops appeared to have any activity inside. Some were boarded up, sparkling piles of glass lingering where a window should have been. It unnerved her that more than one shop appeared to have been broken into and left in disrepair. And everywhere was so empty. She should have been bumping shoulders with the throngs of a heavy crowd as advertisements inundated the streets from open doorways and stores. But it was like the dead of night, silent and unmoving. She already longed for the disordered chaos of a city.

Cassidy reached an edge of the road that came up to a gazebo sheltering a fountain. The water had long since dried up, leaving greenish rust along the bowl. The road veered off to the right, where a crevasse cut off the edge of the town. A little bridge built across it connected a field with a lone church standing in the middle. The grass was a dull shade, but plentiful, and the sun reflected off the structure's white walls. Cassidy stopped at the intersection and listened for any sign of life. Nausea settled in her gut in the absence of it. Since the town had been abandoned, it didn't show up on Corporation maps, so her chip was useless for navigating. Could the man she was looking for really be here?

She finally came up to a saloon that had its vast double doors propped open. Her stomach growled in anticipation. A bartender stood behind the half-moon bar, shelves of alcohol sparkling under the light. Tables and stools were scattered around the room, and two patrons occupied the tables closest to the bar. They eyed Cassidy up and down as she approached the bartender, hands drifting to the weapons at their waists.

"Howdy," she called out, causing the bartender's eyes to snap up from the glass they were polishing. Cassidy shifted. She had never been this far west, so she assumed they spoke a certain way, like she'd seen in movies. Maybe she'd gotten it wrong.

"Didn't hear you come in," the bartender said in apology. "What can I get for you?"

Cassidy decided to forgo the food. "Just directions to the ranch. Please."

The bartender did not reply as their eyes took on an unnatural glow. Android, then. They began transmitting the data, and she scanned the information as it scrolled in front of her. The beginnings of a crude map materialized, but the interface was nothing like the Corporation-generated maps she'd learned to read, and she had trouble making sense of it. Before she could analyze the rest of the transmission, her focus was interrupted.

The man nearest to her grunted, his dark beard so gruff and unruly she couldn't see his mouth beneath it. Two empty glasses with rings of condensation littered his table, and he cradled a third. It was ungodly early, but ever since recovery pills hit the market, fools like him would drink themselves sick, take a pill to sober up, and do it all over again. A pill couldn't regrow a liver fast enough, though.

His speech was slow compared to what she was used to, and it took her a second to register what he was saying to her. "What do you want with the ranch?"

Cassidy straightened. "Is there a problem with me asking?"

"Depends. I'll ask again: what do you want with the ranch?"

"That's none of your business."

"I'm just wondering why a shiner—and a stranger, at that—would come up here and ask about the ranch."

Cassidy bristled, not used to the term being directed at her. She flexed her fingers instinctively, the gold of her implants reflecting the bar lighting. "Maybe I'm curious. What's it to you?"

"We don't want your kind of trouble here."

Cassidy's brows drew together. "*My* kind of trouble? You don't know me."

The bearded man spat, "I know your ilk. My brother gave his life in your pointless war. We don't want your business here. We have trouble enough as it is."

"I'm not Corporation." Her laugh was brusque. "Far from it."

The bartender glanced between them, calculating, but did not intervene. If they determined that an altercation was imminent, they would step in. That reassured her, and she took a deep breath. "I'm here for work."

She projected her messages with the ranch owner, Willa, indicating that she'd been offered a job as a hand with lodging and pay. Her fingers flexed at her side as she scrolled through for the bearded man to examine.

His posture relaxed as his hand drifted from his weapon. "Well, alright, then. I'm sure you can understand my asking. Folks don't come to California for much besides trouble—especially not people looking like they came straight from a Corp catalog."

She crossed her arms over her chest and took a breath in through her nose, so her temper wouldn't get the better of her, then glanced at the bartender. "Can you finish transmitting those directions?"

"Hurry it up," the other patron snapped. "Need the bot to make me a better drink. Thought 'roids were supposed to do things perfect." The end of his sentence came out sharp enough to send spit flying.

Androids were not programmed to have reactive emotions, so she supposed the comment didn't insult them. But it still left a strange sourness in her mouth.

"Cool it" came from the man who had been questioning her as he turned back towards Cassidy. "You can call me Butch, by the way. I assume we'll be seeing more of each other." He held out his hand.

"Right." She shook it, surprised he didn't flinch when the cool metal of her hand met his. "I'm Cassidy."

"Hope you find it alright here, Cassidy."

"Thanks. And for the help." She nodded her head to the bartender, but if they registered the praise, they didn't show it. She went back out the way she came, the faint twang from the jukebox following her onto the street. The whole interaction had set her nerves on edge.

Unable to waste any more time, Cassidy continued towards the bridge, as the map directed. She imagined that in the olden days, it might have crossed over a significant stream. But the Corporation's industry had changed the way the planet behaved; there were some parts of the world that hadn't seen rain in a generation. It seemed like California was such a place. The river was clogged with rocks and chunks of dirt stuck together, so it almost ran dry. Along the small ditch were weeds sprouting pretty little yellow flowers.

Past the bridge, the field was empty, save for the lone church. It was pristine, newer than any of the buildings in the thick of town. The front part of the church gathered in a tall point with a bell hanging above an intricate stained-glass window. The building stretched back and adjoined with a long, rectangular room that was much less ornate. Tall windows lined each side, letting the day's sun in, and Cassidy watched a small group gathered inside.

A woman in a simple baby-blue dress stood in front of a semicircle of children sitting on the floor. There were only six children in front of her. Empty desks and chairs filled the space behind them. Cassidy watched the animated way the teacher gestured with her hands as she spoke, and the way she would tilt her head to the left at the end of each sentence.

Although tiny, the classroom looked exactly like what she had pictured growing up. The art on the walls, the knapsacks strewn about, and even the threadbare rug under the teacher's feet seemed perfect to her. Her Corporation schools had looked nothing like this, all modern, sleek metal and gleaming white that felt too sterile now, seeing what an old classroom looked like. A sudden sense of nostalgia, or something more abstract, surged through her. Cassidy often encountered places or experiences that reminded her of home, but standing outside such a normal, innocent moment, all she felt was longing. She hadn't known that this was something she had missed out on.

She shook off her thoughts and kept going, following the low river through the opening of the valley. After about another forty-five minutes of walking, she reached her destination. She took a minute to breathe, leaning against a tree that bordered the area. Her legs were throbbing from all the walking, and her headache had only worsened.

Neither sensation was unusual. Cassidy was ill—inexplicably so—and had been for the better part of six years. She had good days and bad days, but her first day on the job was not the time to be on a downswing. She needed to pull herself together before she met her new boss. If everything went well, she wouldn't be around for too long, but she still respected the importance of a first impression.

CHAPTER 2

THE RANCH OCCUPIED A wide stretch of land, surrounded by mountains with broad, flat peaks. The land housed so many buildings, sheds, and plots of vegetation that Cassidy didn't know what to make of it. How she'd learn the ins and outs of it all was daunting to consider.

A faint light emanated from a barn in the distance, so she headed towards it. Inside, a woman stood in the farther pen. Her onyx hair was pulled back in a long braid, leaving pieces around her temples and neck. Her dark brows were drawn together in concentration, and her amber skin glowed under the lamp orbs hanging from the ceiling slats. She bent down towards something blocked from Cassidy's view. Cassidy was surprised by how young the woman looked, expecting someone a decade older, at least. But she looked nearer to her own age—thirty-two, at most.

Cassidy walked closer, transfixed by the woman's serene concentration. She was staring so intently that she did not notice the dark well that dipped down in front of her, and her ankle rolled wrong as it landed in the small pit.

"Shit," she muttered as she pitched forward off balance, catching herself by flailing her arms in the air. The woman chuckled, one brow raised, her full attention now on Cassidy. The back of her neck heated from being so clumsy and already cursing in front of this stranger.

"Best mind the cat pee."

"The what?" Cassidy stuttered.

"Cat. Pee."

Cassidy had no idea why cats would pee anywhere they wanted. She sniffed the air and wrinkled her nose.

"You get used to the smell," the woman replied. "You Miss Frisk?"

"Cassidy," she answered and walked to the gate with her arm outstretched, but the woman held her hands up with a sheepish smile. Her gaze stuck on Cassidy's cybernetic hand. "Don't want to do that. I've been at this all morning. I'm Willa. We spoke on the Net."

"Right," Cassidy replied and craned her neck over the pen to see what she was talking about. She found Willa surrounded by baby sheep and some older-looking ones. The babies were adorable, with soft and fluffy wool. Some even had the tiniest beginnings of horns. The older ones creeped her out a bit—something about their eyes.

"What are you doing?"

"Feeding the lambs."

"Don't they do that themselves?"

"They're not synth, so the mommas are pretty hit or miss on raising their young."

Cassidy whistled. Organic animals must mean a whole lot of unnecessary work and complications, but there was no way to have synth factories outside of the Corporation. Cassidy herself hadn't eaten non-synth food in years.

She glanced down at the sheep huddled together on one side of the pen. "Why don't the moms all feed the babies?"

"It's their nature, I suppose," Willa responded.

Cassidy thought it might have more to do with the decades-long exposure to radiation, but she wasn't going to debate with the woman. The silence stretched on as Cassidy tried to come up with something intelligent to say, but she didn't know a damn thing about sheep.

"So, is this where I'll be working?"

"When I need you to. But for the first few days, I'll have you follow me around to get a feel for things." She eyed the bag Cassidy gripped by the strap. "You got some other things you'll need to set down?"

"Nope, just this."

"You travel light. I like that," Willa said in approval, but Cassidy sensed that the compliment came from a place of surprise. "Let me show you where you'll be staying, and you can change into something more comfortable." She exited the sheep pen and pressed her thumb to the pad to lock it.

Cassidy shuffled in behind her broad steps, looking down at her outfit apprehensively. She must have seemed more like a city slicker to these people than she realized in her leather jacket and dark-wash jeans. Wordlessly, she followed Willa back out towards one of the buildings she'd passed earlier.

Willa motioned for Cassidy to scan her chip on the door's lock. She reached for the handle, which scanned her chip and programmed itself to open for her, then she stepped inside. The light hardwood floor was covered with homey-looking rugs in reds and oranges, and a cow skin bordered the bed. It was a small room—only a dresser, table, and chair, with far fewer amenities than her modernist apartment in Chicago.

Willa frowned as she lingered in the doorway. "I'm sure it's a lot less than you're used to. If it's not to your liking, you're welcome to try and find something in town instead."

"This is fine, thanks."

An awkward beat stretched between them. Cassidy had never been very good at hiding a lie, but they both pretended to accept her statement as it was.

Willa examined her nails, but her eyes were trained on Cassidy with a spark of interest. "What's Chicago like?"

"Busy. Windy." She didn't want to talk about the things she missed while it was still so raw. She also wasn't ready to talk about why she'd needed to leave. She hoped she'd have everything figured out and would be long gone before that conversation came up.

Willa laughed, but if she was disappointed by Cassidy's vague answer, she didn't show it. "Well, we've got the wind, but not much else. I'm sure you've seen nearly the whole town on your way here." Cassidy grunted in response. "I always wanted to travel," Willa continued, "see what other places are like. Haven't had the means yet."

"Maybe in the future." She felt for Willa, but she knew her type. Once they made enough excuses and set down roots, it was hard to move on. Cassidy doubted Willa would ever leave her ranch or her town, but she found no point in saying so.

"Well, I'll give you a little bit to get settled. Why don't you meet me in the house at nine thirty? It's the building right in front of this one."

"Alright," she replied as Willa eased off the door and shut it behind her. Cassidy sighed and sat down on the bed. It creaked under her weight. She wasn't unfamiliar with the bizarre sort of feeling that came with living in a new place. But this time, her disappointment was rooted in being forced to some backwater town that seemed both stuck in time and like it was at the edge of the world. She'd find none of the things she'd grown used to in Chicago.

The fact that she hadn't slept on the train caught up to her, so she decided to take a quick nap.

Cassidy awoke a few minutes before nine. Grumbling, she stretched out and ran a hand over her face. She took off her leather jacket—a ridiculous choice for a California summer—and left the room.

She circled to the front of the house, kicking up clouds of dirt as she went. A small wooden porch lined the side that led to the front door. A sun-worn rocking chair sat in the far right corner, and some bizarre leafless plants scattered the railing and steps. Cassidy kicked off her boots, and the screen slid open once it sensed her.

The inside of the house matched her room, only bigger. A living room with vast, bright windows greeted her, with a hallway on the right leading to rooms out of view. To her left were short stairs to an L-shaped loft above. Mismatched furniture spread out to make a seating area, and full bookshelves framed the windows. Rosemary and honey hung heavy in the air. It wasn't Cassidy's style, or like any place she'd been in before, both strange and comforting all at once.

"Cassidy?" Willa called out from the right.

"Hi," Cassidy called back.

"I'm over in the kitchen."

She followed her voice to the first room down the hall. The walls were painted a cheery yellow, and everything from the dish towels to the spoon rests had farm animals on them. It was charming in a way, like the kind of kitchen Cassidy would expect a grandmother to have. Something savory-smelling bubbled away on the stove.

"Hungry?" Willa asked, putting the spoon down on a cow-shaped spoon rest.

"I could eat," Cassidy downplayed, though the sharp ache in her stomach said otherwise.

"Great, it'll be ready in a few minutes." Willa turned back to the stove, humming under her breath as she shook some spices into the pot.

Cassidy stood behind her, unsure of what to do. It'd be polite to offer to set the table, but she worried that would be too formal for a quick and casual breakfast. Instead, she idled around the U-shaped kitchen counters to the other side, where a small table sat in front of bay windows. They faced the base of the mountains, dry and mottled with dark green and gray bushes. The whole landscape had a similar tone to it, as if someone had brushed over it with sepia. It was so dull and monotonous compared to the vibrancy of Chicago. Cassidy turned back around to find Willa staring at her.

"Not like the city, huh?"

"Less color, for sure," Cassidy hedged. Willa scoffed, but didn't reply.

"So," Willa said as she brought over two steaming bowls and set them down, sitting to Cassidy's right, "you grew up in Chicago?"

Cassidy stalled, not sure how much information she was ready to share. "Since I was about eight. Moved in with my grandma. I hadn't left until now."

"You've heard what it's like out here?" Willa asked. Cassidy nodded. "And you still came?"

"You're the one hiring. Can't complain that someone took you up on it."

The silence between them stretched, and Cassidy wished she'd gotten the better of her temper and held her tongue.

Willa broke the silence. "You ever regret that?" She nodded in the direction of Cassidy's left hand, wrapped around the fork halfway to her mouth.

"What, the synth?" Willa hummed in assent, and Cassidy continued, "It's hard to remember being without it. But it makes things easier for sure."

"I can see why folks come to rely on it, working against what's natural to have an advantage."

Cassidy winced. There were people who got more and more tech until they were almost androids themselves. Shiners. It wasn't something the body or the brain could handle, and it never ended well.

"It can be hard to find the limit, for sure. No one around here has tech?"

Willa shook her head, derision apparent. "Not around here. There's another town, Mariposa, a ways away, and I've heard they've got more going on. But it's only rumors; no one's ever been out that way."

Cassidy filed the information away for later; it might be the exact place she was looking for. She'd seen the name Mariposa during her research, but ended up in Bell Valley based on Willa's job offer. She hoped she hadn't made a mistake.

Willa drew her from her thoughts. "What are you hoping to get out here?"

Cassidy saw no point in telling her the real reason, so she settled on "You had a great offer. Plus, I've always liked animals."

Willa scoffed and stood, her chair scraping against the hardwood floor as she rose. Damn, the woman ate fast. "Well, we'll see how you feel about that once you've done some real work. People don't last in California. Leave the bowl in the sink, and follow me out back."

Cassidy tried not to scowl at her tone. She shoveled the remainder of her breakfast down and did as instructed, slipping her boots on at the front door and circling to the back of the building.

Willa walked a few paces ahead of her, her dark braid swishing in rhythm with her steps. She'd braided in pretty red beads the color of fresh clay. They stopped at a shed next to two boxy coops housing a mix of chickens, roosters, and doves. Willa opened the shed and waited for Cassidy to come closer. It wasn't quite big enough for two people, so she lingered under the doorframe.

"You're gonna be checking for eggs. You'll do it once in the morning and again in the afternoon." She handed Cassidy a robust wicker basket with a wide and worn handle. "Today, we'll each take a coop, but normally you'll do both on your own."

"Okay," Cassidy replied, retreating backward so Willa could walk back in front of her.

"While you're in here, check the water and feed. They dispense automatically and sanitize themselves. They need to be refilled about once a week."

Cassidy peered into the coop closest to her. The bottom had a row of wooden boxes with some sort of fill inside, and the back was lined with levels of boxes and posts. She snapped her gaze back to Willa as she realized she was still instructing.

"You're also gonna clean everything out once a week, so it makes things easiest to do it all on the same day." She directed Cassidy to the front of the gate, where the coop opened. "They wander out during the day, so don't worry if they get past you. Be careful they don't peck your ankles."

Cassidy blinked. Realizing that was the end of Willa's spiel, she turned to unlatch the gate. Sure enough, birds flooded past her. She dodged a mean-looking rooster on his way out.

"How do we get them back in?" she wondered aloud.

"Most of 'em come back in their own time. They're used to it by now. If not, you can pick them up and put them back in."

Cassidy imagined there was more to it than that, but she hoped it wouldn't come to it. She suspected that the rooster would get a thrill out of running her all around. She walked inside and picked up a few eggs nestled in the hay on her left.

They were varying sizes and colors, but she supposed that was normal. She had expected the perfect white synth eggs, so seeing them in different colors was a novelty.

From there, Willa led her through a variety of other tasks in her new routine. They worked quietly, and Cassidy tried a few times to break the ice, but Willa didn't grace her with more than brusque answers and asked no questions of her own.

After Cassidy weeded in the garden until her cuticles were split and bleeding, Willa turned towards her. "That's fine for today. If you want lunch, I'm sure you can find something in town. Dinner will be ready around seven."

Cassidy perked up, eager for some free time. "If you're sure?" Willa nodded and headed towards the stables. Cassidy wasted no time heading back to her room to Connect. She had a lot of work to do.

CHAPTER 3

As soon as Cassidy sat on the edge of her bed, she Connected to the Net and waited as it materialized around her, ready to cede to her commands. She had no idea where to start, which was how she'd gotten to this point in the first place. The last doctor she'd been to had promised her answers, and then vanished into thin air. She'd been diving the Net for months, looking for any sign of him, and the only lead she had left was California.

It was illegal to work on synth if you weren't under the Corporation, which meant going to their hospitals and their doctors and using their medicines. But Cassidy had tried all the conventional options, and now the only choice left to her was something different.

She knew she wouldn't be able to find information in the traditional way; the Corporation Net Corps regularly scrubbed unwanted information. California had its own local Net, but the only caveat was that you had to be within the coordinates the IP covered to access it. If she could have avoided moving to California, she would have, but there was no way around it.

Cassidy started diving the Net the way she normally would, bits of binary and lights swirling past her field of vision at a breakneck pace. She was no longer in her room; she was in a galaxy of ones and zeros in colors the organic eye could never comprehend. She sifted through data until she came upon arrest records, work histories, and anything that could lead her to a clue. Nothing, until she found an article from an independent site deep in the server. It was inconsequential, talking about recent bandit raids across the valley. But there was a section discussing new medical supplies that had been stolen from a clinic, and it was the closest mention to a doctor Cassidy had found since her search began. She bit back a curse as she found the rest of the section redacted. She'd have to find the original, then. She noted the author of the piece and the address for the journalism offices and ended her session on the Net. Gathering her things, she headed out before Willa could decide she should be working after all.

Cassidy followed the path through the valley, which spat her back out at the church/schoolhouse. It was about half past noon, which she guessed was some kind of recess, as the small group of children were out in the field surrounding the building. A few were playing tag, laughing and shrieking, while the rest sat among the beige grasses, eating their lunch. As Cassidy continued on her path, she was intercepted by the schoolteacher, who seemed to come out of nowhere.

"Hey there, stranger," she sang as she stepped in front of Cassidy, causing her to pause. Her dark hair was split into two braids that reached past the floral bodice of her blue dress. Rosy cheeks and a smattering of freckles across her nose made her look much younger than Cassidy suspected she was.

"Hi," Cassidy replied, looking side to side for a new viable path.

"Don't suppose I can help you with anything?"

"Not really. I'm just going into town."

The teacher's hazel eyes narrowed, assessing. "You from around here?" Her gaze lingered on the glint of Cassidy's synth hand. Cassidy realized at this point that she'd probably be getting an interrogation from every person in town. She sighed. She thought small-town folks were supposed to be friendlier.

"I just started at the ranch," Cassidy replied, hoping it was an acceptable enough answer for her to be on her way.

The woman's posture relaxed. "Oh, that's such a relief! I didn't know Willa finally found someone. She's been needin' the help."

Cassidy stood there, shifting her weight back and forth between her feet. She wasn't sure how she should reply.

"Oh, right," the teacher continued, as if Cassidy had conveyed something meaningful with her silence. "I'm Annabelle. And you are...?"

"Cassidy," she replied as she shook Annabelle's outstretched hand. The woman had a surprisingly strong grip for such a willowy schoolteacher.

"I hope you don't mind my questioning you. It's just that

I'm responsible for all the kids, and I can't just let strangers by like it's nothing."

"Of course," Cassidy replied, and she did understand. Annabelle's questioning made much more sense than what had happened earlier at the bar.

"What are you going into town for?"

Cassidy tried to think on her feet. "I'm running an errand for Willa."

"On your first day? Well, you'll certainly get the hang of things, then. But if you need help finding anything, come see me. I live and work here at the church."

"I appreciate it."

Annabelle smiled. "So, where did you come from?"

"I—"

Before Cassidy could get into it, a bell rang out. All the children gathered their things and headed back inside. Cassidy let out a breath she didn't know she'd been holding.

"Oh, shoot." Annabelle frowned. "I'm not trying to be rude, but that's my cue to get back."

"No problem."

"It was a pleasure though, Cassidy. I hope to see you again soon."

"Likewise," she replied, watching Annabelle and the last few children flutter back into the schoolhouse. She could have sworn there was another adult figure, but they were walking too briskly for her to get a comprehensive look. She only caught the brim of their white hat disappearing behind the building.

Cassidy continued into town with the soft sounds of the classroom fading out behind her. At midday, things had picked up a bit, but not by much. A few shop doors were propped open for the people milling about inside. The barber was wiping down some chairs in front of their window and did a double take at Cassidy as she walked by. She passed a couple coming out of an apartment, and they looked at her up and down. Everyone was noticing her, and it was starting to creep her out.

She came to a multiuse building with four placards on the door, the names flickering as they projected into the air. One of the units was vacant, but it appeared that the journalism office was still here. She tried the door, but it was locked, and the bio-scanner was programmed to only open for employees of the rented spaces. She sighed, taking a beat to think things through. She hadn't decided how to approach the whole endeavor, but she hadn't planned to be so direct. The less people knew what she was after, the better. The normal thing—the right thing, even—would have been for her to ask the author directly for the information they had. But as suspicious as the folks she'd encountered so far had been of Cassidy, she was just as suspicious of them.

She'd left the Corporation without fulfilling her payment plans on her implants, clearing her medical debt, or providing notice through the proper channels. She'd just disappeared. If someone were inclined to turn her in, they'd receive a good chunk of credits for their trouble. So, despite the wrongness that settled in her gut, she'd have to go about things a different way.

Each office had a one-way camera to telecom with, so Cassidy rang the other two businesses, hoping at least one would answer. After she stood around for five or so minutes, the therapy office on the ground floor answered the call.

"Hello?"

Cassidy put on an embarrassed smile and held her backpack under her arm, so it appeared more like a satchel. "Hi, I'm so sorry. I'm supposed to deliver a package to the office above yours, but they forgot to give me temp access, and they're out for the day. I'll be behind on my quota if I have to come back. Do you think you could buzz me in?"

The person on the other end paused, and Cassidy shifted in place. After a beat, *"Yeah, no problem. One sec."*

Cassidy's smile was genuine as the locked door clicked open. "Thank you so much." She breezed up the stairs before her cover story could be questioned and headed down a long hall. There were only two doors at the end, each bearing an LED of the business name and door number. The journalism office was on the left, and through the fogged glass, she verified that no lights were on inside. Perfect.

She used her ocular implants to scan the door handle. It seemed like there was a basic alarm system attached. If she was quick enough, it shouldn't matter. A town so small wouldn't have a very quick police response time, she hoped. Using her organic hand, she turned the knob to the point of breaking, then stuck a synth finger under the gap to release the lock. She didn't hear any alarms yet, but she knew to be quick.

Inside the offices were rows of cubicles separated by holo-screens. There were two private offices to the left and a break room to the right. She examined the cubicles, finding most of them to be out of use. There were no nameplates, data pads, or any personal touches on any of the desks. She turned towards the private offices, noticing that one had personal items strewn across the tabletops.

The office had a simple key lock she was able to pick with her synth hand. They must have put all their trust in the tech lock on the front door. The inside of the office was dark with the blinds shut, but she let it be, as she didn't want to risk anything being out of place. With her ocular implants, she could see just as well anyway. She walked up to the three monitors framing the corner of the table. There was no way she could try hacking the system without leaving a trail, so she shuffled through the contents of the drawers beneath them. All she needed was a printed copy, or a holo-pad with the unredacted article on it. She'd even settle for research notes or a business card mentioning a doctor.

She went through three useless drawers before the shrill ring of an alarm filled the office. She glanced around, hoping something would catch her eye, but she had no time. Dashing back out, she closed both doors behind her. She paused in the middle of the stairwell to make sure no one would see her exiting the building, then reemerged onto the main street. She kept her pace even, despite the thin layer of sweat settling along her brow and neck.

Cassidy hurried back to the ranch before Willa could notice she'd left the property. If anyone looked into the break-in, she'd need to have a solid alibi of being at work. Still, she was frustrated that she'd risked discovery on her first day, only to not have any results. She'd have to think of something else. There was no way she'd give up so fast, but she was too disoriented to think of a new plan.

The sun was absent by the time she got back, and Cassidy

realized she'd never done her second round with the chickens. Yet it seemed Willa had taken care of the task herself, with all the chickens and one nasty rooster back in their coops for the night. She hoped she hadn't been too foolish in going off the property on her very first day. If Willa fired her, there was no chance she'd be able to stay and look for the doctor without an income.

Cassidy headed to Willa's house to see if she could help with dinner. Willa hadn't said anything about whether they would share all of their meals or not, but Cassidy hoped it was only a first-day thing. She had no need of regular mealtime company.

On the way over, Tom, the barn cat, sauntered into her path for chin scratches, which Cassidy obliged. With her grandma being allergic, she'd never had the chance to have one as a pet.

After Tom had enough attention, she continued on to the main house. Entering through the back door, she could hear the rhythmic creak of the rocking chair on the front porch. All the windows were open to let in the nighttime breeze. She could smell something herbal roasting in the kitchen, her stomach grumbling as she continued past. In all her scheming, she'd forgotten to eat lunch.

Willa sat in the chair nestled in the corner of the porch and had her feet propped up on an overturned apple crate. She was reading an old thriller. Cassidy hadn't seen a paper book anywhere in Chicago. It was smaller than she'd imagined them to be.

Cassidy slowly sank onto one of the steps, not wanting to disturb Willa's focus. Willa held her page with her finger and glanced up.

"So, what do you think?"

"Of what?"

"The work, the ranch, the weather, anything."

"Oh, it's nice."

Willa chuckled at Cassidy's diplomatic response. "That's polite of you, but really. Do you think you'll be sticking around?"

"It's different, but I can handle it." Cassidy might not like the dusty town, but she wasn't much for quitting either.

"Good." She paused. "I'm surprised."

"Surprised?"

"Well, you don't seem like the type."

Cassidy's shoulders raised. "The type to what?"

"I figured you city folk would prefer an office to a barn, that's all."

Cassidy smiled bitterly. "Not sure why you think you know me so well, considering we just met."

"I know enough. You think you're the first person to try their hand in the wastelands?" Willa's short laugh dripped with derision.

"Why'd you hire me if you didn't think I'd be cut out for it?"

Almost under her breath, Willa muttered, "As if I had a choice..."

"Have you always been this friendly?" Cassidy's smile was anything but kind.

"Beats being a Corpo cog."

Cassidy stood. "The Corporation is a lot of things, but at least they teach people manners."

Willa's gaze was intense enough to burn. "You know what? Might be better if we keep things professional. You can fix yourself dinner, but let's not pretend to be friends."

"Fine by me."

Willa got up, folding the page in on itself and leaving her book on the seat of the chair. Cassidy closed her eyes and took a breath in, counting down from five. She should have guessed the ad was too good to be true; she didn't have the luck to score a decent job and a decent boss. Her instinct was to skip town and try her luck in Mariposa, but the idea of making money for rent stayed her impulsiveness. She'd just avoid Willa and enjoy the free housing until she found a solution to her problem. This wasn't a forever situation, but it'd be a long few weeks or months until she was done with it all.

Cassidy sat on the porch, waiting for Willa's footsteps to fade away. A vulture circled in the distance in smooth arcs until it touched down somewhere she couldn't see. When she was certain Willa had left the kitchen, she stalked in and grabbed a plate as fast as possible, retreating back to her room. She dug into a rich stew, full of flavor that warmed her from the center of her chest and throughout her entire body. She would miss meals this good, but she didn't want to suffer through another fight for it. She wasn't the greatest cook, but she'd been taking care of herself long enough that she could at least manage something edible.

When she returned to Willa's house to clean her dish, all the lights had been dimmed, and soft music drifted from a closed door at the end of the long hall. A gentle, warm light filtered out of the cracks around the doorframe, bouncing off the hardwood floor. Cassidy almost had a mind to knock and apologize when she remembered who had started their fight. If Willa wanted to make baseless assumptions about her, then Cassidy would leave her to it. California would be a distant memory sooner or later, and being on good terms with folks wouldn't change that.

She settled back into her room and decided to ping her friends. They'd stopped pinging her after the morning's train ride, so she was due to get back to them. She tried calling the comms of her old roommate, Alexa, letting it ring for two minutes until she gave up. She tried her old bar coworkers, Nate and Vera, next, and was similarly ignored. It should have been around 10:00 p.m. back in Chicago. She knew they'd be out, but it was only a Tuesday, and she'd hoped they were doing something more subdued, so they could take her comms.

She sighed, not even bothering to ping the last few of her friends. When they went out, they tended to *indulge,* so much so that even before Cassidy moved, she'd started to fall out of sync with them. She'd done the partying, the drinking, waking up in someone else's bed with the last twinges of a high. It felt like she was growing up, or at least growing out of it, faster than they were.

She worried her lip as she sat in her empty, foreign room. How would she fit in when she got back? She hoped she'd find the doctor who could help her and return cured, but what then? Suddenly, it seemed like she'd left herself behind when she got on the train two days ago. The person they knew was almost certainly not the person who would be returning, and the first seeds of doubt planted themselves in her mind that whoever she was when she left California would not be welcomed into the crowd anymore.

CHAPTER 4

THE NEXT AFTERNOON, CASSIDY decided to check out the local clinic on her lunch break. Willa hadn't said anything about remaining on-site for breaks, so she'd enjoy the freedom while she had it.

She already knew from the Net that the one doctor employed there was not who she was looking for. But maybe the man she was looking for had worked there at some point, or had been in contact with them. Doctors outside the Corporation were small in number; it'd make sense for them to have some kind of system of their own.

The clinic in town was not a sprawling complex, like Cassidy was used to, but just a small office above the barbershop. The waiting area was compact and decorated more like a lounge than a medical facility. No receptionist, or even an android, sat behind the lobby desk; there was only a scanner for her to place her hand on so it could read her chip. She didn't have an appointment—didn't want one, really—so she tried calling out.

"Hello?" Silence, so she tried again. "Excuse me?"

The sharp clack of heels grew from down the hall, until the door next to the check-in counter slid open. A tall woman with dark hair and a sharp look in her eyes walked through, her mouth already tensed in annoyance. "Is there something wrong with the scanner?"

"No, I—"

"Have you not been to a clinic before?" Her gaze drew down to the gold of Cassidy's hand. "You must know how this works. You check in. You wait. When it's your turn, you get called back. You don't call for me."

"I'm aware," Cassidy gritted out through her teeth, skin prickling from the doctor's tone. "I'm not here for an appointment. I just have some questions."

The doctor crossed her arms. "We have holo-consultations on the Net."

"I don't need medical help." *Not from you, anyway.* "I was hoping you have information on a physician. I'm looking for Doctor Thorne?"

Something briefly flashed across the woman's face, but she schooled her expression quickly. "I'm not familiar with the name. And I'm the only doctor in town."

"Do you know the doctors in Mariposa?"

She sighed. "There are only two clinics, and neither of them have a doctor by that name. Is that all?"

Cassidy bit back a retort. "Yes, thank you for your time. I'll let you get back to..." She glanced around at the empty waiting room. "... work."

The doctor huffed and turned back around without a word, and the door slid shut just as fast. This room was so different from the ones she'd been in over the past six years, the sterile Corporation hospitals she was so familiar with that they felt like a second, unwelcome home. She thought back to the last time she'd been in one of those waiting rooms.

Cassidy had been at the hospital almost every week the last few months after her symptoms started to worsen. She'd read all the holo-magazines and memorized the pattern of the floor. She was restless and stifled by the lack of progress so far.

"Cassidy?" A nurse android peeked into the waiting room. "I'll take you back now."

Cassidy wordlessly crossed the room, packed with people who had been waiting much longer than her. She tried to ignore the heat in their stares, but their eyes burned into her back as she followed the android down the hall.

She scanned her chip without needing to be asked and followed the gesture of the nurse to wait in a sterile white room. She'd been in enough of the different offices to know they all looked the same. Everything was branded with the Corporation's logo in the same signature ice white. It was not a welcoming environment, but Cassidy didn't need to feel at home. She just needed to feel better.

A sharp knock reverberated through the door before it creaked open, and Dr. Thorne stepped inside. They'd done this enough that there was no need for formalities.

"Your last tests were promising. We were able to rule out your hand and ocular implants as damaged in any way. Your nervous system modulator seems to be intact as well."

"So, what does that mean? More tests?"

The doctor smiled, as if it were an inside joke between the two of them. "More tests. That's the only way we're going to figure this out."

"Alright," Cassidy sighed, already connecting her palm to the med-bed scanner, "have at it."

Cassidy was poked and prodded over the next few hours, slipping into a mental dissonance over what had become her life. It was the fifth week in a row she had been to the office just for testing. Each time, they focused on a different theory the doctor had. Each time, it ruled something out. She supposed that was a better outcome than finding more problems, but they hadn't resulted in anything like the doctor promised. She had to be patient, she was reminded often, but what she was losing faster than her patience was hope.

Once she finished changing out of the Corporation-issued top and bottoms, the doctor came back in.

"I've already made your appointment for next week, so we can go over what we found. My office will ping you if we need you to come in sooner."

"Alright, thanks, Doc."

She got a ping two days later, asking her to come in the next morning to discuss her results. Being pushed forward—it was either good news, or news no one wanted to hear.

That night, the doctor pinged her directly, which was far outside protocol. The messages were choppy and full of mistakes. The only one she could decipher well enough read, *DON'T LOOK FOR ME*. Confused and alarmed, Cassidy wiped the messages.

When she checked in the next day, she sat in the waiting room for over an hour. By the time the android led her back, she was one of the only people still waiting. The same knock sounded at the door, but a woman stepped through instead.

"Hi, Cassidy, I'm Dr. Vishnu."

"Hi. Sorry, my appointment is supposed to be with Dr. Thorne?"

The woman barely registered the comment, already setting up her scanners and files across the wall. "Dr. Thorne is on leave."

"What? For how long?"

"I'm not at liberty to discuss that with patients."

Cassidy was taken aback, but the doctor continued with scathing professionalism, "I'll be running the next tests on his behalf."

"But I was here to discuss my last test results. Are we not doing that first?"

Dr. Vishnu scrolled through Cassidy's file before responding, "I see that your test results from the twenty-eighth were discussed with you under Doctor Thorne."

"Those weren't the most recent tests. We did more on the ninth."

"I'm not seeing anything else in the file." She paused, seeing that Cassidy wasn't moving. "Please connect to the scanner, so we can get started."

"No, I'm sorry. I'd rather wait until Doctor Thorne is back."

The doctor let out a quick breath of annoyance, but recovered her composure. "Very well. I'll have the office contact you when he returns. You'll still be billed for this visit."

Cassidy cringed; her Corporation insurance wouldn't cover these visits for much longer.

Cassidy left the clinic, nerves jumbled by the way she had been treated. Worse still, she'd run into two dead ends. What if Dr. Thorne wasn't off grid in California, like she thought; what if he was dead, or worse? For him to have vanished from under the Corporation so suddenly, what had really happened to him? It was starting to feel like she'd come to California for nothing, and she wasn't sure how she could go back.

There were more abandoned states on the East Coast, but that would mean crossing the country and starting over with credits she didn't have. No, he had to be somewhere in California. Cassidy couldn't stand the thought that she'd left everything behind and come to such an inhospitable place for nothing.

CHAPTER 5

CASSIDY'S TRAINING CONTINUED TO fly by, but she'd made no progress on her search after hitting the last dead end. She was frustrated and doing her best not to let it seep into her interactions with Willa. Things between them didn't need to get any uglier than they already had. Another problem came from spending all of her time at the ranch. Cassidy had always been a social animal. It was grating on her to only see one other person day in and day out. It didn't help that Willa avoided her past providing instructions or barking out tasks to complete.

Cassidy figured she'd head to the saloon for some food and beer. If she couldn't convince folks to warm up to her, she might as well drown her sorrows. It was an old habit of hers she'd thought to leave behind in Chicago, but she had no reason to be on her best behavior anymore. Her boss was a jerk, the people in town distrusted her, and she wasn't a permanent fixture by any means. So, maybe she deserved to get a bit sloppy and just forget for one night.

The best part of leaving the Corporation was that her debt stayed where she'd left it. The Corporation didn't use credits, opting instead for bits that were useless outside their system. So, if financial freedom was the only joy she'd gain in the wastelands, then she was determined to enjoy it. She'd only received one paycheck from Willa thus far, but having few other expenses meant she could indulge.

She took the more direct route to town for fear of getting lost, not having ventured off the ranch at night yet. A borrowed bandana wrapped her face. Willa estimated that a sandstorm was due any day, judging by the harsh winds that preceded it the entire week. But the thin cotton did little, save to keep her from swallowing the bugs and dust swirling through the air. It was miserable, despite the true storm being days away.

Even with the worsening conditions, the saloon was bustling. It was the liveliest she had yet seen the town by far. Music and conversation drifted towards Cassidy as she approached the patrons spilling out nearly to the front porch. The nightlife in this sleepy town didn't compare to her old bar in Chicago—not that she expected it to. But it would do. The dim lights afforded a modicum of privacy for the groups of people scattered around the space. Cigarettes, whiskey, and the tang of something more illicit wove its way through the tables to where Cassidy stood.

With the increase in patronage and the lower lighting, no one paid her any mind as she took a seat at the bar. She rolled down her bandana and enjoyed an unobstructed breath. A different man was behind the bar this time, cracking jokes with a customer down at the other end of the arched counter. His greased hair and silver rings caught the lights that hung above the bar. He turned around and saw Cassidy sitting there, flashing a too-wide toothy grin her way. "Well, hey there, darlin'. I'm Dean." His grin, however, faltered when he saw the glint of her synth hand resting on the bar.

"Need something?" he said, looking her up and down.

She scoffed at his change in tone. "A drink, to start. What's on the menu?"

He nodded his head towards a flickering menu projected above the rows of bottles. "Corp don't teach you to read?"

Cassidy's face burned. "Didn't see that, sorry."

"Yeah. See, we have to figure things out for ourselves around here. Better get used to it."

Her mouth turned down. "It was an honest mistake."

"We've gotten folks like you before. Expecting us to cater to them, like they're better than us."

"You're doing a lot of projecting, there, buddy."

He leaned forward towards her, arms resting on the countertop. "I'd watch the attitude if I were you, shiner. There's a whole lot of us and only one of you."

Cassidy looked around the bar. The few patrons closest to her were turned away, but made no attempt to hide that they were listening. The fact that no one intervened or tried to defend her said it all.

The bartender turned to help another customer to her right, and Cassidy scampered off to a table in the back before the situation could get worse. She took a deep breath in through her nose and held it, waiting for the anger to abate. Calming, she looked around the room, desperate to salvage the night somehow.

To her left were three people sitting around a square table littered with drinks and cards. They hadn't touched either since Cassidy sat down, instead talking quietly amongst themselves.

A patron came gliding in, dressed head to toe in black to match their hair, and sat down in the empty chair with a sigh. "Sorry I'm late. Hope I didn't hold things up for too long."

"That's alright" came from the woman who was sitting to their left. Her pale skin was offset by her dark, sharp bob that seemed far too modern for California. "Everything okay?" Her voice affected the same slight accent all the Californians seemed to have.

They took a long draw of the drink already ordered and waiting for them. "Work stuff. The new alarm system has been giving me trouble."

The woman frowned, tucking a strand of her cropped black hair behind her ear. "They never found out why the last one went haywire?"

"The company said it was a break-in." They laughed, leaning back in their chair. "I told them bandits don't usually read the paper."

Cassidy's entire body went still. Could her luck have turned around so soon? She surveyed the patron again, supposing they could be a journalist type. But were they the author she'd been after? Either way, she needed an in with them.

She sat still, wondering how she'd be able to break into

their group without being forceful or pushy. The man sitting closest to her gripped his cards tightly, white knuckles framing the hand. She examined them over his shoulder, hoping her stare wasn't too obvious. His hand was terrible, but he confidently raised the bet by almost double. Cassidy smiled to herself. If she was patient, maybe the man would keep betting poorly until he'd have no credits left.

The round ended with the woman winning. Much earlier than Cassidy expected, the man threw his hand on the table and stood, his chair scraping against the floor with the force of it. The woman whistled and shook her head, grinning at the third player sitting across from her. His deep skin glowed in the warm saloon lighting. He wore a simple green button-down that did little to hide the wide breadth of his shoulders. He rolled his eyes and shrugged, a knowing smirk on his face. There was a camaraderie in the gestures and glances amongst one another, but no one made a move to continue playing. She needed to act before they decided to call it for the night.

"Need another?"

All three heads swiveled towards the sound of her voice. The woman squinted her almond eyes, assessing. The other two were looking at her as well, but not in the way she expected. Unlike the mistrusting look of the others in town, their gazes were open, curious. After a moment, the woman nodded her head, turning towards the vacated chair. "Wouldn't hurt."

Cassidy stood, sinking into the empty chair. Each player's bet was displayed on the table with little holochips.

"What's your name?" the woman asked.

"Cassidy."

"I'm Mara. You're new in town."

It wasn't a question, but Cassidy answered anyway. "Yeah, working at the ranch."

"Willa's place?" came from the man in green on her left.

"You know it?"

"It's not like there are many to confuse it with."

Cassidy laughed to play it off. Of course, thinking back, a town this small wouldn't have more than one ranch. And of course, everyone knew one another. She wasn't used to it.

"And you are?"

"Finn. And that's Sam."

Sam nodded their head in acknowledgment, their gaze never leaving their cards. Cassidy's entire attention focused on the name. She was certain it was the same name as the author whose article she'd tried to find.

"Alright. So, what are we playing?"

"Hold 'em," Mara answered. "You familiar?"

"Some."

Mara's eyes dropped to Cassidy's synth hand and trailed the rest of her. "Your synth make you a cheat?"

"Mara..." Finn cut in, exasperated. The way the other two tensed made it seem as if the woman often had trouble holding her tongue.

"Nope." Cassidy tamped down her annoyance. "So, you can't use that as an excuse if I kick your ass."

The mood around the table diffused a bit, and Cassidy looked at the two cards in her hand. Pocket sevens, which wasn't too bad. She had to decide how reckless she wanted to be. She needed to impress them enough to invite her back.

She was a stranger to these people, so she hoped their lack of familiarity would work in her favor.

Mara bet twenty-five credits and called, and Finn followed suit. Sam laid out the first cards: an ace, a ten, and a four. Cassidy glanced at Mara, but her expression was inscrutable. Finn was easier to read. The way he kept scratching his left ear made Cassidy think his hand wasn't a winner. But that wouldn't help with him being after her.

For the turn, Mara decided to call, so Cassidy thought it'd be best to test her theory by raising it to forty. Finn sighed and folded. She fought off the smug smile threatening to appear.

"Oh, this one is bold." Mara laughed.

"Just trying to make an impression."

"I'll say," came from Finn, lips turned down after being bet out of the round.

Sam put the last card down on the table, their hazel gaze bouncing between Cassidy and Mara. As for Mara, she drew out her move, trying to make Cassidy sweat. When they revealed their cards, it turned out Mara had the better hand. Cassidy parted with a sizable chunk of her credits.

"You've got a pretty good bluff."

Cassidy assumed Mara meant this as a compliment. Sam hummed in agreement.

"Thanks. You're pretty hard to read yourself."

"You're a much better loser than Finn—"

"Hey—"

"—or Holden."

"The one who stormed out?"

"Mm-hmm," Mara replied, drawing the sound out and

making her distaste clear.

Finn cut back in, "We only played with him a handful of times. I promise the rest of us are more fun."

"Hey." Cassidy held her hands up. "You don't have to convince me."

"Why don't we play something a bit more relaxed? No more bets." Mara nodded to the bar. "You drinking? How about a round on me for being a good sport?"

"I won't argue with that." Cassidy was relieved she'd be able to have a drink after all.

Mara got up and headed to the bar. Finn stretched out and leaned back in his chair, whistling along with whatever song had come on.

"You all come here a lot?" Cassidy asked the both of them, but only expected Finn to answer. She wasn't sure if Sam had said a word at all. But they were a very attentive listener, nodding along and laughing when it was appropriate. Cassidy wondered what it would take to draw them out of their shell. She'd have to try harder to get them to talk with her.

"We try every other week or so. Sam here has been extra busy lately with work, so we haven't gotten together in a bit."

"What do you do? If you don't mind me asking." She hoped the question didn't sound as forced as it felt coming out.

"I do the newspaper and Net site for the town."

"Oh, cool! I didn't know there was a newspaper." She paused for effect and added, "No offense."

"None taken. You're new, after all." Sam shrugged, ending the conversation. It was the most they'd said the entire night, which was enough for Cassidy.

Before they could lull into an awkward silence, Mara returned, arms full of pint glasses and a little bowl of peanuts. Cassidy jumped up to help her distribute it all before it spilled.

"Thanks." Mara smiled as she leaned down to place a glass in front of Sam.

"Sure." Cassidy returned to her seat and held hers up in salute. "Thanks for the drink."

"Happy to have someone new to play with."

"It's nice to have someone around with a decent poker face" came from Sam.

"*I* have a good poker face," insisted Finn.

"But an obvious tell," Cassidy chimed in.

"What? Do not!"

"No, you do." Mara cut in, looking between them. "Why do you think you always lose?"

"Oh, man..." Finn was so upset that Cassidy couldn't stop the laughter bubbling from her mouth. Soon they all joined her, even Finn, his broad shoulders shaking.

They played a few more rounds and had a few more drinks. Cassidy found she enjoyed spending time with them. She could see herself joining them on weekends—playing cards, getting meals, and whatever else they did to entertain themselves around town. She'd almost felt guilty about her ulterior motives for joining them, but she was trying to survive, after all. She wouldn't be in town long enough to make meaningful friendships; she knew that. But drinking, playing cards, and laughing with them was the first time she'd felt like her old self in a while.

CHAPTER 6

THE SANDSTORM CAME, JUST as Willa predicted. Their tasks were cut short to limit their exposure, but the animals still had to be tended to. She shadowed Willa with each animal to learn what they needed and how to act around them. Only the horses made her a bit nervous, based on the sheer size of them. She let Willa do all the hands-on work when they went into their corral.

The weather was biting, and it made traveling between outbuildings all the more difficult. The wind whipped at Cassidy's hair and clothes, threatening to upend anything she tried to carry. How anyone lived with this being a regular occurrence seemed insane to her. She had no idea why these people went to so much trouble to live in such inhospitable and inferior conditions. The Corporation wasn't perfect, sure, but it was better than this.

By late Friday, the winds subsided, and they resumed their normal duties, along with the arduous task of cleaning sand out of every crevice it had wedged into during the storm. Willa gave Cassidy the easier tasks with the sheep and the cows, saving her from having to deal with the horses. Cassidy admired and respected them, she just didn't want to be too near to them.

Best of all, she got to cultivate the greenhouse. Cassidy's fondness was obvious in the way she lingered to examine new blooms and pluck old leaves from some of the established growth. But she was surprised that Willa had picked up on it and afforded her that small kindness.

She was almost finished potting after lunch when she launched into a tremendous coughing fit. Her hand came away with specks of a silvery gray, looking molten against her pale skin. Seeing the inhuman sheen of implant fluid immediately kicked up her heart rate. Her vision started to speckle black with panic when Willa came in through the doorway.

"Everything alright?"

Cassidy quickly wiped her hand on her pants and straightened up, "Yeah, fine. Some water went down the wrong way."

Willa paused for a moment, looking down. "Right. Well, whenever you're done, start working on shearing before you lose the sun."

Cassidy smiled, somewhat forced. "I'll be right over."

It wasn't until she was alone and cleaning up her tools that she realized her faux pas; she hadn't brought her canteen into the greenhouse with her.

After her first full day of being independent, Cassidy entered the kitchen to make dinner and found Willa packing different foods into a cryo-basket on the counter.

"Going somewhere?"

"Thinking about a quick hike." Her hand hovered over the basket for a moment. "You can join, if you want."

Cassidy surprised herself by responding, "Sure, nice weather." Though she wouldn't admit it if asked, she was lonely. She hadn't heard from the folks she'd met at the saloon, and people in town still kept their distance from her. She and Willa hadn't gotten off to a good start, but Cassidy had a newfound interest in fixing things between them.

They passed the barn and started to hike up one of the hills bordering the property. The steepness of the hill was hard on her joints, and she was out of breath by the time they crested. The peak was wide and flat enough for them to sit. A tall old willow reached across half the clearing, fallen leaves littering the ground below. The branches hung so low that the trunk was barely visible.

Willa set down the basket and got to work laying out all the food, the lid hissing open as the temp seal disengaged. Cassidy wordlessly sat down, taking in the view. The sun was setting earlier and earlier each day, so they were right on time to catch the pink and orange streaks leaking out across the sky. The day was warm, but as the sun was leaving, it cooled down rapidly.

Willa finished arranging their feast and settled down next to Cassidy, her legs stretched out in front of her. There were various sandwiches, fruits, homemade cheeses and jams, and an unopened bottle of whiskey. Cassidy wrinkled her nose. The Corporation stopped selling whiskey after the war, seeing as it was so popular in the abandoned states. It was such a strong symbol from the war that making or selling it resulted in a fine, and even jail time in some cases. She'd tried it once at a secret speakeasy back in Chicago, but found the liquor too thick and smoky.

"This is one of my favorite spots," Willa said as she grabbed a sandwich for herself and handed one to Cassidy.

"How'd you find this place?"

"One of the goats got away one day. Just jumped straight over the fence. I spent the entire morning looking for her, until I heard her bleating up here."

Cassidy laughed. "You're kidding."

"It's funny now, but I was so worried. When I finally sat down to catch my breath, I noticed how peaceful it is up here." Willa poured herself a glass, handing the bottle to Cassidy. A silence stretched between them before Willa glanced at her. "You're taking to the work well."

"I like it. More than I thought I would."

Willa cracked a small smile. "Yeah?"

"Yeah. Didn't think all the dirt and bugs would agree with me."

"Well, I'm glad. It's nice to have the help. I..." She sighed. "I'm not in the habit of apologizing, but I feel I owe you one."

Cassidy shook her head. "It's fine."

"I judged you before I even knew you." She chuckled. "You've been proving me wrong ever since."

"I think we both said some unwarranted things. Truce?"

"Truce."

"So..." Cassidy took a small bite of the sandwich. "What do you do for fun around here?"

"Well, I like reading and hiking. But there's plenty to be done around the ranch, so..." Willa trailed off, mouth turning downwards.

"So, you don't get out much," Cassidy said with a grin, teasing. She wouldn't judge her for being hardworking.

Willa chuckled. "Yeah, you could say that."

"How long have you lived here?"

Willa's voice filled with pride. "My whole life. It was my momma's ranch, and I took it over when she died."

"Oh, I'm so sorry."

Willa waved her hand dismissively. "It's alright. She had been sick for a while. It was better to know she was at peace. And this was all a while back, anyway."

"Is this what you always wanted to do? Own a ranch?"

"Well, I knew it's always what I would end up doing. My family's been on this land for generations. And I do love it. But if things were different, I'd have liked to run a restaurant. It's something I've always gravitated to, feeding people."

"Yeah, I get that."

"What about you?" Willa countered, pivoting towards her.

Cassidy's palms started to dampen. Having Willa's full attention made their conversation feel real and intimate in a way Cassidy wasn't expecting.

"What *about* me?" she tossed back, hoping to get out of answering somehow. It was cowardly, with how forthcoming Willa had been, but she was a coward all the same.

"Living in such a big city, there must've been something that stuck with you."

"Well..." Cassidy paused, weighing how truthful she should be. Her answer was inconsequential, really, but this would be taking a hammer to her walls. She wasn't sure if she wanted them to come down. "I've always liked photography. Not as a career or anything, but it's fun to do."

"Oh, are you any good?"

Cassidy scoffed, "Well, I..."

Down at the bottom of the valley, near the north edge of the fence, dark shapes were moving in their direction. There was nothing past the ranch—no one that lived there, anyway. "What is that?"

A sharp, staccato sound rang out across the valley.

Willa looked in the direction of Cassidy's outstretched hand before cursing and rushing to her feet. "Move. Now."

"What's the matter?"

Cassidy started to gather their things as Willa headed back the way they came. "Leave that stuff, come on," she barked out, leaving Cassidy to scramble behind her.

Cassidy tried to match her pace, rocks loosening under her boots and skittering down the hill. One wrong step, and she'd be joining them. "What are we doing?" She raised her voice so it would carry.

"Can you shoot?"

"Shoot?" Cassidy echoed with incredulity.

"Yes," Willa shouted, "a gun?"

"No, I've never." The only time she'd ever even seen a gun was in the movies.

"Fine. Make sure the barn and stable are locked, then go to your room and barricade the door. I'll find you when it's safe to come out." Willa didn't even sound out of breath as she shouted off the instructions.

There was no time to process, only act. They reached the

bottom of the hill, and Cassidy raced to the barn. An eerie calm settled over her as she used her entire body weight to throw down the latch and lock the door. If she stopped to think, she'd shut down; too many thoughts vied for her attention for her to make sense of them.

The stables were closest to the edge of the property where she'd seen movement. She hadn't watched where Willa went, hoping the other woman could take care of herself. Based on how fast she'd acted, this wasn't the first time the property had been threatened. But by what? Cassidy ran with her eyes resolutely forward, scanning for what lay ahead. She didn't know if it was beasts or bandits or worse, but she pumped her legs faster and faster, hoping she wouldn't find out.

The horses, intelligent as they were, sensed the danger plucking at the air. They whinnied and bucked frantically, and Cassidy couldn't corral them back into the stable. They were the most valuable animal on the property by far; Willa would certainly fire her if she left them to their fate. Taking a deep breath, Cassidy vaulted over the secondary fence and into the main corral. She crouched and held her hands out in front of her, advancing slowly. She'd been taught how to approach them under normal circumstances, but she hadn't been given the kind of training for a situation like this.

The smaller horse, a deep brown mare, bolted into the pen out of sheer luck, but the pale stallion galloped away to the back of their enclosure. Cassidy tried every trick to get the horse to approach her, to no avail. She crouched down in his line of sight, beads of sweat stinging in her eyes, when a sharp crack broke the silence in the air. She looked left and right, not trusting the way sound traveled in the valley to tell her which way it had come from. The horse took off with the shock of it, finding shelter on his own. She flung the stable doors closed and bolted to the back of it to get out of the open.

She stood pressed against the back of the building, chest heaving with the effort, as the thudding of hooves and shouts grew closer and closer. She turned the corner to see three riders, faces covered with wide-brimmed hats and masks, leaping over the fence surrounding the property. They were headed straight for her. Cassidy's thoughts bounced between hiding and running. She was too far away to make it back to her room without them seeing her, but the stable was the first place they were likely to head.

The orange glow of their guns cut their silhouettes against the darkening horizon as they grew ever closer. Another shot rang out, up into the sky. Willa stood ahead of them, dead center of the property, with the gun now aimed in their direction, stance wide and shoulders squared. Her braid came loose in sections, whipping across her face as she shouted towards the intruders, "Turn back around, or the next shot will be in one of your skulls."

The bandit in the middle sat atop a horse twice the size of the two flanking it, expression occluded by their deep red cowl. The one next to him was indistinguishable, but one far in the back stuck in Cassidy's memory. The all-white outfit, complete with a wide-brimmed white hat, jolted her recognition. She was certain that was the man she'd seen at the church. And on the train? She couldn't get a clear look at him with the pace they were galloping in her direction.

Willa did not budge. Cassidy shut her eyes, not wanting

to see her felled—or worse. Another shot rang out, and Cassidy's insides went cold. The footfalls of hooves broke from the steady beat, and one of the horses neighed frantically. The air split with the high-pitched whir of a gun being recharged, and she dared to peek back around the stable. A rider was down, their horse crying out as it lay on its side, limbs wild in the air. The two remaining riders turned, dust kicking up behind them as they retreated toward the horizon. The horse and the man all in white shone like a star as they headed towards the wastes beyond the ranch.

Willa advanced on the rider, whose leg was trapped under the dying animal. The deep color of blood spread over his denim until it mixed with the dirt below, creating a sickly color of mud. She pointed her gun at his head, the bright flashing on the trigger indicating that another shot had been charged. "Are there any more of you?"

The harshness of her tone did not prompt the rider to respond. For all the pain he must have been in, he did not cry out, only met Willa's stare with hard and unflinching eyes.

"So be it," she said as the shot rang clear through the center of his forehead.

Cassidy jerked back at the sound of his body thudding against the ground. She had never seen death so violent, and never so close. In all her life, she hoped to never see such a scene again. Her body was shaking like a calf, and try as she might to stop, it would not. Slowly, she came up behind Willa, who had lowered her gun to her side and stared out at where the two remaining riders had fled.

"You didn't give him a chance."

Willa looked over her shoulder at Cassidy's broken voice,

mouth turned down in a hard line. "They wouldn't have given us a chance either." She turned and walked back in the direction of her house, past the carnage without a thought. "Welcome to California."

CHAPTER 7

WHEN CASSIDY WENT OUT to start her chores the next morning, the bodies of the horse and the rider were gone. The only sign that Cassidy hadn't dreamed the entire thing was the brown mess of dried blood in the dirt. She made a wide circle around the area, not wanting to disturb the ground there. She had no idea what Willa had done with them or how she'd moved them on her own, but she was grateful she hadn't been asked to help. Being a bystander to death was one thing, but to touch it directly felt like playing with fate. Death already loomed over her shoulder more than enough.

When her work was done for the day, she was too shaken to sit by herself in her dark and confining room. She needed to be around people, have a drink or two, and push the entire incident to the recesses of her mind. She pinged the group she'd played cards with and hoped they'd take her up on the offer. If not, she was prepared to drink alone, as long as it meant shaking loose her thoughts. They messaged back within the hour and agreed to meet up, despite the short notice.

Cassidy came up to the saloon just as a patron came flying out the windows on the lefthand side of the building. Shattering glass, shouts, and cheers poured out into the evening air. A burly, bearded man in a cowboy hat and flannel stomped out onto the porch and right up to the patron strewn among the broken glass. He raised them up by their collar and held a fist in the air to strike—again, it seemed, judging by the bruise already forming around their left eye. Before he could strike, another man came bustling out the doors, both halves swinging with the disruption.

"Stop, please!" he cried as he came between the man's fist and the patron. "We'll leave you alone. I'm sorry. They've had a few too many."

The man hesitated, then sighed and released them, letting them thump back down onto the wood. "Whatever," he muttered, "not worth it, anyway."

The group of onlookers dispersed as the man turned to head back into the saloon, and the two patrons hobbled towards the road to town. When Cassidy got inside, activity had resumed as normal, and if she didn't know any better, she'd presume fights like that were commonplace in Bell Valley.

Mara and Finn were already inside at the same table Cassidy had met them all at the month before. As she approached, Finn shot up and wrapped her in his massive arms.

"Sorry, he's a hugger," Mara interjected.

"I'm picking that up, yeah."

Finn laughed, the sound reverberating from where her ear squished against his chest. "Good to see you! I'm glad you reached out."

"You too." She took her seat to Mara's left. "Is Sam coming?"

"Yeah. Things were busy today, so they're coming straight from work."

"Oh, anything going on?"

"Nothing I've heard about. Sam is pretty secretive about their pieces until they go live."

Cassidy respected that. It was such a small town that if enough gossip spread, there would be no one left to read the news.

Mara stood. "I'm going to grab a drink. Want to come with?"

Cassidy glanced at the bar to find Dean behind it again. She winced. "Eh, I'm okay for now."

Mara threw her hands up in the air. "For the love of god, not you too!"

Finn glanced over and put an arm around the top of Cassidy's chair. "She has something of a vendetta against Dean. I'm sure you can guess why."

Mara's expression hardened. "I really can't stand that bigot. He was on Finn before you. Give me a second... Beer?" Mara stomped over to the bar without waiting for an answer and started shouting at Dean, her finger right in his face. It was too loud inside to hear what she was saying, but Dean didn't even have the good sense to look embarrassed. All of a sudden, they both looked her way and Cassidy's shoulders shot up to her ears. Mara waved her over, and Finn slapped the back of her chair.

"Better do what she says," he said. Then seeing Cassidy's expression, he added, "She means well."

Cassidy pushed up from the table and made her way over, wishing the moment would end. She reached where Mara was and hovered behind her.

Mara cleared her throat. "Well?"

Dean turned to her, smarmy grin in place. "*I'm sorry* if I made you uncomfortable. That wasn't my intention." He held out his hand. "Truce?"

Cassidy sighed, knowing he was full of shit, but wanting it to be over. "Sure."

His grip was bruising, as if he could squeeze his apology right back out of her. Her blood boiled at being subjected to this. Their drinks were already on the bar, so Cassidy grabbed hers and made a quick retreat, Mara scampering behind. She was grateful she'd ordered a bottle, so he couldn't have spit in it or worse. She hadn't wanted his bullshit apology in the first place. Turning to Mara, she said, "Feel good about yourself now?"

Mara's brows creased. "What?"

"You didn't need to do that. If I wanted to, I would have."

Mara's dark hair fell into her face as she shook her head. "He shouldn't act like that."

"Like what?" Cassidy spat. "The same way as you?"

"That's not fair."

"You have no idea how people treat me here, and you're just going to make it worse."

Mara held her hands out in front of her. "Geez, I was trying to help."

"What makes you think I wanted your help?"

"Wow, okay. Noted. Sorry."

Cassidy sat down and popped her bottle cap off on the edge of the table, trying to calm her temper. Just as things were settling between her and Willa, here she was picking another fight. She couldn't afford to cut herself off from this group until she got what she needed from Sam. She'd apologize to Mara when her blood wasn't running so hot through her veins. It didn't help that Mara wore a petulant frown and refused to look in Cassidy's direction.

"So..." Finn leaned forward, either oblivious to the tension or doing his best to push past it. "We want to hear all about the ranch."

"I'm not sure it's all that interesting. I take care of the animals and crops and stuff."

"How's it working with Willa?"

"She's a decent boss."

The sentiment hung in the air for a moment. Both of them expected her to have more to say.

"And she's ... doing well?" Something shone in Finn's dark eyes, like concern.

Cassidy had no idea what to make of that question. "As well as anyone. I didn't know you all knew her. Small town, I guess?"

"Well," Mara interjected, done sulking, "she used to be in here a lot. She was a ton of fun." The end of her sentence had a bite to it, implying that Cassidy was anything but. Before they could get into it again, a shadow fell over the table.

"What are we talking about?" Sam asked as they sat down.

They ran their fingers through their dark hair, the glow of the lantern in the center of the table accentuating the pale purple crescents under their eyes.

"Cassidy was telling us how Willa's been. Wouldn't it be nice to invite her next time? It's been too long since we've seen her."

"Oh." Sam's mouth turned down at the sides. "Sounds good."

Finn continued, unaware of the shift. "We all should have tried harder..."

The conversation moved on, leaving Cassidy's head spinning. What had happened between them and Willa?

"Now that we're all here, how about we get started?" Mara brandished two decks of cards.

"What are we playing?"

"Do you know blackjack?"

Cassidy nodded. "Works for me." She looked to Finn and Sam, who were already setting up their holo-projectors for betting.

They played several rounds, and Cassidy even surprised herself and won two in a row. They had a good time joking, talking about the latest small-town drama, and enjoying their drinks. Cassidy had a steady buzz by her fourth beer, her movements slower and less constrained by gravity. Things wrapped up about three hours later, and they said their goodbyes.

Cassidy hung back to walk with Sam. "Hey, which way are you heading?"

They pointed west, in the direction of the clinic. "A bit outside town."

"Mind if I walk with you?"

They gave her a quizzical look, but nodded for Cassidy to follow as she tried to match their long, quick strides.

"How was work?"

"Busy. I've been working on this story, but I'm not sure it's going anywhere."

"Does that happen a lot?"

They tilted their head, considering. "I'd say about fifty-fifty. This town has more going on than you'd expect, but most of it has already been reported on in some way."

"That makes sense." She picked her next words carefully. "You do all the reporting?"

"For a while now."

"Wow, seems like a lot."

"It can be. In a town like this, everyone knows everyone. It can get ... awkward."

"Oh, I bet. Isn't there anything to report on outside town?" She hoped all the questions didn't come across as anything other than curiosity.

"Sometimes. There's really only Mariposa to the east; the rest of the state is abandoned. And bandit gangs don't sit down for interviews." They both laughed, though Cassidy's own sounded hollow to her ears.

"Ever been to Mariposa?" She tried to keep the tone of her question even, not too eager. "For a story, I mean."

They shook their head. "No, not yet. It's a long way to go, and nothing has been worth it so far."

Cassidy didn't know where to take the subject from there, so she left it alone, despite her inhibitions being lowered enough to tempt her to do otherwise. After about ten more minutes of walking, they stopped outside a fence surrounding a dark blue cottage-style home. It had a big oak tree with a swing affixed to the thickest branch, and a large building behind it to the right.

Sam looked at her for a moment, considering. "Do you have a minute?"

"Sure." Cassidy followed them back past the house to another structure.

"I know you mentioned liking photography, so maybe you'll get a kick out of this." They brushed their index finger over the handle to unlock it and led her inside. It looked to be a personal darkroom, the eerie glow bathing the walls in cherry red. Several sizes of photos hung off fishing line across the ceiling, and different worktables with a variety of equipment lined the space.

"This is incredible! Is this all for the paper?"

"Some of it is. Some is a personal project I'm working on, and the rest is for fun."

"How'd you get all this stuff?"

"It's mostly cobbled together with junked tech. Finn is the one who did all the hard work; I just told him what I wanted."

The setup was impressive, considering the resources they had. Cassidy made a slow circle around the room, weaving between the lines of photographs. Sam took a strong interest in portraits and architecture. She picked out a dozen different buildings from town among the collection.

"If you ever want to develop something here, let me know."

"That would be awesome, but I don't know how. I've only ever done digital."

"I'd be happy to show you. I taught myself too. Something

about the old-school technique adds a depth to a piece you can't create digitally."

"I agree."

Before she finished her exploration, a knock sounded at the door.

A head popped into the doorway, messy brown curls falling over a forehead that was wrinkled in surprise. "Hey, I thought I heard you get back. How was— Oh, hello."

Sam gestured between them. "Cassidy, this is Alex, my partner. Cassidy's been joining us for cards."

Alex stepped farther into the room, a wide grin bringing out the dimples in his cheeks. "Nice to meet you, Cassidy. I take it you're a fan of photography too?"

"Yes, hi. It's nice to meet you. I'm sorry, I didn't mean to intrude."

He waved his hand dismissively. "Nonsense. This is Sam's space, anyway. And all their friends are welcome."

"That's nice, thank you. And this is fantastic, Sam, thank you for showing me. But I should probably leave you to it. It's about time I got something to eat."

Alex shrugged. "I could fix you something quick, if you'd like, no need to run out. We eat late when Sam goes out."

"That's so kind of you, but I should be heading back." She inched towards the door before he could offer anything else.

A look passed between the two of them, the simple intimacy and understanding novel to Cassidy. She was almost envious.

"Of course. I hope to see you again soon though."

"And ping me about developing whenever. It'll be fun."

"Definitely. Thank you again. And it was nice to meet you,

Alex."

They both bid her goodbye, arms around each other as they retreated into the house. Sam hunched over as they leaned down to kiss the side of Alex's head. Cassidy sighed as she continued down the road. Sam was much more open than she'd initially expected them to be. Offering their darkroom, introducing their partner—it was all too familiar for Cassidy. She couldn't forget that she was just here to get information about Dr. Thorne; there was no reason to get attached.

CHAPTER 8

CASSIDY PICKED UP HER pace in the brisk nighttime air. It was late enough that she heard the owls coo from their roosts. The alcohol buzzing in her blood made her mind light and carefree. She wasn't paying attention to where she headed, but she did find her way home. She was already unlacing her boots out front when she realized she wasn't alone.

The last thing she expected was Willa, draped in moonlight on the roof of her home, head tilted up towards the sky. The bottle in her hand twinkled with movement as it caught the light. She was so lost in thought she hadn't noticed Cassidy clambering back.

Cassidy's feet stopped before her mind made sense of it. She was surprised to find herself curious—curious about this person who made it so clear how little regard she held for her, and curious about someone whom she had seen kill.

She walked to the railing of the front porch and used it as leverage to swing up to the roof. In her state, it was less than elegant, but she made it up on the second try. Willa didn't look her way. She wordlessly passed Cassidy the bottle of dark liquor—already a third empty.

"What's going on?" Cassidy took a polite sip and gave the bottle back to Willa. Her head was already swimming enough to caution her intake.

Willa took a long drink, the column of her throat working it down. She placed the bottle between them. "I haven't been completely honest about the situation here."

"What do you mean?"

"I should have said so in the ad. Or the day you got here, and..."

"Willa, it's alright. You don't owe me anything."

Willa turned to Cassidy with a sad smile. "After everything that happened last night, I haven't been fair to you. And I regret it."

"You've already apologized for that."

As if she didn't hear her, Willa continued, "I'm sure you can guess I haven't always been on my own out here. I ran things with my husband."

Husband. The word hung in the air between them. It was like all the alcohol Cassidy had consumed settled at the pit of her stomach. She had never seen Willa wearing a ring or seen pictures of anyone who might be that to her.

"You're married."

"I was... Am. I... Well, he's been gone for about a year and a half now."

"Oh, you divorced?"

"No, he died." Her voice caught on the last word.

"That's terrible."

Willa glanced back up from where her gaze had been focused on her lap, but she was looking past Cassidy now, her expression vacant. "We had been fighting all the time then. One night after a fight, it got especially ugly. He stormed out to get some air—and that's when the bandits came."

"Bandits?"

"We've dealt with them a lot, being so far out of town. Last night was the first time they've been here since."

"That's what you meant? About them not giving us a chance?"

Willa laughed, or sobbed, the sound indistinguishable to Cassidy. "They didn't even ask anything. Just shot him and left."

"Why would they do that?"

"It's such a stupid reason, and I..." A tear leaked from the corner of her eye.

Cassidy panicked. "It's okay, forget I asked. That's awful, I'm so sorry."

"After everything that happened last night, it brought it all back. That's why I..."

"I get it."

"I don't want you to think I'm evil, or a killer. But I've seen what it takes to survive out here. You don't live long without giving up a part of yourself."

"What are they after?"

"Anything they can get their hands on, I suppose. If you think it's bad here in town, the wastes are worse. No shelter, food, water. All kinds of weather and disease. We're a damn oasis to them."

"Why don't they just live in town? No one's making them live like that, right?"

"They prefer that way of life," Willa scoffed. "Think we're lesser for having law and order. But just because we're in the wastes doesn't mean we have to live like animals."

"Has it always been this bad?"

Willa nodded. "Last couple years or so, yeah. They split off into a few gangs. For a while, we thought they'd have enough trouble among themselves, but they still come out here to bother us."

"And the cops don't do anything?" Cassidy's question was hesitant. So far in her time in California, she hadn't seen a single officer.

Willa's laugh was dry. "We have a sheriff. What few deputies there were died in the war. No one ever came forward to replace them."

Cassidy kept her wince to herself. It was no wonder they struggled with so much crime. "You never thought about moving?"

"Move where? Most of us have gone our whole lives outside of the Corporation. I wouldn't know how to live like that."

Cassidy chuckled. "Once you get used to it, it's not so bad."

"Why'd you leave, then?"

Shame burned in Cassidy's gut against the truths she didn't dare speak. Even with Willa being so vulnerable with her, it wasn't something she was ready to return.

"Do you have anyone to help you out? Someone to talk to?"

"I don't get into town much anymore. With everyone knowing... I don't like how they treat me. Like I'm going to lose it on them."

"I don't blame you." A lot of pieces were clicking into place—about the town, and the way they talked about Willa. It was awful to think Willa had been carrying all of this and the burdens of an entire ranch all by herself.

"I know I was being selfish. I didn't want you to treat me like that too. But after last night, you deserve to know what you've signed up for."

"I understand. And you won't get that treatment from me."

Willa fixed her with a glare. "I know you say so, but pity is part of human nature."

"My life hasn't always been so great either. We all have our shit. It's not going to be a problem." She reached out and placed a hand on Willa's shoulder. They weren't like that—she hadn't even shaken her hand when she first arrived—but she wanted her to know she meant it.

"No one sticks around this place. I hope you'll consider staying."

"Can't get rid of me that easily."

They let the moment sit. Surrounded by so much tragedy, Cassidy couldn't help but be grateful for their newfound friendship. It wasn't obvious at first, but Willa was a genuine person—more genuine than anyone she'd ever met.

Willa looked her in the eyes, pleading. "I promise there's nothing else I haven't told you. And I'm sorry this took me so long."

"It's alright. You hardly knew me."

"Still, I don't know."

She ignored the tears leaking out of the corners of Willa's

eyes. "Thank you for telling me. I'm sure it's difficult to bring back up."

Willa squeezed her hand, still resting on her shoulder, then dropped it into her lap. "It is, but I feel better with you knowing."

Cassidy drew her own hand away too, the sudden loss of contact amplified by the chill in the air. She shifted to stand, assuming Willa wanted some space.

"Cassidy?"

"Yeah?"

"I'm sorry I was so awful to you. I never..." She ran a hand down the side of her face. "I've never had anyone around here besides him. I didn't want to replace him."

Cassidy cocked her head to the side. "Then why did you?"

"This is the only ranch. And I was too ambitious. People gave me grace for a while, but the food was coming in slower than they needed. I could either hire help, or starve the whole town."

"There was no other option?"

She smiled sadly. "I was ... stubborn at first. But when I got around to asking, the answers were the same. Everyone else has their own burdens. No one has the time to help as much as this place needs. Until you, anyway."

"That's a lot of pressure."

"Maybe so, but it is what it is."

Cassidy nodded and continued towards the edge of the roof.

"Hey," Willa called, and Cassidy stopped to turn towards her. "Whatever brought you here, I'm glad for it. Thanks for listening."

"Of course. See you in the morning."

"Yeah."

The climb down was much more difficult for Cassidy than it had been on the way up. Though she was far more sober than when she'd arrived, her steps were heavy and clumsy, and her mind was elsewhere. She got back to her room and laid in her bed, still dressed, staring into the unseeing dark. She couldn't sleep, only think about what Willa had told her.

Cassidy had experienced loss, more than most of her friends back in Chicago—more than anyone she'd met. There was finally a person to understand her and her pain, but what did that matter? She wasn't meant for this life. She was playing at settling down, when it was only a matter of time until she'd be drawn back to the city. It was where she belonged. She couldn't help but wonder if she belonged in two places, or if maybe she was becoming someone else entirely.

CHAPTER 9

THE FOLLOWING WEEK, CASSIDY swallowed her pride and asked Willa to teach her how to shoot. She'd underestimated the woman's mettle, and with things thawing between them, a lesson or two shouldn't be unbearable.

They met at the back of the property, next to a row of cacti that towered to near Cassidy's height. Along the parallel fence were empty bottles lined up for her to practice on. Willa leaned up against the length of the fence, a foot propped up on the middle beam. She drained the contents of a beer before lining the bottle up in the already plentiful row.

Cassidy's palms itched, and she was suddenly certain she'd embarrass herself in front of Willa. She shouldn't care, but after seeing her in action, she did not want to be found lacking. It was clear how little Willa thought of city folk, and out of sheer pride, the last thing Cassidy wanted to do was prove her right. Willa held out a rifle-style shooter, plasma activated and fully charged. Cassidy held it gingerly, nervous she'd brush a finger over one of the numerous buttons that would set off a blast.

Willa chuckled to herself and came up behind Cassidy. "Hold it up like you're not afraid of it." Cassidy raised her arm so quickly that she nearly elbowed Willa in the throat. "Easy there." Willa's hand gently glided over the joint, relaxing it into a more acute angle. "The synth hand is your dominant?" Cassidy nodded. "Alright, you want that on the trigger here." She dragged Cassidy's fingers into position. The implant had enough nerve receptors for her hand to function naturally, but touch wasn't supposed to feel like anything. She shivered all the same as Willa's slender fingers rearranged hers around the trigger.

"What do the different buttons do?"

"Different blasts, mostly. The one closest to you is a single shot, and you can hold it down to charge a stronger blast. The ones in front are at different burst speeds."

"So, like, more than one?"

Willa laughed. "Yeah, a few more than one." She stepped back, and Cassidy felt her absence chill the air around her. "You want to give it a shot?" They both snorted at the unintentional wordplay.

Cassidy tried to keep a strong stance, like Willa demonstrated, and trained her gaze on the bottle dead center. She took a deep breath in and released the trigger, sending off one bright orange shot. It whizzed past the bottle and towards the horizon until it eventually disintegrated in the air.

She looked back at Willa, expecting to find her expression mocking, but she was patient as she came over and corrected Cassidy's stance. "Try again. Now that you have a feel for the kickback, adjust your aim."

It took seven more shots for Cassidy to hit the bottle, but Willa let out a hoot when she finally struck true. "Alright, now show me that it wasn't dumb luck and do it again."

They worked through the bottles until there were only two left, and the sun had dipped too low on the horizon for them to continue.

"You're getting there. A few more sessions, and you might hit the targets on the first try."

Cassidy laughed in disbelief. Where was the uptight, judgy woman she had met?

"But," Willa interrupted her thoughts, "we used up all the beer for this. Can you go to the store and grab another case?"

Cassidy saluted and headed towards town.

The grocer was emptier than usual; only one other patron lingered through the aisles as she grabbed her case of beer. She checked out with the sole cashier. "Quiet night, huh?"

She gave Cassidy an odd look. "You could say that."

Cassidy took her beer and headed back towards home, wishing she hadn't tried to make any awkward small talk. The stores she went past were shut down early too, blinds drawn and doors boarded up. Willa hadn't mentioned another storm rolling in—at least, she didn't think so.

She'd made it halfway back from the grocer when the faintest hint of smoke drifted through the air. At first, she thought it must be an overactive chimney in the autumn chill, but as she reached the road, a deep orange glow had the shadows of the surrounding buildings dancing along the path. Frantic shouting and activity grew as she got closer, so loud that it overwhelmed her senses. She surveyed the area, looking for a source. Thick black smoke billowed from the left-hand side of the church. The flames were spiking so high they seemed as tall as the mountains.

She took off running, abandoning her case of beer on the road. There were already a handful of people out in the field, and a steady trickle of people coming out of the apartments across the way. Two men rushed out of the door ahead of her with several buckets between their arms. They stopped a few feet ahead, glancing around.

"This way!" she shouted and took off towards the path of the stream under the bridge that still held a small river of water. She hoped they'd heard her over the commotion and were following. Once she reached the closest section of running water, she bent over to catch her breath, the two men not far behind her. She held her hands out for a bucket and filled it to the brim. Water sloshed over the sides and onto her clothes as she ran back towards the church. The grass crunched underfoot, spurring her on. If the fire spread to the field, the whole thing would be ablaze in a matter of minutes. She passed the bucket to the closest person, who passed it down, and so on. The line spat out an empty one, and she ran to fill it. She kept seeing flashes of white: the church as it burned, a hat, an all-white outfit. But the chaos was unfolding too rapidly for her to keep her attention on any one thing for too long.

She ran back and forth, past the point that her body was

capable of being pushed, as more people joined the effort. She wasn't as close to the blaze as some, but she was slick with sweat, nonetheless. Her hair stuck to her neck and the sides of her face, and her shoes were caked in mud from the dry dirt mixing with all the water that spilled as she ran. The pain in her joints was increasing rapidly, but she couldn't rest, or she'd never get back up. For a while, it seemed like the flames were only growing, and she feared it would overtake the whole town. But after seemingly no change, the flames started to recede, and the smoke grew lighter and lighter until it resembled a puff of smoke from a cigarette.

With the adrenaline keeping her upright, she walked around to the side of the building to inspect the damage. It was worse than Cassidy thought. Not only had the beautiful stained-glass window melted away into nothing, but what she hadn't seen was that the left side of the building housed the rectory. The scene was haunting. Black ash covered what remained of the structure and bed. What looked to have been a dresser was reduced to rubble. Of the four walls, only two remained intact. A cross hung perfectly on the back wall, as if spared from the blaze. It was hard to tell if there were any personal effects, as almost everything except the larger structures had been burned away.

She stared at the stained, exhausted faces that mirrored her own, wondering what to do. A woman sat in a pale green nightgown, hugging her knees and facing away. The pallor of her skin under the moonlight made her look like a ghost. She appeared impossibly small. The moonlit glint in her hair was incredibly familiar to Cassidy.

"Annabelle? Are you okay?"

Annabelle didn't look up at the sound of her voice, just wordlessly shook her head.

You weren't supposed to ask a lot of questions when someone was in shock, but it was like the adrenaline had her brain going at double speed. She couldn't stop the words from pouring out. "What happened? Was anyone hurt?"

"Don't know, and don't think so," said a voice Cassidy was hoping to never hear again. Dean came around to face her. In all the commotion, she hadn't seen that he was there. He bent down near Annabelle, taking on a softer tone than he'd ever use with Cassidy. "It'll be alright, darling. Nothing that can't be rebuilt. We'll find you a place in the meantime."

Cassidy gasped. The thought that Annabelle had been sleeping in the very spot that was now a pile of debris made her stomach churn. Things could have been so much worse. She unbuttoned her jacket and draped it over Annabelle's shaking frame, the shock and chill instantly setting in as it left her body. Dean nodded at her, something close to respect coloring his expression. She backed away to the edge of the crowd. There would be enough people fussing over Annabelle without her adding to it.

"Cassidy?"

She turned to see Finn walking towards her from the apartment building across the street. He seemed so out of place in his plaid flannel pajamas that Cassidy had to fight the urge to laugh.

"Hey, Finn. Long time no see."

Finn was too preoccupied to laugh at her weak attempt at a joke. "How long have you been out here?" He looked her over for any sign of injury, though it must have been hard to tell under all the soot and ash. "You must be freezing."

"Oh." It was setting in how late it was. She still hadn't eaten dinner.

"Hold on, let me get you something."

"No, don't go to the trouble."

Finn rolled his eyes. "Cassidy, please. I live right over there. Just give me five minutes."

She did as he said, not able to move anyway. He was back in less time with a thick black sweater in his arms. Once she'd gotten it on, it was almost to her knees.

"Great, that's better. Do you want me to walk you home?"

She stared at him for a second; she must have been more out of it than she realized. "I'm okay, Finn. Thank you for the sweater."

He looked ready to argue, but sighed, "Alright. Ping me when you get home. We'll talk tomorrow, yeah?"

"Yeah. Thank you."

His gaze branded her until she made it out of the clearing. Her feet dragged and her head throbbed; she was sure all that smoke inhalation had done her no favors. Worse still was that she'd have to shower before bed, or risk ruining her sheets. Smoke and soot and dirt clung to her in places she didn't want to think about. That was not how she'd expected to spend the rest of her evening.

She had barely gotten through the gate before Willa bolted off her front porch.

"Cassidy?"

"Hey. What are you doing up?"

"I never heard you come back. I know it's none of my

business, but I was worried something had happened."

"Oh. Kinda. There was a fire... The church ... I tried to help."

"Oh my god." She wrapped an arm around her and sat her down on the first step of the porch. "Hold on one second." She disappeared into the house and returned with a glass of water. Between how she and Finn were acting, someone would think it was *her* building that burned down. "Is everyone alright?"

"Annabelle is shaken, but she's okay. The front part of the church is pretty wrecked though."

"That's awful." Willa was rubbing slow, soft circles on her back, making her eyelids heavy. She might have responded with words, but it was like a slush coming out of her mouth as her head tipped forward.

Willa muttered something under her breath, slinging Cassidy's arm over her shoulders so she could bear her weight. "Just had to run towards the fire, huh? You look awful." Willa's voice sounded so far away. Cassidy didn't bother trying to hold a conversation at that point.

Willa laid a few towels out on the couch and eased Cassidy onto it. She'd be guilty over the mess when she regained her senses. Willa pulled her shoes off and slid her legs onto the cushions, draping a heavy blanket over Cassidy, who was still in Finn's sweater. Cassidy thought she left, but she returned a few moments later and began wiping a damp washcloth across her face. The cool water made her jump, but Willa calmed her and kept cleaning.

She finished and went to withdraw her hand, but Cassidy caught it at the wrist. She hadn't meant to, didn't know what to say, but she gazed into Willa's eyes, feeling her pulse thunder beneath her grip. Willa ran her other hand over Cassidy's fingers, then gently laid her hand back down on her chest.

"Get some rest. You'll probably feel even worse when you wake up. I'm just down the hall if you need me." Her footsteps echoed across the hardwood floor. She didn't even make it to her room before Cassidy succumbed to sleep.

When Cassidy awoke, her entire body was weighed down with pain. She glanced around, remembering how Willa had carried her in the night before. She sat up and stretched, testing her strength. Willa had left a glass of water on the coffee table in front of her, and she drank it down eagerly. Her throat burned like she'd raked her nails along the inside of it, and she coughed the last few gulps down.

"Cassidy? You up?"

"Yeah," Cassidy croaked out in a voice she barely recognized. Between the smoke and shouting, her vocal cords could only produce a shrill, crackly tone. It was so faint that she wasn't sure Willa heard her, so she stood to go down the hall.

"Oh, hi," Willa said, appearing in the doorway. "Sit back down before you fall over." Cassidy sank back into the cushions obediently, and Willa joined her on the opposite side. "Glad to see you're up. Thought you'd sleep for longer though."

"Time?" The sound raked out of Cassidy's body painfully.

"Just past eleven."

"The work?"

Willa shot her a mildly annoyed stare. "I can do it myself. If you try to work the next couple of days, I'll lock you in your room."

Cassidy sighed, not wanting to be treated like a child. Willa meant well, but being mothered never sat right with her. She hadn't gotten enough of it growing up to get used to it. Since every word clawed its way out of her raw throat, she just nodded in understanding.

"Great. I'll fix you breakfast." Willa wandered off into the kitchen, the sounds of pots and pans clanging mixed with her gentle humming.

Cassidy must have fallen asleep again, because when she opened her eyes next, there was a plate of eggs and toast laid on the table next to a fresh glass of water and a little pile of pills. The food was lukewarm, and she knew Willa had already gone back to the grounds by then.

Cassidy ate quickly. She hadn't eaten in so long that her stomach cramped, unused to the fullness. Setting down the remaining triangle of toast she had been working on, she examined the pills. She searched for the tiny letters on the side to see which ones Willa thought she needed. *V* for "vita pill," sort of a catchall for basic ailments, along with *P* for "pain" and *R* for "recovery." The latter would be useful on account of all the smoke she'd inhaled. Cassidy was grateful that Willa kept a well-stocked medicine cabinet, swallowing them all at once and finishing her breakfast.

She dropped the plate and utensils into the speed washer

and put them away, then made her way back to her room. It killed her not to be working when she knew Willa needed the help. Since they had begun evenly splitting their duties, Cassidy realized how hard it must have been for Willa to manage things by herself. Begrudgingly, she laid down on her bed and picked up the book she'd been working through. Her mind was hazy, like it had been covered in a film which made it hard for her to focus.

She drifted off again, and when she woke, it looked like she'd missed the brilliance of a sunset, the sky a murky blue. She glanced down to find she was still in her clothes from the night before. In her sleep, she must have removed Finn's sweater, since it lay in a crumpled heap at the side of her bed. She took a quick shower, already steadier on her feet, thanks to the meal and medicine Willa had provided for her. She was sitting on the foot of the bed, trying to untangle her hair, when a knock sounded at the door.

CHAPTER 10

"Cassidy? You awake?"

Cassidy dried her damp hands on her pants and went to the door. Willa was standing outside with an annoyed expression, but it melted a bit when Cassidy opened the door.

"Hey, are you feeling any better?"

"Yeah, a bit. Thanks for breakfast." Her voice was still raspy and a bit strained, but it was only slightly uncomfortable to speak compared to the pain earlier.

"That's great. Listen, I know you've been resting, and I tried to delay it, but the sheriff has a few questions for you."

"The sheriff?"

Willa rolled her eyes. "He said he's talking with everyone who was there last night."

"Right."

"I can tell him you're still asleep, if you want."

Cassidy gave her a small smile. "Thanks, but I'd rather get it done with."

"Okay," Willa said as she turned, "come on, then. I have him at the house."

Cassidy straightened herself up as best she could, but she was in loose linen loungewear, and her hair was still damp and unruly from her shower.

Willa introduced her to the man sitting in the living room, Sheriff Cole, who sat with a rigid posture in front of an untouched cup of coffee. His beige uniform was starched almost to excess, so it sat stiffly against his body. He was clean-shaven and younger than Cassidy had expected, late thirties at most. Cassidy went to shake his hand, and his grip was gentler than she was expecting.

"Evening. I'll try not to take up too much of your time; Willa mentioned you're still recovering." His glance in Willa's direction looked almost nervous. Cassidy nodded and sat to his left in the deep green armchair bordering the edge of the coffee table.

"Let's go through your account of things."

"Okay..." Cassidy described everything she remembered. She expected him to interrupt her with questions, or at least take notes, but he did neither. She stopped after she recounted how Willa had helped her inside, the back of her neck heating at what she left unsaid.

"Did anything that happened seem unusual to you?"

Cassidy laughed dryly. "I'm not sure how that sort of thing usually goes, but no, I don't think so. Although..." She paused. "Town was awfully empty last night, and places were boarded up like for a storm."

The sheriff sighed. "There've been rumors of gangs roaming nearer to town, but I had hoped they would keep heading past us."

"You think someone could have done this on purpose?"

"Bandits have been a thorn in our side for too long now. I reckon they were after the donation box, and things got out of hand."

"Was anyone going to tell us about these rumors?" Willa cut in, tone sharp. "Or just hope we'd fend for ourselves?"

Sheriff Cole shook his head sadly. "I'm sorry, Miss Ghera, for how things have been for you. If we'd had any way of getting someone out here, we would have. But with just me and the deputy, we can't be everywhere at once."

Cassidy cleared her throat, unable to let the next thought go, angry on Willa's behalf. "It's already happened." She paused, unsure how honest she should be about the incident. "Bandits rode up here some weeks ago."

"They came here? For what?"

Cassidy glanced at Willa, whose expression was too murky to read. "Not sure. They got scared off before they could do anything." She'd leave out the fact that not all three of them had ridden away.

"And you have reason to think they meant you harm?"

Willa scoffed. "Why else would they come here, armed?"

"If you see suspicious persons again, ping my chip directly, and I'll come check it out." He held out his palm for Cassidy to scan his data, adding his personal contact to her logs.

Cassidy crossed her arms. "And if I see someone? What can you do?" She hadn't meant the question to sound so harsh, but she didn't know why they bothered having a sheriff or any kind of law if the bandits were left to their own devices.

Sheriff Cole sighed. "The best I can, miss."

She instantly regretted her tone. She couldn't imagine trying to keep a whole town safe from the elements along with gangs of bandits.

He stood, shaking both of their hands and tipping his hat as he went out the back door. "Have a good evening."

Cassidy mulled over what he'd said. She couldn't shake the insistence that there was more to it, that the bandits were after something else. She didn't dare mention the man she kept seeing, all in white, who seemed to appear wherever there was trouble.

Willa broke her train of thought. "You okay? You have a weird look on your face."

"Still tired, I guess." Cassidy felt a bit guilty for not opening up to her, but she didn't want Willa to think she was losing her mind too. She stood. "Need help with dinner?"

"You relax. I'll call you when it's ready."

Cassidy was sure she wouldn't be able to take another day or two of being looked after; it made her itch with restlessness in a way she didn't understand. She'd have to convince Willa she was well enough to get back to work. Still, not wanting to pick a fight, she resumed her position in the armchair.

They ate a silent dinner. Cassidy had too much on her mind to hold a conversation. But a shift had occurred between them. Maybe it was Willa taking care of her, teaching her to shoot, or opening up to her that had changed things. But Cassidy was beginning to enjoy her presence, the low-maintenance way they could be around each other. Willa didn't need to fill the silence, like so many Cassidy usually surrounded herself with. It was nice to just be together.

Cassidy couldn't find the time to get off the ranch for the next few days. Her suspicion was right: Willa had been drowning in the work, despite Cassidy only being out of commission for about a day. By Friday, she had finally caught up on things, so she contacted Sam to see if they wanted to help her develop some of her photos. Her original plan had derailed too far, and she needed to get back on track. Find the doctor, get cured, and get out. The longer she went without progress, the longer it took her to return to her life in Chicago.

She pinged Sam, and they agreed to meet up after dinner. Sam was a night owl like her, which she appreciated. Her first visit had been spur of the moment, but now that she'd made plans in advance, she headed out on the ranch to gather things for a little basket. Her grandma instilled her with impeccable manners throughout her childhood, so she knew she couldn't show up empty-handed. She trimmed some basil and kale and picked the first pomegranates that had turned a pretty magenta color.

She couldn't make the trek without passing the ruins of the church, unable to look away from the destruction as she came upon it. It was the first time she'd been back since that night. And although it was dark, she could still make out the ugly, eaten wood of what was once there. It was heartbreaking in a way Cassidy hadn't anticipated. She'd never been one for religion, organized or otherwise, but the thought of something that meant so much to others being destroyed made her chest ache. The Corporation had religious halls, but they were stark, ugly things. Cassidy better understood the draw of practicing when it was done in as beautiful of a building as the one in Bell Valley. And now it was gone.

She continued past the church, the gnarled remains sinister under the glow of the late autumn moon. The chill in the air was sharper than it had been earlier in the season, and Cassidy's light jacket did little to insulate her. So far, throughout living here, she had continually underestimated the weather in both its hot and cold moments. The dust and storms were a whole other issue she hadn't adapted to either, and probably never would. Her pace quickened to make up for the chill, and she found Sam and Alex's place with less difficulty than she was expecting, remembering which was theirs by the distinct navy color.

As she approached the fence, a black-and-white blur leapt off the porch and launched in her direction. Cassidy's brain was so overloaded with animal-handling knowledge that she couldn't remember if she should crouch or stand firm, look it in the eye or not. Before she had the time to decide, it cleared the fence and bowled her over. Her tailbone and elbows broke her fall as she was met with an onslaught of sniffing.

Alex came bustling out next. "Ranger, no!" He ordered the dog to retreat and sit as he offered Cassidy a hand up. "I'm so sorry. We're still working on his manners."

Cassidy brushed off the back of her pants. "No harm

done." Now that he'd settled a bit, she leaned over to scratch behind his ears. "How long have you had him?"

"About five months. He's our first dog together, so we're trying to work on boundaries and everything. It's kind of practice."

"Practice?"

"Oh, well, we're hoping to adopt in the next few years."

Cassidy beamed at him. Everything she learned about the two of them made her heart thaw a bit more.

"Oh, I almost forgot..." Cassidy tried to reorganize the basket she'd made, picking up a few pomegranates that had rolled away from her. "A few things from the ranch. Thank you for welcoming me into your home."

Alex's eyes lit up as he clutched the basket to his chest. "This is incredible, thank you. Willa's stuff is the best."

"Agreed. I hope you enjoy it."

Alex looked down at the basket before replying, "How is Willa doing these days?"

"Getting on, I think." Her neck grew hot at her lack of familiarity. With the amount of time they were spending together, she really should have a better answer to give.

"Well, I shouldn't keep you. Sam can be particular about sharing their friends." He turned with a wry smile. "And they've taken a liking to you."

She entered the darkroom, the hiss of the door the only sound to announce her presence. The initial adjustment for her eyes was as jarring as the last time, despite her implants.

"Hey. I'll be finished with this in a second." Sam faced towards the table and leaned over a tray that had some sort of liquid in it. They hunched over so severely that Cassidy's neck hurt from looking at them. After a few minutes passed, they pulled out their photo and placed it on a line near the back of the room to dry. They finished tidying the corner they had been working in and turned towards her. "Okay, ready to get started?"

"Sure." Cassidy had five photos in mind she wanted to develop, so she'd scanned them onto her chip in advance. She also brought her camera, just in case they needed to access the raw files directly. "What do you need?"

"We'll do a few together, then maybe you can do some on your own. Send whichever one you want to start with over to the printer."

"Printer? Doesn't that kind of, I dunno, defeat the purpose?"

Sam laughed. "The printer doesn't have any ink, only the data from the photo. So, it'll have to be developed to display the image."

"Right. Makes sense."

Sam walked her through the process, which was full of technical steps and required good attention to detail. Cassidy wasn't quite sure she'd be able to do it without Sam's help. For the first two photos, they kept the conversation focused on instructions. Sam was passionate about it all—but that bled into the way they instructed her with an overabundance of detail and technicality. Cassidy found she couldn't hold a conversation and keep up with the process so she abandoned the former in favor of paying attention.

They hung up a photo of Tom, the barn cat, when Sam took a step back. "Alright, want to try one on your own?"

"Yeah, why not?" Cassidy wasn't confident that she could

complete all the steps as well as Sam, but she adored the results, so she wasn't ready to call it a wash yet. She began going through the motions while Sam leaned against an adjoining table, tapping tools or materials she needed whenever she appeared lost.

"So," Cassidy started, when she got to a step where she was confident enough to chat, "I'm sure you heard about the fire."

"Terrible. Poor Annabelle. Finn's already started rebuilding though."

"That's good, at least."

"He said you were there?"

Cassidy poured the required chemicals into the tray as Sam's eyes followed. She put the lid back on the last bottle. "Yeah, I caught the middle of it. Just tossed a few buckets around."

"He was pretty worried about you. Said you looked ready to collapse."

"Oh, it wasn't so bad. I feel awful though. I pinged him, but I need to stop by to thank him in person. And he lent me a sweater I need to return."

"Sounds like Finn. He won't hold it against you."

Cassidy paused, using the next step to gather her thoughts. "Did anyone come to speak to you?"

"For the paper? I'm usually the one to go ask the questions."

"No, the sheriff came by. Asked me what happened."

"Did he?"

She glanced at them sideways. "Yeah. Is that not normal?"

"I don't know. I thought it was a wildfire?"

"He didn't think so. The whole thing is weird."

"Is there something bothering you?"

Cassidy laughed, but it came out harsh. "Probably imagining things." She was sure Sam would dismiss her suspicions about the man as well. And she was determined to secure their help in finding a solution to her illness. She didn't want to ask too much of them and risk their refusal.

She hung up the photo she had been working on, the darker colors already beginning to develop.

Sam shrugged. "Hey, it's as much for my own curiosity. But we don't have to talk about it. So, what have we got?" They got up and went to inspect her work.

"Oh, uh—"

"These are great! You have an interesting perspective." They went down the line until they got to the one she had just finished developing. Cassidy's ears heated at the attention they were giving them. "What are you going to do with them?"

"Not sure yet. Maybe hang them in my room."

Sam smiled. "They should be ready within the next hour. Why don't we have a drink in the house while we wait?"

She followed them into the house, the front door opening into a small entryway and living area. The walls were a deep green, with interesting black-and-silver furniture. It was the most urban-looking place she'd been in since she left Chicago, and she felt instantly at home.

"Wow, cool space."

"Thanks. It was Alex's first, but he let me mix things up a bit." Sam led them into a kitchen with a sleek black island with bar stools along one end.

Cassidy sat down as Sam grabbed two beers from the fridge. "I like it. How long have you been here?"

"The house? Two years. The town? Five."

"Oh, I thought you grew up around here."

Sam joined her, leaning across the opposite side of the island. "I'm from New Jersey, originally." Ah, that made sense; New Jersey was one of the better-off abandoned states on the East Coast. "Went to college with Finn a while back, and he pinged me one day to tell me about the job at the paper. Moved here and crashed with him until I got situated."

"I didn't know you two went back so far."

"Yeah, he's a great guy. And I owe him a lot."

"Oh yeah? For the job?"

"And for introducing me to Alex. Finn had done work for him a handful of times and set us up one day. He knows I'm pretty hopeless with that kind of thing, so he didn't even tell me it was for a date."

"You must have been mortified."

"At first, yeah. I was planning to make an excuse to leave. But then we clicked, and it's been natural ever since."

"Ugh, it'd be annoying if I didn't like you both so much," Cassidy teased.

"What about you? What brought you here?"

"I saw Willa's ad and figured it sounded like a great deal, lodging and all."

"Yeah, but going from a city like Chicago, living in the Corporation, to this? That's a pretty big change. Didn't you hear the stories about the wastelands?" They ended their sentence with a smirk.

She laughed. "Everyone keeps asking me that. You all

must think I'm insane for coming out here."

"Well, it's not for the weather, the ambiance, or the general life expectancy." They huffed in amusement.

Cassidy set down her drink and ran her finger along the lip of the bottle. "To be honest, I came here for something else."

"I don't mean to pry, if you don't want to talk about it."

"No, I just... I don't want you to hate me."

Sam laughed incredulously. "Why would I hate you?"

"I think I should start at the beginning."

So, she told them—all of it. Her illness, the clues about Dr. Thorne, "visiting" their journalism office. The only thing she kept to herself was her suspicions about the man in white. "I'm sorry about the last part. I never thought I'd meet you. Or like you."

Sam's smile was as sharp as a razor's edge. "I would have never known it was you if you didn't say anything. I'm almost impressed."

"You're not mad?"

"You didn't steal anything?"

"No."

"Break anything?"

Cassidy shook her head.

"Then there's nothing to be upset about."

Cassidy looked down at her drink, the lump in her throat forming against her will. "I don't think I deserve that, but thank you. And I'm pushing my luck here..." Her laugh was dry as it came out. "... but do you think you can help me?"

Sam sighed. "Oh, Cassidy. The journalist in me can't leave this alone."

Cassidy rubbed at the back of her neck. "Honestly? I was kinda hoping you'd say that."

Their toothy grin glowed under the hazy overhead lights. "Let me do my thing, and I'll ping you if I find something."

"If you find anything about a Dr. Thorne, that would be amazing. I keep hitting dead ends."

"No promises, but that is my specialty." They winked. "I'll do my best."

"Sounds good. Thanks, Sam."

"That's an awful situation to be in, I'm sorry. I promise I'll help you if I can. But I hope you don't regret coming here."

"Nah, I don't."

"Good. We all like having you around."

"Everyone has been great, and I'm really glad to have met you."

Sam smiled, and they lapsed into a silence so different from when they had met. It was companionable, and it was exactly what Cassidy needed. They went back to the darkroom one final time, so Cassidy could take down her developed prints.

"Let's do this again sometime."

"I appreciate you helping me and being so understanding. Seriously, Sam, you're the best."

"Anytime. Enjoy those."

"Say bye to Alex for me?"

"You got it."

She returned through the little gate, with no sign of Ranger this time. Cassidy took her time heading back to the ranch. She wanted a snack for the rest of her walk back, and she looked to stop in somewhere for something small. As she should have expected, most of the stores in town closed by nine. That only left the saloon, and Cassidy had no desire to risk running into Dean again on her own. She didn't think their interaction after the fire meant he'd suddenly be civil with her. She'd already walked past half the buildings she wouldn't normally pass, so she decided to cut down an alley to save time.

About halfway down, she started to hear the faint sound of footsteps, but thought nothing of it. But as she continued on, the footsteps got louder, much quicker than they should have. Pinpricks sparked along the back of her neck, and she started walking faster. She was being ridiculous, but she couldn't shake the sensation of being watched. The unease in her stomach grew until it was too much to ignore. She stopped suddenly and turned around, facing a man about four feet away from her. He was dressed in all white, with a wide-brimmed hat and a dark beard covering the bottom half of his face. His neck shimmered with the traces of a gold implant that continued down the collar of his button-up shirt.

A step forward from him, and a step backwards from her, on and on, but she was running out of room. The alley didn't run through like she'd hoped, but was closed off behind the neighboring storefronts, littered with wastebaskets and old cardboard boxes. She glanced behind herself to see how much room she had left, and when she turned forward again, he was in front of her, much too close for comfort.

She steeled herself to speak, but was hit with a sudden and strong shock along the base of her skull. It spread across her temples and down her neck. The sensation was so sudden that it knocked her to her knees. Only the heel of her hand stopped her from falling over completely. Her vision flickered around the edges before it went out.

She came to lying on the ground, the cold and wet of the pavement seeping into her clothes. As she propped herself up, the sharp twinges of her headache pulsed. She looked back to find she was alone again. She scanned the ground with her ocular implants, but the only set of footprints traceable were her own. Her limbs were both too light and too heavy. How much time had passed? She'd left Sam's at about ten, and it was barely past eleven. She must not have been out for more than a few minutes.

She slowly stood up by bracing her hand against the wall for support. The tips of her fingers ached, cold against the brick, and her implants tingled like the remnants of a static shock. The walk home would be anything but fun in this state.

Cassidy couldn't understand why he'd left her there when she was at her most vulnerable. Whatever he'd wanted, he'd had the privacy and the opportunity with her passing out. She frantically patted herself down and found she still had all of her belongings. Why, then, was he following her, threatening her? Had he done something to her implants, or were they acting up as a symptom of her illness? The questions all surged through her mind until they melded into one confusing tangle of fear.

By the time she made it back to her room, she was covered in a layer of cool sweat that wracked her body in shivers. She ripped off all of her dirty clothes and wrapped herself in her bed blankets just to stop shaking. Once the initial shock and adrenaline wore off, she realized how scared she was. She hated the tendrils of fear that snaked through her veins. All the tech and implants in the world couldn't save someone from being human, from being mortal. What a false hope it all was.

CHAPTER 11

CASSIDY FELT LIKE SHIT for the next week. She tried to rationalize otherwise, but she was getting worse at a pace more rapid than she had before. As much as she'd grown to like and respect Willa, they were already too close. Living and working together, spending their meals together as of late... She had to keep some distance before things crossed a line. But she needed help, fast.

There were only two people she trusted to help her and who would keep this to themselves. She pinged Finn and Sam separately, asking them to meet the next day. In her desperation, she hadn't thought much of it, but she cringed at how late it was, hoping she hadn't disturbed them. She crawled into her bed, thankful that she was at least exhausted enough to drift to sleep and be numb to her problems for a little while.

She asked to meet with Finn first, since she hadn't seen him since the fire two weeks ago and was long overdue to return his sweater. They met up at the little coffee house, the wastelands' version of a café. It was charming, small and built out of the owner's home. They didn't offer all of the fancy lattes she was used to ordering in Chicago, but they had rich coffee, which was all Cassidy really needed. Despite it being late November, they sat outside and enjoyed the sunny morning. Finn sat across from her, wearing the sweater she had laundered and returned, saying he was too lazy to stop home and drop it off. He sipped on Earl Grey tea.

Cassidy was always fascinated to learn about how people were at different times of the day. Like how Finn loved mixed drinks, was terrible at card games, and was the definite storyteller of the group. But what she was pleased to learn was how he liked his tea, how many times he rubbed the nonexistent sleep from his eyes as they talked, and how he was much more of a morning person than she was.

"It's mostly because of my work," he explained. "Construction always starts early."

"Is there a lot of construction to be done in a town as small as this?"

Finn's smile turned downwards. "Take the fire. Whether it's weather or bandits, there's always something needing work around here."

"Do you like the work?"

He beamed, his smile so disarming that Cassidy was smitten, and she didn't even swing that way. "It's what I've always wanted to do. Work with my hands. Create something out of nothing—things that help people."

"You're sure helping Annabelle."

Deep red dusted across his cheeks. "She deserves it."

"Oh my gosh! You like her!"

Finn stiffened, teacup halfway to his mouth. "What? Why do you say that?"

"You're so easy to read, Finn. Come on."

"I don't. It's nothing."

Cassidy's features softened. "Hey, I'm not trying to tease you. I'm sorry if I made you uncomfortable."

Finn sighed. "No, it's fine. And you're right. But it doesn't matter."

"Why not?"

"You've seen her. She's the nicest and most beautiful person I've ever met, and we've grown up together our whole lives. If something were meant to happen between us, it would have already."

"You don't know that. And you're a catch, Finn." He laughed as she continued, "Have you ever put yourself out there? Told her how you feel?"

He sighed again. "Of course not. I see her all the time. It would be so awkward if she turned me down."

"So, you'd rather pine after her from a distance for the rest of your life?"

"I don't know what I'd rather. And enough about me. You wanted to meet up to talk about something, right? It seemed kind of important."

Cassidy crossed her arms over herself. "Let's wait for Sam." She checked her chip for the time. "They should be here soon."

Finn stared at her uneasily. "Alright."

Cassidy steered clear of bringing Annabelle up again, but the back of her mind was already working. If there was one thing she loved, it was matchmaking, and she was talented at it too. She'd have to find a way to finally get them together.

Finn was telling Cassidy about a new video game he thought she'd like, and she was nodding along, enjoying his enthusiasm. Video games had never been her thing, but she enjoyed the way Finn talked about his interests—wild gestures, and expressive brows. She let her eyes wander a bit until they stuck on a man a few tables behind Finn, visible over his shoulder.

It was the man from the alley; she was sure of it. The hat was unmistakable, yet she still hadn't seen much of his face. She warred with herself over whether to confront him or not. What would happen to Willa if word got out about what happened, what she'd done? Cassidy's feelings about the woman were all mixed up, but she didn't want anything bad to happen to her.

Cassidy focused her oculars to scan him for an IP—a means of identification—but got no results. She tried two more times and fought down the rising bile in her throat at the thought that her implants were malfunctioning too. That, or he had an encrypted IP that was untraceable, something she didn't want to consider. To have that done made him either incredibly important or incredibly dangerous.

Finn noticed the way her attention drifted. "Cassidy?" He glanced behind his shoulder aimlessly. "Is something wrong?"

"Sorry. I thought I recognized that person behind you."

Finn did a double take and laughed. "Well, it's a small

town. That's bound to happen."

Cassidy faked her own laugh, but when her gaze drifted back to the spot behind Finn's shoulder, she found that it was empty.

Sam met them outside about twenty minutes later, when their drinks were down to the dregs and Cassidy was in tears over Finn's story about a ridiculous work accident they'd had the other day. Sam's dark clothes contrasted with the cool tones of their skin so sharply that they looked like they'd escaped from an old black-and-white movie.

Cassidy saw them coming first. "Morning," she greeted them, and Finn turned around in his chair to face Sam.

"I'm surprised we got you up so early."

Sam sat in the vacant chair between them. "Well, you know me. Couldn't resist a bit of intrigue."

"Thanks for coming, Sam. Any news?"

"I wish I could say yes, but not quite." Cassidy couldn't stop the frown that pulled on her mouth, and they continued, "Well, it's not a total lost cause. I have a lot more to do before we give up."

Finn crossed his arms, leaning back in his chair. "Does anyone want to fill me in?"

"Right. Sorry." Cassidy gave him an abridged version. If anyone could help her, Sam could. But Finn was smart and resourceful, and they might need a fresh pair of eyes.

"God, Cass, I had no idea. Whatever you need, I'm there."

Her smile was weak, but genuine. "I appreciate both of your help."

"Of course," Finn replied, "that's what friends are for."

Something in that rang true, and she wished she could

believe it. But once she got what she wanted, she'd be on her way. She didn't have the heart to tell them that, though.

Sam leaned over and rested a hand on her shoulder. "We'll figure it out, okay? So, don't worry about it in the meantime."

"So, how does this investigating thing work? Can we do it over lunch?"

Cassidy laughed. "We just had breakfast."

Finn shrugged, nonplussed.

"Well, want to come by the ranch?"

"You cooking?"

"Usually do."

"Alright, I'm in." Finn, not hard to convince, stood up.

Cassidy hung back. "Sam?"

They stood for a moment, head hung in thought. "Alright. But, uh, why don't you ping Willa first?"

"Yeah, good idea. We don't have guests that often; she may want to tidy up a bit."

On the way, she contacted Willa and asked to have guests for lunch. It was odd, having to ask permission, but even though she lived and worked there, it wasn't her space—not really.

CHAPTER 12

As they approached the gate, Cassidy stopped them. "So, uh, one quick thing... I don't want you to lie or anything, but let's keep this whole thing vague, okay? Willa doesn't know anything about it."

Sam and Finn glanced at each other. "Sure." Finn smiled. "If that's what you want."

Cassidy opened the gate for the two of them and let them pass. "Have either of you been here before?"

"Just once." Sam pushed their hands into their pockets, expression clouded.

"Well, I haven't." Finn continued with a wide smile, "How about a tour?"

"My pleasure." Cassidy wondered if he was intentionally good at maintaining the mood, or just had coincidental timing.

She led them through the property, showing off the crops and greenhouse. They spent the most time at the barn and stables; everyone was always more interested in the animals. Funnily enough, Tom was the biggest hit, despite cats being the most common animal they had by far. But she couldn't deny his charm as he wove around their legs and meowed in short, croaky beeps. He was her favorite too.

Finn was occupied with the horses when Sam pulled her aside. "Can we talk?"

"Of course. Something bothering you?" The answer would be yes, she was certain, but she hadn't figured out why yet.

"You know how I told you sometimes work gets awkward?" Cassidy nodded, and they continued. "Well, something happened a while back with me and Willa."

"About the ranch?" They nodded, then Cassidy's eyes widened. "Oh, with her husband?"

"He was so involved in the community, I couldn't ignore his passing. But Willa is so private."

"So I've noticed. But you wrote about it?"

"My job is to represent and report on the town. If I make it personal, then it's not journalism anymore."

"But he can't have been the first to ... pass like that. Why would that make her upset?"

Sam cocked their head. "How much did Willa tell you?"

"That it was bandits, and it was sudden."

Sam stuffed their hands in their pockets. "There's more to it than that, but I don't think you should hear it from me."

Cassidy couldn't help the curiosity that hummed through her veins. "So, she got mad about whatever you found out?"

"We were friends, and there was a level of trust there that

I broke. I've always been very committed to my work, but sometimes I focus too much on the bigger picture. By telling the story the way I thought was best, I ended up hurting her."

"Is that why you don't want to see her? You feel guilty?"

Sam glanced at her. "You know, if you ever get sick of the ranch, I could use you at the paper. You're more perceptive than you let on." Cassidy chuckled as they continued, "You'd be right though. I haven't seen her since. She denied my pings in the weeks after, so we didn't even have a chance to talk. I don't know if she'd listen now... I don't deserve it."

Cassidy put a hand on their arm. "I'm sure she forgives you, if there's even anything to forgive."

Sam smiled thinly. "I guess we'll see."

They hadn't come across Willa, despite having traipsed across the entire property, so Cassidy figured she was in the house, doing some last-minute tidying. She took them around to the porch, so they could take off their shoes, and she slid inside to get a read on Willa before they both joined her.

"Willa?" She followed the sounds she heard distantly and found Willa in the living room. The space, already tidy, was now immaculate. She had laid out several blankets and pillows, leaving the couch barely visible underneath. "I wanted it to be a casual thing. I didn't mean to stress you out. I can take them somewhere else..."

Willa faced away, but turned to Cassidy with a smile. Her hair was up in a messy bun, small baby hairs and loose pieces caught in the surrounding light from the midday sun. "No, it's fine, I just haven't had company in a while. Well, you know, besides you. That's different. I wanted to make sure everything looks nice and..."

Cassidy smiled, amused by her excited rambling. This was a side of Willa Cassidy hadn't seen before.

She returned outside, where Sam and Finn were chatting softly. "Come on in." She led them to the living room, where Willa was waiting in the armchair. She shot up when they entered.

"Oh, my goodness! It's been so long." She went to hug Finn. "It's so good to see you both."

Finn returned her embrace. "It feels like it's been ages. You look great."

She beamed at him and stepped around to face Sam.

They stood back a bit, lingering in the doorframe. "Hey, Willa."

She didn't move to hug them, but didn't seem unhappy to see them either.

"Hey, Finn," Cassidy jumped in, "how are your chopping skills?"

"I'm pretty proud of them. Need help?"

Cassidy shuttled him into the next room, hoping Finn would get the idea. She started taking out pans, chopping boards, and utensils while Finn leaned against the counter. He ran his fingers through the holo-calendar, watching it shift around his movements. "What's on the menu?"

"I was thinking beef stew?"

"Sounds good to me."

Cassidy handed him a knife and instructed him to dice all of the vegetables while she started adding the meat and broth to the pot. She'd had an overreliance on tech cookware in Chicago. Learning to cook the old-fashioned way with Willa's equipment had expanded her cooking skills immensely.

She and Finn found an easy rhythm together, working at the same speed and weaving around the other when they needed to move about the kitchen. Willa and Sam still hadn't joined them, and Cassidy couldn't decide if that was a good or bad sign. But she didn't hear any shouting, so she assumed they'd be able to mind themselves while lunch got made.

Finn dumped in the rest of the prepped ingredients, and they took their time setting the table, folding the napkins into ridiculous shapes and stacking silverware into a giant pile. She couldn't help but ask, "Do you know the deal with those two?"

"Only what I've guessed. Sam seemed upset, but I thought they were being empathetic. Are you saying something happened?"

"I don't know if it's for me to say ... and Sam didn't give me the full story."

"I get that." Finn was disassembling their fork tower so he could put them at each table setting. "But it's so rude of you to lead me on. Now I'm curious."

Cassidy laughed. "Well, if today goes okay, maybe Sam will feel more comfortable talking about it. How long do you think we should give them?"

"When is lunch ready?"

Cassidy glanced over at the timer; fifteen more minutes. "Not much longer. But we should let them sort it out before we all have to eat together."

Finn grimaced. "Good idea." They each fiddled with the utensils sitting in front of them.

Cassidy couldn't help but feel the whole day had been about her thus far, and she wanted to hear more from Finn. "So, you grew up around here?"

A gentle smile floated across his face. "Yeah. My parents, my sisters, and me."

"Do they still live here?" Cassidy hadn't met them if they did.

Finn glanced out the window. "No. My dad passed away in the war. Then my mom and baby sister moved to Tennessee. I have a lot of cousins over there."

"Oh. You ever visit?"

He laughed dryly, "Not as much as I should. They moved because they couldn't stand to be here without my dad. It's kind of the opposite for me, I guess? I hate seeing them in some new place. It makes everything so real."

"I get that." When Cassidy's grandmother died, she had moved away before she could really afford to. "You have another sister?"

"Yeah. My older sister, Cynthia, is a big-shot lawyer in Boston. She does Net crime stuff."

"Very cool. You keep in touch?"

"As much as we can. Surprisingly, she's anti-tech. One of the few things we have in common."

Cassidy gave him a once-over. Apart from his chip, he was all organic, like everyone else in town. She had somehow become the minority here with all of her tech.

He broke her train of thought. "You have any siblings?"

Cassidy honestly wasn't sure. "Uh, no. No family at all." Her grandmother had been her only real family, anyway. She might have half-siblings out there from her mom—wherever she was—but no family who mattered to her. She certainly hadn't mattered enough for them to ever find her or make contact.

"Well, you've got all of us. That counts for something, right?"

"It does." She felt warm and tingly at the notion. Even if she could only have them for a short while, she was grateful for their newfound friendship all the same.

By then, their lunch had been ready for about ten minutes; it was getting ridiculous to keep waiting.

"Be right back."

Finn nodded, staying put as Cassidy got up. She peeked her head around the corner into the living room and found the two of them huddled together. Sam was at the edge of the couch, and Willa was in the armchair, the rug bunched up from when she scooted closer to them.

"Hey, you two, ready to eat?"

Sam was laughing about something and turned to the sound of her voice. "Sorry to leave it all to you, we were catching up."

"Please, Finn and I had it covered." Cassidy lingered in the living room as everyone else filed in around the kitchen table. The sound of scraping chair legs and dishes clattering drifted towards her.

As she went to join them, she had the strongest sense of vertigo, and her vision whited out. She tried to steady herself, but it was like she was back on the hypertrain, rocking despite the ground being steady beneath her. She crouched over, fighting back the groan that was pushing to escape her lips as a bout of nausea took hold.

"Cassidy? Are you coming?" came from Willa.

"Yeah. Coming." Her words sounded strangled to her ears, but hopefully no one else could tell the difference. When she righted herself, she was overheated, and a thin layer of sweat coated her forehead. She wiped at it before entering the kitchen. Only Sam was facing the door and saw her as she walked in, her face white. Their eyes widened in alarm. Cassidy shook her head a fraction and moved to sit down.

"This looks great," they supplied, as a way of justifying their reaction.

"Yeah." Willa was already serving out heaping portions to everyone. "Thanks for making everything."

Cassidy shrugged. "It was nothing, just some chopping."

As they chatted about their lives, work, and the town, Cassidy did her best to stay alert and chime in when it was appropriate. But despite her efforts to stay present in the conversation, she kept drifting back to her worries. Every little twinge in her body felt like proof that she was declining even further.

When it was time to walk them out, she knew she had to impress on Sam how important it was that they find anything, any direction to go in.

Sam was already a step ahead of her. "Something happened right before lunch, didn't it?"

"I'm getting new symptoms. Worse ones."

Finn kicked a loose rock. "Shit."

Sam met her eyes, and she felt anchored by the determination in them. "We're gonna do whatever we can. Don't worry, okay? We'll figure out something soon."

"Please take care of yourself, Cassidy. If you get worse,

then ping me. I live a lot closer than Sam. I can get you to a physician, if that's what you want."

"Thank you. Both of you." She squeezed both of their arms. "I'm sorry to dump this on you."

"Please." Sam rolled their eyes. "Stop apologizing. That's what we're here for."

"I don't want to be a burden. You know I've got your back too, right? You both?"

"Duh. Now..." Finn wrapped an arm around Sam's slim shoulders. "I'm walking this one home. Say thanks again to Willa for me. It was nice to see her again."

"Same for me. And thank you for bringing us back together."

Cassidy was glad to have eased Sam's burdens a bit. It was the least she could do in return for what they were trying to do for her.

The rest of the week went by quickly enough, but Cassidy was plagued with a myriad of odd symptoms and ailments. Most would only last part of the day or a few days at most, but it was troubling. Sleeping became more difficult, as she would get random muscle spasms and shocks that would draw her back when she'd almost reached the precipice of sleep. Since she was sleeping less, she filled the time with walks around the area and practiced her photography. She and Sam hadn't done any more developing, but whenever they did again, she'd have a huge backlog to work through.

Amidst that, Finn messaged the group to meet up, since it had been so long. They chose to meet on a Saturday night at the saloon, per usual. Cassidy wondered if it'd be awkward, since they had been meeting without Mara. Her meddling with Dean still plucked at something in her temper.

When Saturday rolled around, Cassidy headed out to the field towards the saloon. The church had been coming along quickly. Finn was doing incredible work, but Cassidy mourned what it would never be again.

Before Cassidy could get to the bridge, though, she heard the distant sound of galloping. It wasn't uncommon to be on horseback around town, but there was no good reason to be going that fast. Hooves thundered against the ground as the sound grew closer and closer. Cassidy raced to the brush along the river for cover. She'd feel ridiculous if it turned out to be an ordinary townsperson, but after what happened in the alley, she was on higher alert.

Crouched down, her entire body felt like it was buzzing, like mornings when she drank too much caffeine. Her vision narrowed in at the edges, and panic took root in her chest. It was not the time to lose consciousness, but she had little say in the whims of her tumultuous body. She wavered, as if swaying with the breeze, before it all went dark. The last thing she saw was the tall, strong legs of an all-white horse slowing to a stop at the end of the bridge.

CHAPTER 13

CASSIDY CAME TO, THE lights of her consciousness returning dimly back to life. She was flat out on the grass, still
just as dry as the summer's day she'd arrived, and the day
she feared the whole area would be set ablaze. Among the
ever-changing weather, dangers, and opinions of California,
it seemed that damn grass was the only constant. Cicadas
buzzed around the clearing like a synthwave beat.

She tried to ease herself up, but felt a slight pressure at
the center of her chest. Panicked, she looked down to find
a pointed all-white boot resting on herself. Cassidy's eyes
snapped up to a face, obscured by a wide-brimmed hat. Only
the dark outline of a beard and a wolfish smile were visible,
even from her angle below him.

"Ah, you're back." He said it so fondly, as if she'd been on a
vacation—as if his foot weren't weighing her into submission

in the dry grass. "You're hard to get a hold of."

Cassidy gulped, unsure how to proceed. She had no interest in engaging in conversation with this man, but she had little choice. Her hip felt mockingly bare where a firearm should be. She no longer thought it an overreaction that everyone else in town always carried some kind of protection with them.

She tried her best to stall. "Where are your friends?"

His mouth turned down. "You know what happened to one. The other decided he wasn't cut out for this line of work."

"And he left?"

A harsh smile replaced his frown. "Something like that."

"I guess this is the part where you start monologuing at me?" She flexed her synth hand tightly.

"Cute." The block heel of his boot ground ever so slightly into her sternum. "You have something that doesn't belong to you. I've been hired to collect it."

"You must have the wrong person. I have an embarrassingly small collection of things. Nothing to warrant a..." She coughed from the weight of him on her airway. "... person like yourself."

He clucked his tongue in disappointment. "You're only making this harder for yourself, Cassidy."

A small tendril of fear snaked through her at the confirmation of her name. She'd had the irrational hope this was all some outlandish misunderstanding.

"So dramatic."

He sighed like a long-suffering parent. "You can cooperate, or I can take what I need."

"And what would that be?"

"Don't play coy. It's insulting to us both." He paused.

She used that moment to take her balled-up fist, full of genuine badlands dirt, and flung it up towards him. It wasn't a perfect plan. Rivers of it rained back down into her face, but enough made it up with the wind to have him spluttering, altering his center of balance. Not waiting for him to compose himself, she rolled to the left and bolted upright. Her head swam with the quick and choppy movements, but she was able to stumble farther into the clearing.

If she'd had a horse too, then things would be a lot simpler. As it stood, she could only hope he wasn't able to track her in time. She'd be overtaken too quickly. She careened through the brush, mindful of every sound she made. The only chance she had was getting back to the ranch. After their last attempt, she hoped he wouldn't dare try trespassing on Willa's land again.

Cassidy ran in such a convoluted pattern that she disoriented herself, only able to regain her bearings when she followed the brightest star north. Her muscles burned with the effort; everything she'd heard about adrenaline rang false. She hoped she'd keep enough stamina to get to the ranch before she collapsed. Her face stung, full of tiny little cuts she received from passing branches. She could have sworn the stomping of heavy boots came at her from all sides. Her heart raced as she was unable to differentiate which direction she was being chased from.

She came up to the ranch from a different angle than she was used to, fighting to get her bearings. She knew she wouldn't be safe until she was within the gated perimeter, and locked in her room for good measure. It was a small blessing that Willa was enough of a homebody in the evenings that she wasn't out to see her arrive in such a state. It was wrong, with all that she already kept from her, but she couldn't burden her with this. Not with how dangerous things had become.

Cassidy risked a glance back as she catapulted over the lower edge of the fence near the field of crops. Everything in the distance was dark and unmoving, putting her mind at ease. Thanks to her pursuer's bizarre commitment to his fashion sense, she'd be able to spot him from a healthy distance. But it seemed she'd shaken him after all. Once she was certain he wasn't coming after her, she bolted back to her room and leaned against the door as it slid closed in what felt like slow motion. With the whole ordeal over, every sensation that her brain had pushed away came flooding back to her in a rush.

Her limbs burned and cramped, joints especially hot to the touch. Her head pounded, and the skin on her face stung like she'd been raked along a bed of nails. Worst of all was the comedown from all the fear and anxiety, making her limbs shake and her heart beat in an uneven rhythm. She wasn't sure if she was going to pass out or throw up, but she wished she could unscramble the mess in her brain and think things out. Now that she knew what dangers she was facing, she had to come up with a plan. What right did she have to drag her new friends and such a battered town into her mess? It was clear the man in white wouldn't give up until he got what he was hired for.

Everything had gone to shit too fast. She didn't even have

a lead on where Dr. Thorne could be. She crawled into bed and threw the covers over herself as best she could. Her body shook, but whether from the sweat that had settled across her skin or the adrenaline crash, she wasn't certain.

She considered reaching for the emerald crystals still hidden in the pouch of her bag, but decided against it. As harrowing as the night had been, she didn't feel as though she'd reached her limit yet. It had taken her months to wean off her nightly use back in Chicago, and there was no telling how strong the effects would be without her previous tolerance. And in case the man was still lingering about, she needed to have a sharp mind. But she craved something to abate the gnawing fear growing inside of her, settling on an early night's sleep instead.

For the next few days, Cassidy's whole body ached like she had a nasty hangover, without any of the fun of actually earning one. Willa kept giving her concerned looks and asking if she was okay, which she tried to play down.

"Is there something you're not telling me?" Willa gave in one night at dinner.

"No," Cassidy lied. Willa fixed her with a hard stare, so she relented. "I don't know, honest. I made an appointment with the physician for Thursday."

Willa's shoulders relaxed, so Cassidy hoped that'd be the end of it. It was a small mercy that she'd let it go for the time being. If she asked more questions or figured out that

Cassidy was being followed, then things would get much worse.

Cassidy didn't want to visit a doctor when she knew what the answers—or lack thereof—would be. She'd been to so many Corporation doctors that when they couldn't come up with results, they labeled her as "drug-seeking" and banned the pharmacy from prescribing anything to her chip number. She'd been dealing with the agony for long enough and hoped her visit wouldn't raise any suspicions with the town doctor. They'd already had enough tension with their last meeting.

The waiting room was as empty as the first time she'd visited. She skimmed the net while she waited. The holo projecting from the chip in her palm made the surrounding skin bluish and sickly-looking. Net skimming was shallow, but more acceptable in public than a full dive. She was halfway through Sam's latest edition, browsing the missing persons posters after the most recent bandit attack, when the door across from her slid open.

"Cassidy?" a voice called from somewhere beyond it.

"Uh... Coming?" Cassidy assumed it was the physician from before, and no one else was there, so she crossed down the hall towards the voice. There were a few closed doors until she got to two rooms that were open at the back. The one on the left was bright and stark white, looking more clinical than the rest of the space by far. It had a few monitors and a med-bed along the wall. The room to her right was darker, lit by the various screens and equipment in the space, surrounding one piece of machinery. Cassidy had encountered plenty of Arachnae machines before. A surgeon would control the machine via a screen, and dozens of robotic arms could perform several surgical procedures at once with exact precision. She was surprised a town as small as this warranted one or had a doctor trained in the technology.

The doctor was waiting for her in the white room though, so she didn't linger. She hoped things wouldn't be awkward after the way their first interaction had gone.

"Cassidy?" she confirmed, tapping on a monitor to pull up the forms Cassidy had filled out when she made the appointment.

"Yes. Hi." Cassidy wasn't sure if she was supposed to sit on the med-bed or not, so she lingered in the doorway. It was unclear whether the physician remembered her from their interaction all those months ago.

"Please sit and scan your chip on the bed." The physician resolved her awkwardness, gesturing to the reader attached to the bed rail. Cassidy held her palm on it as she got comfortable. The med-bed was modern too, so it would be able to do most of the scans and analysis that she was used to getting in Chicago. It'd be able to detect anything going wrong in her body, whether synth or organic. At least, it *should* be able to.

"Tell me what happened," the physician, Dr. Sara, asked without looking up from her perusal. A wash of embarrassment crested over Cassidy as she realized she hadn't gotten her name before.

She relayed what happened to her and answered all of her questions about what she was doing before, and how she felt after, even though Cassidy had submitted all of this information before her appointment. However, she did play off all her running as exercise, rather than how she was running for her life. She didn't bother getting further into her medical history, since those records were withheld on Corporation servers. And she wanted to see what the doctor would make of her without any bias.

Cassidy tapped her fingers over the smooth apparatus of the scanner. She still hadn't been instructed to remove her palm. "You don't think my implants could be rejected, do you?"

"No." Dr. Sara's oculars glowed as she examined Cassidy's records. "Rejection of any margin occurs within two years. It's uncommon for them not to take after that period." She sighed. "You look healthy, and your optics don't reveal anything abnormal." She turned to face Cassidy. "You've made quite the life change. How are you taking to it? Are you stressed?"

"Are you saying I had a panic attack or something?"

"You tell me. Has anything been bothering you lately? Everything is physically sound, so the only other avenue to consider would be mental."

"No, I'm fine. Things have been going well."

The doctor, unconvinced, returned to the monitor. "I've scanned you the details for our local psychiatrist. Or you can find someone on the Net. But there's nothing medically wrong with you, so I'm afraid that's all I can do." She paused. "Coming to California could be classified as a mental health crisis, if you're designated as a danger to yourself or others."

Cassidy fought back the urge to laugh. Coming to California was the opposite of a suicide mission, but she understood what it looked like to someone else. She transferred the credits as she left. Even the consultation fee was ridiculous. She thought back to the days when she didn't have any tech, and how much less everything cost. The surcharge for synth was criminal. She was lucky to be off Corporation servers, so her previous medical debt hadn't followed her to California, or else the fees would be raised even higher for the "risk."

The doctor's assessment hadn't been reassuring, and Cassidy knew she wouldn't be able to see her again. It wasn't like she could have misinterpreted anything; the tech did most of the work anyway. So, her dismissal of her symptoms meant there was no second chance. Her meager hopes of finally getting results were dashed. At the rate she was declining, she'd hoped something would have shown up on the scans. Could it all be in her head after all? Cassidy had never been prone to anxiety or worry, but things could change. She knew that better than most.

CHAPTER 14

IT WAS SUPPOSED TO be a lazy Sunday for Cassidy. She only had to feed and clean up after the livestock, and she'd be done for the day. It'd take her to noon at the latest, so she had most of the day to herself. Normally, she'd waste the day surfing the Net and go out for drinks with whoever invited her. But in this small, sleepy town, she had to entertain herself, and California's Net was so small that she'd already dived through it front to back in the months she'd been there.

As she stepped out of her room, she caught Willa going around the corner.

"Oh, hey."

Willa popped her head back around, her usual French braid swinging around to rest over her shoulder. "Good morning. I was hoping to catch you, but I didn't want to rush you."

"Oh? What about?"

"Well, seeing as it's a Sunday, I thought once we're finished up with everything, we could take another hike." She added quickly, "That is, if you don't have any other plans."

"No, that sounds great! I was thinking I should take my camera out somewhere today."

"Perfect. You want to head out after lunch?"

"Sounds good to me."

After a light meal, Cassidy got a bag together with her camera, an extra battery, some water tablets, and an extra pair of socks. She grabbed her bag and met Willa out in front of the main house.

"So, where did you have in mind?" Cassidy asked as she fiddled with the strap of her bag, needing something to do with her hands. She enjoyed spending time with Willa, but she was used to larger group gatherings. She didn't have much experience interacting with people one-on-one.

Willa interrupted the anxieties tangling up her thoughts. "Well, I had a few ideas. If you want something easy, we can head to the poppy field east of here. Or, it's a bit more of a trek, but if we follow the river up the mountain, we can go to the waterfall there, which is pretty incredible."

"Let's do the waterfall."

Willa grinned. "I was hoping you'd pick that. It's about two-and-a-half hours each way, so I grabbed us some snacks."

They set off. Cassidy didn't bother taking out her camera at first; the crossing into the field was one she was already used to and didn't find exciting to photograph. But after they passed the schoolhouse and started up the base of the mountain, she powered it up.

Willa, who was in front, guiding them, glanced behind herself and laughed. "We're not even at the best part yet."

Cassidy snapped a quick photo before she lost her smile, then took another of the mountain's profile looming above her. "I know."

They went up with Willa pointing out native flowers and plants for Cassidy to take photos of and explaining their uses. Being a green thumb as well, Cassidy was shocked by how much information was new to her. She was impressed with Willa's vast knowledge of local plant life. She was explaining the medicinal uses of willow bark as Cassidy snapped a photo of the sun breaking through the spaces between the leaves.

She took another photo of Willa as she was deep into her spiel. The light bounced off the glossy twists and turns in her hair and dusted the russet peaks of her collarbones. She went to snap another, but wasn't as subtle as she thought.

"Hey, none of me." Willa didn't sound put off by it—embarrassed, maybe.

"Too late. Plus, you could use some. Don't think I didn't notice the lack of personal photos you have at home. It's like you kept all the stock photos in the frames."

"I don't want to hear judgment on my decorating from a person with only one pair of shoes."

"I thought you liked that I travel light."

Willa wrinkled her nose. "Not *that* light. It wouldn't kill you to have some variation."

"Coming from a person who has a dozen flannel shirts," Cassidy shot back, looking pointedly at the plaid shirt Willa was wearing and owned in every color imaginable.

"Don't bring my flannels into this."

She held her hands up. "Hey, you started it."

Willa laughed and bent down to pick a sprig of baby's breath that sprouted between the weeds. "Truce, please. If I have to bring up your taste in music, it's gonna get ugly."

Cassidy gasped as she tucked the flower behind her ear. Willa's gaze stuck to it as Cassidy replied, "There's nothing wrong with synth-pop. I've seen you tapping your feet when you think I'm not looking."

"I would never." She cracked a grin. "Come on, or we'll never get there before nightfall."

"Sure. You don't want to admit you like my music."

"Just about as much as I like your cheesy action movies."

"Yet you asked to watch a cheesy action movie on Wednesday."

Willa paused for long enough that Cassidy knew she'd won. "No comment."

They wove higher and higher, and when Cassidy was about to give in and ask how much farther, they turned a corner, and it was like the sound barrier broke. The rush of water met her ears, so loud that she was surprised she hadn't heard it sooner. She could hear the birds chirping and trees rustling before it all came into view.

The water was much clearer up here than it was by the time it washed down to town. It sparkled as it flowed down the mountainside until it met in a small pool below. There were more willow trees, as well as some fruiting trees Cassidy didn't recognize.

"What are these?" She pointed to the one nearest Willa.

"Oh!" She immediately started piling the greenish,

roundish fruits in her arms. "Quince. Terrible to eat as is, but they'll make fantastic jam or pie."

They each went about their own business for a little while. Cassidy experimented with lighting and angles as Willa gathered different fruits and plants. Now and then, she'd let out an excited little "Oh!" under her breath, and Cassidy would try to take a picture of her without getting caught. She'd have to stop before she creeped her out.

They ate crackers and cheese at the edge of the lake, their feet dangling in the water. When they were done, Willa began to unbutton her flannel.

"What are you doing?" Cassidy turned away as the tips of her ears heated. The zipper of Willa's jeans sounded too loud in the space between them. They fell to the ground like a slap across the face as Willa stepped out of them, leaving her in only her underwear.

"You didn't think we'd come up here to not get in the water?"

"I only brought an extra pair of socks," Cassidy replied dumbly.

"Well, then don't go swimming in all your clothes." Willa laughed.

Cassidy was aware of every muscle in her body, but as if they were not in her control. Her head moved on its own. Her eyes glanced up against her will. Slowly, she traced from Willa's bare feet and up her ankles to her calves, strong from her hard labor, across the backs of her knees, and to her thighs, where Cassidy's gaze got caught as Willa turned around with an amused expression. Cassidy was bright red by then, matching the soft nasturtium blooms Willa had gathered earlier.

"Well?"

"Huh?"

"You getting in?"

Cassidy cleared her throat. "I, um..."

"Come on. Don't make me swim all by myself."

Cassidy nodded, swallowing her trepidation. She didn't dare break eye contact with her for fear of where her eyes would land next.

"Right, okay. Crap," Cassidy whispered to herself. She wasn't even sure what pair of underwear she had thrown on that morning. She shucked off her overshirt, and by the time she pried the collar off her head, Willa was submerged in the water. The splash didn't even reach her ears. She stood so she could take off her pants. As she checked to make sure Willa wasn't looking her way, she stopped, entranced.

Willa unbraided her hair and ran her fingers through the tangles. The strands were sheeny and heavy. Cassidy had never seen it loose like that before. She swallowed thickly and made quick work of her pants, not bothering to fold them like Willa had. In only her tank top and her underwear—a newer pair, thank god—she dove in loud enough that Willa would know she'd joined her. She reemerged and brushed her hair back from her face.

Willa was smiling. "See? Isn't it nice?"

"Yeah, it is. Can't remember the last time I've been swimming."

"I used to come here a lot."

"Why'd you stop?"

Willa paused, water dripping from the gentle point of her

chin. "I don't know. Wish I hadn't. But now we can both enjoy this."

Cassidy couldn't stop staring at the way Willa's hair framed her face, the color her skin glowed under the sun. Had she always looked like this?

Willa must have felt the weight of her stare. "What?"

"Nothing."

"I'm surprised a city slicker like you knows how to swim." Willa splashed at her playfully.

Cassidy smiled as she dodged. "I learned when I was growing up, just don't care for it."

"Really? I could swim all day if I was able to. I love the feeling of being in the water."

Cassidy sighed dreamily. "It's probably the closest we'll get to what it feels like to be on the moon."

Willa twisted her face up. "See, that's not for me—the planets and all that. The one we've got is enough for me."

"Seriously? You don't even like the stars?"

"They're alright..." At Cassidy's expression, she amended, "Well, I guess maybe I haven't appreciated them properly."

"Our next outing will be stargazing, then."

Willa nodded, then did some laps around the oblong pool while Cassidy idled in the center. She didn't have the muscle strength or dexterity to manage anything else. She ran her hands back and forth through the water as the bubbles collected between her fingers. After about five laps or so, Willa popped up in front of her, wiping her face of excess water.

"You—"

"This—"

They both laughed, gesturing for the other to continue.

"This is cool. Great idea," Cassidy said.

"Thanks. Although if I had known you aren't much for swimming, I wouldn't have insisted."

Cassidy would let her think it was the swimming that made her so nervous. "Nah, it's fine. Feels nice after all that walking."

"Speaking of, you think we should head back?"

"Guess so, if you're ready?"

"Yep," Willa replied, popping the P at the end of the word. She passed Cassidy, bare arms brushing hers for a second as she headed for the bank. Cassidy had no choice but to head in the same direction as Willa rose out of the water. Her skin started to pebble from the cooling late afternoon air. Cassidy swam after her, slower than necessary, so she wouldn't crowd her.

Her vision traced the long lines of Willa's body as she bent down to retrieve her folded clothes. Their eyes met briefly as she straightened back up. Her brown eyes looked almost black, and there was something apprehensive about her expression. Cassidy figured she wanted privacy, so she veered left to get out on a large, flat stone that jutted out from the water. She'd left her clothes in a pile next to Willa's, so she'd have to busy herself with something until she was done. She figured she'd try to pull her hair off her neck, wringing it out and trying to tie it into a bun. Her hair was the longest it had ever been, still only barely past her collarbones, but she found it unruly all the same. After she wrapped it around itself for the third time, Willa cleared her throat from behind her.

"Need some help?"

Cassidy sighed, "Sure. Please."

Willa settled in behind her and began untangling the mess Cassidy had made. The ends of her hair brushed the tops of her shoulders and the skin above her tank top as Willa worked. She was acutely aware of how little she was wearing, and what she did have on stuck to her tighter than any clothing she usually wore. Willa, on the other hand, was entirely dressed, making it such a stark difference.

Willa began pulling sections of her hair together, and Cassidy closed her eyes as it sent tingles across her scalp. No one had ever done her hair before, and she hadn't expected it to feel so good. Willa hummed as she worked, the tune familiar to Cassidy, but she was unable to place it.

And all of a sudden, Willa was done, and Cassidy was warm and buzzing all over. She wished she had taken a little bit longer.

Cassidy cleared her throat. "Thanks."

"Of course."

"What were you humming?"

"Hmm... Can't remember." Willa's voice was light and teasing.

"It sounded familiar."

"Did it?"

"Like that new Zee Melody song you said is trashy."

"Couldn't be."

Cassidy turned her neck to look back at Willa, who was still crouched right behind her. "Whatever you say. How's it look?"

"Looks alright." Willa smiled as her eyes roved all over

Cassidy's face.

"If I get home and see you made me look like a moron, I'm putting in my two weeks."

Willa rolled her eyes. "It looks nice, I promise. So dramatic. Here." She passed over a bundle of fabric. "I brought your clothes too."

"Oh, thanks."

Willa nodded in response and walked back to their bags. Hers looked ready to burst from what she'd gathered. "Hey, can I put some of this stuff in your pack?"

"Sure. Just put my camera on top." Cassidy struggled to get her clothes back on, since they were sticky and stiff against her still-damp skin. She straightened up to see Willa clicking through her camera. "Any you like?"

"They're all great. I didn't realize you were taking half of these though." A deep blush spread across her nose and forehead.

"I can delete them if you want. I don't get to practice on human subjects much. I hope that's okay."

"Well, if it's to help you practice..." She lingered on one frame, then gingerly set the camera back down where Cassidy requested. "Ready?"

"Just about. Your bag's not too heavy, is it?"

"No, I'm fine." Willa slung it over her shoulders and turned around slowly, hobbling her way back to the path they came in on.

Cassidy burst out laughing. "Did you leave anything for the animals?"

"Very funny."

"You sure you can get down okay with all that?"

Willa turned around and winked. "I'm tougher than I look."

Cassidy knew that was true.

CHAPTER 15

CASSIDY WAS GROWING TOO close to Willa. The fondness she had for the other woman had snuck up on her. Maybe, if she cured herself and fixed her baggage, she'd be able to pursue a friendship—or wherever they were headed. But it wasn't fair for either of them to grow close when Cassidy's life was still too turbulent. After the waterfall, her stomach was always in knots around Willa. She needed some distance to regain her footing.

She pinged Finn and Sam to have another card game night. She wanted a drink and her friends' laughter to keep her mind off Willa. They decided to meet at Sam's instead, and included Alex to even out their group. It was a win for Cassidy—no Mara, no Dean, no nosy townspeople to sneer at her tech. The long walk there couldn't be put off, and she needed to stop by the grocer to pick up a gift to be polite. She left as the sun streaked orange and purple across a murky sky.

Something in the air didn't feel right; it was just off. A too-sweet aroma enveloped her as she made her way to town.

A vulture circled along her path like a vengeful cloud, until it swooped down in the distance and met land. Cassidy's steps built the sick anticipation in her gut as she neared where it had landed in the distance. Buried among the pale grasses, the vulture was crouched down towards something enshrouded in the field. Carrion was streaked on its maw as it drew its head up to glance at her. Dark, emotionless eyes met hers before it continued its meal.

Cassidy moved as close as she dared and peered down at the bird. Her stomach immediately dropped, and she fought to keep her lunch down. A small rabbit, maybe a baby, lay torn open in the field, dissected by the bird's vicious beak. Despite the gruesome way it looked on the earth, its eyes were peaceful, its face relaxed, as if it had only been resting. Cassidy lurched away to let the bird finish its meal.

Her breaths came quicker and her vision swam as she righted herself. When the sweetness of decay hit her nose, she lost the battle with her nerves and heaved into the bushes beside her. Her throat burned and her gut cramped as she wiped at her mouth with the back of her hand. She walked the short distance to the active part of the stream to wash, hoping the water wasn't too polluted.

Death had never gripped her so strongly before, taking a hold of her senses like that. Even the death of the bandit hadn't shaken her as bad. The late afternoon was comfortable, but she shivered anyway, unable to stop her mind from flashing back to the rabbit. The death at Willa's hands had been clean, quick, and out of sight. Something about being a spectator to the reality of it all made her uneasy.

She took a deep breath to straighten up and get a hold of herself. If she continued spiraling, she'd be late, and Sam or Finn was bound to ask after her. She couldn't handle explaining her reaction to this. She'd been flirting with death for the better part of six years; she was supposed to be used to it. Cassidy wished she didn't have to walk the rest of the way alone, longing for someone to lead her mind away from her train of thought.

Once she arrived outside of Sam and Alex's house, she rolled her shoulders back and put on a dazzling smile. To her, it was harsh and brittle, but it would pass any outside scrutiny. She was the last to arrive. The living room was bathed in moody lights that drew the eye into the center of the space, where a large folding table was set up. Sam leaned over beside the empty chair to shuffle the decks while Alex bussed trays of snacks and drinks between there and the kitchen island, where the food sat prepared. Finn was playing with Ranger in the backyard. Cassidy could only hear his bright laughter and the dog's excited barking as they raced back and forth. She smiled to herself. It seemed Ranger finally found someone who was a match for his own energy.

Sam looked up at Cassidy's arrival. "Ah, welcome!"

Alex came from the kitchen and pulled her in for a hug. It was then she realized that she'd never made it to the grocer to pick something up for them. She fought the shame that burned in her gut and hoped that it didn't show on her face as Alex released her.

"Hey, this looks pretty official for being thrown together at the last minute."

Sam laughed. "Alex has been waiting for the chance to host something like this. We've had this stuff in storage for years." Alex laughed along, not minding the teasing.

Finn hadn't heard her arrival, so Cassidy went out back to say hello and bring him in for their first round. The grass stretching across the backyard was a beautiful green in comparison to the dry field around the church. Just the thought of that tan shade of grass drew Cassidy's mind back to earlier events, churning her stomach. Finn had just thrown a ball across the clearing for Ranger to chase after, and he turned towards Cassidy with his arm still in the air. "There she is." He smiled. "Ready to get started?" He gave her a hug around her side and crouched down as Ranger returned with the ball. "Alright, boy, that's enough for now."

The three of them padded back towards the house, Ranger trotting behind them with his tongue hanging out of his open mouth. Finn dropped the slimy ball in a basket near the step leading to the door. "You're quiet. Everything alright?"

Cassidy shook her head before smiling. "Yeah, long day. Sorry."

Finn patted her on the shoulder and continued into the house, accepting her lie because he was a good person. Every time Cassidy told an outright lie or a half-truth to one of her friends, her heart shrunk a little. But that was the rot that seeped into all of her relationships eventually, something she planted and harvested. She didn't know any other way.

Back in the house, everyone waited around the table, already sorting out cards and setting up their betting chips. Cassidy sunk into the chair between Finn and Alex, waiting for Sam to deal all of their cards. As surrounded as she was, her mind eased the vise grip it had on her, and she relaxed into her seat. They set up for poker, Cassidy's favorite. The first round was a warm-up, everyone focused more on their cards than on the company.

Finn tugged on his left ear again, and Cassidy knew she had to put him out of his misery. "Finn..." She laughed. "You've gotta sit still. Otherwise, we'll know you have a bad hand."

He looked over at her with a wide-mouthed expression. "Are you serious? I thought you were joking before! I have an actual tell?"

"Well, yeah," Alex answered sheepishly, "even I picked up on that."

"No way! I bet Sam told you, didn't they?"

"We do tell each other everything," Sam cut in, "but I'm afraid your poker face hasn't come up yet."

Cassidy patted Finn's shoulder. "Hey, you can work on it. Can't help you with the bad cards, though."

Finn grimaced and folded, dramatically keeping his hands flat on the table. "This whole time..." he whispered, more to himself. "I can't believe all the credits I've lost."

Cassidy couldn't believe no one had ever told him before. Poor thing. She tried to keep him from dwelling, and she folded as well, so they could move on to the next hand. "So, Finn. Sam tells me you're the reason these two are together."

"I don't know if I can take that much credit, but I will."

The whole table laughed, and the fond look between Sam

and Alex didn't escape Cassidy's notice. Their quiet intimacy had always stuck with Cassidy, in the way they innately seemed to understand each other. She thought about the little habits she and Willa had started to draw from each other. Before coming to California, Cassidy had never been a fan of reading—hadn't picked up a holo-book ever since her grandmother would read to her at night—but she found herself reading the books Willa left for her, and she'd started buying her own in town so she'd have something to swap with her.

What used to be so foreign—the comfortable touches and knowing glances—now seemed in the realm of possibility. But whether it was friendship or something more, Cassidy wasn't certain. She also wasn't certain she could afford either—definitely not the latter. But a small, selfish part of her wished that such connection was possible for her, even for a short while. She tried to picture love like that when she was healed and well, but only saw deep amber skin and onyx hair braided with pretty beads. She only saw a person who talked to their plants and knitted as much as her grandma had.

The familiarity should scare her, snap her out of the lull California had put her in. She was getting distracted from the reason she had come out here in the first place. But after the cyclone of emotions she'd experienced throughout the night, she was tired of fighting it. She'd go back to building up her walls in the morning, but she just couldn't do it yet.

Before she knew it, she was heading home with an armful of leftovers and a medley of thoughts that were more confusing than comforting. Her mind was elsewhere as she broke into the edge of town, surrounded again by the humble rows of shops and apartments.

She saw movement out of the corner of her eye as she walked along the dirt path, and she tensed. It was still early enough for folks to be out and about, but the presence behind her felt pointed, trained on her. Her muscles coiled like a spring just before release, and she glanced at her periphery again. A bit of tension seeped from her body at the realization that they weren't wearing any white. She wanted to laugh at the way her paranoia warped her perception of even the most mundane thing. But still, she was being followed, and it was no less unwelcome. Abruptly, she turned left, past a flower shop brimming with bouquets and seed stands. The road was narrower, and most shops were beginning to close for the day. If she was still being followed, then she'd know it was intentional.

The footsteps continued steadily behind her, and she warred with the choice of turning to confront them, or picking up her pace until she made it back to the ranch. She was cursing herself for choosing to turn down a less populated path. It was clear that her recent experiences with danger had not sharpened her survival instincts in the slightest. Cassidy was too on edge to do the smart thing, so she stopped mid-step and turned to face the person behind her.

They were only a few paces behind, following the shadows of the buildings lining the road. The shade could not hide the frown on Mara's face as she reached the distance where Cassidy had stopped walking. She looked paler than the last time Cassidy had seen her, her posture less confident as she stood in front of her with her hands in her pockets.

"Mara?" Cassidy cocked her head to the side. "Are you

following me?"

"Did you just come from Sam's?" The accusation was clear.

Cassidy sighed. "I don't see how that's any of your business."

"So, you did." Mara's face fell.

"What do you want, Mara?"

"I'm trying to apologize." The way it came out made it clear that wasn't something she was in the habit of doing.

"You already did. We're good."

Mara crossed her arms over her chest. "Are we though? You're clearly avoiding me."

Cassidy's neck heated at the confrontation. Mara was nothing if not direct. She also wasn't wrong.

"Look," Mara continued, "we clearly got off on the wrong foot. I'm sorry I offended you. I know we don't really know each other yet, but I get ... too involved sometimes. I never know when to quit." She sighed, blowing a short, dark strand of hair away from her face. "Sam and Finn are all I have. I feel like I'm losing them to you."

Cassidy's frown deepened. "That was never my intention."

"I know." Mara smiled sadly. "But that's what's happening."

Cassidy considered her next words. There was more going on than Mara was aware of, but she did have a point. "Okay, I was bothered by what happened at the saloon. But I should've let it go. I'm sorry we've been excluding you." She knew the ache of loneliness, and she had never intended to draw Mara away from her friends. She was surprised that was the case—that they had chosen her—but she knew it was right to mend it.

Mara pulled Cassidy into an unexpected hug, releasing her just as quickly. "Thank you for understanding. I promise to tone it down."

"It's fine." Cassidy laughed. "I'll get used to it, I'm sure."

They stepped apart. "Sorry if I freaked you out. I saw you coming from their direction, and I got so angry. But now that I'm calmer, I realize I was being a stalker, huh?"

Cassidy waved her hand. "Only a bit. I need to get back, but we'll do something together soon, okay?"

Mara smiled. "Okay. Thanks, Cassidy." She headed back the way they'd come, posture more relaxed.

Cassidy continued down the road to get back to her normal route. She hadn't wanted to get into things with Mara, but she'd been far more understanding than Cassidy would have given her credit for. She didn't want to drive a wedge through their friend group, especially when she wouldn't be around for too long.

CHAPTER 16

WHEN SHE GOT HOME, she dropped the leftovers in the fridge as Willa was cleaning up. Willa had spent a good portion of the day working outside, giving her cheeks and the top of her nose a sun-kissed glow. Cassidy stared at the freckles daring to form until she realized Willa had been speaking to her.

"Huh?" Cassidy stuttered.

Willa suggested they go for a walk after dinner, and Cassidy wasn't able to keep the surprise off her face. Willa just shrugged. "It's been a while. I want to see if anything has changed."

Cassidy threw on her boots and bandana before she could change her mind. They were heading towards another dust storm within the week; Cassidy only hoped she'd be a bit more prepared for it than she was for the last one. She'd never forget the grit of the dirt that was wedged between her teeth for weeks, even after rinsing out her mouth a dozen times.

They walked side by side, and she let Willa lead the way. She enjoyed hearing how the stores had changed, what trouble Willa had gotten into growing up, and how she'd pass the time on a free day. She knew Willa had grown up here, but until this point, it had been abstract, far removed. Now she could almost see a teenage Willa going to ring-and-ditch at an apartment and getting caught fleeing because she tripped on the stairs.

"Cassidy?" Annabelle came out of a little apartment a few doors behind them. Her chestnut hair was loose, and her brown eyes had the life back in them that had been missing the night of the fire.

"Annabelle, hi. How are you?"

Annabelle's smile was small, but genuine. "I'm okay. Living with Beth for now."

A flash of guilt crossed through Cassidy, as she had no idea who Beth was, when clearly after all this time, she should.

"That's great. I, uh, meant to check in. Time got away from me."

"That's kind of you. The thought is enough." She smiled wider, but it faltered a bit when she realized Cassidy was with company. "I'm so sorry, I didn't mean to interrupt." She straightened up and held out her hand. "I'm Annabelle. I... Willa?"

Willa shifted behind Cassidy, her posture inwards until she was addressed. "Hey, Annabelle. It's been a while, huh?"

"Oh my goodness! I hardly recognized you. Your hair is so long now! I feel so silly; of course it's you. It's so nice to see you!"

"You too. I was sorry to hear what happened."

"Thanks. Nothing to be sorry for. If I'm being honest, I'm tired of hearing it." Her eyes widened. "Oh, gosh, you must think I'm such a jerk. You of all people..."

"I get it, believe me. You must be looking forward to the renovations being finished?"

Annabelle's smile was eager, grateful to have been let off the hook. "Finn and the guys are doing a fantastic job! They'll be done in no time. It'll be better than before."

"That's certainly a positive way of looking at things," Cassidy cut in.

"I'd like to think so. Well, I don't want to keep you two. But it was such a fantastic surprise to see you, Willa. Please, don't be a stranger."

"Same to you, Annabelle. I'm glad you're alright."

"Thank you. Good night." She disappeared back into the door she'd come from—Beth's apartment, Cassidy assumed. She glanced sidelong at Willa, trying to gauge how she felt about that conversation. She was sure she hadn't been prepared to run into anyone. But at least the person she faced first knew what it was like to have their life turned into a giant pity party. And not that Cassidy would ever voice the thought out loud, but maybe having another tragedy for everyone to whisper about would take the spotlight off Willa a bit. She'd earned it, at least.

"What are you thinking?" Cassidy asked after they started to loop back past the church construction and towards home.

"I feel like kind of an idiot."

"What? Why?"

"I kept from going out because I didn't want to keep being reminded of things, but I think staying away kept me frozen in it. I've known most of these people my whole life, and I just..." She sighed. "Maybe this whole time, I was doing myself more harm than good."

"Healing is a messy process. You can't regret what's already happened."

"You say that like someone with firsthand experience."

Cassidy winced. "Who hasn't been touched by death at this point?"

Willa turned to Cassidy, chuckling. "You sound like a real Californian."

"Well, I'm sure starting to feel like one." They had stopped walking by then. The moon bounced off the surrounding trees and caught in Willa's hair. Wind gusted around them in a high-pitched whine, shaking the surrounding trees like a drumbeat. Cassidy slowly drew her bandana down to breathe in the evergreen air. The dust barely bothered her anymore. "I'm happy to be here, you know?"

"I know." The way Willa was looking at her, she felt like the most interesting person on the planet. Her gaze bounced from Cassidy's eyes to her lips and back around again. Was Willa even aware of where she was looking? Slowly, Willa pulled down her own face covering and tilted her head up the slight distance to Cassidy's, eyes glassy like she was in a trance.

Then, Willa surged forward, perhaps too quickly, pressing her lips to Cassidy's. Cassidy's entire body went still. Willa's lips were soft and unhurried as they explored, but Cassidy's hands rested at her sides. She longed to touch Willa, anywhere, but that would unleash something in her that she wouldn't be able to restrain.

Every soft brush of Willa's hands and lips was like a live wire sparking at her skin. She wondered if she'd ever really been kissed before this moment. She'd never felt such tenderness or care. Usually, kisses were brief, just a box to check off on the list of intimacy. But Willa kissed her like it was the main event, like it was all she ever wanted to do. Cassidy wished she was allowed to feel the same.

They took a breath of air, chests heaving and foreheads resting against each other. Cassidy hesitated to speak, afraid that in doing so, she would break the trance they were both in.

Willa was the one to give in. "You must think I'm a terrible person."

Cassidy pulled away to look Willa in the eyes. She tapped her chin. "Hey, no. Why would you say that?"

"You know my situation. It's all so complicated. Did we ruin everything?"

"No, not at all. Clear your head, then we can talk, okay? But I don't think anything bad about you. I never could." Cassidy tried not to sound too hopeful. She needed to clear her own thoughts and find a way to let her down gently.

Willa returned her gaze with a smile, eyes dipping to her lips that were surely swollen. Cassidy's face heated. She drew her bandana back across her face, glad to have something to cover how bright red she burned.

They walked the rest of the way home with a bit of distance between them. Cassidy's mind was churning with doubt. Had she somehow been leading Willa on? Would she be an idiot for turning down probably the last relationship she could expect to have in her life?

When they worked together the next day, it was like nothing had happened. She was glad they could get along despite last night's developments, but did that mean Willa was expecting a good outcome? Cassidy didn't know if she could turn her feelings off like that. Would she have to move away? Or even quit? She kept busy to quiet her mind, but the doubts crept in anyway.

She didn't have much experience romantically. There were past flings—too many to count—but they were tinged with desperation and alcohol or drugs. One of Cassidy's many stages in processing her illness was a sort of recklessness to beat it to the end first. She'd spent a solid year waking up in places she didn't recognize, with people who were strangers. Among the drinks and substances she'd consumed, she had been sure one of those nights would be her last. After a year of living like she was courting death, she gave up on trying. If she couldn't take herself out by living however she wanted, then her illness deserved the final punch.

But it felt nice to have been so *seen.* So cherished. She hadn't found that in Chicago—probably never would.

The following morning, she took her first two meals out on the ranch, so by the time dinner rolled around, her stomach was in a thousand knots. Willa hadn't asked to talk yet, but they would have to talk at dinner.

Willa, as it turned out, was practiced at steering a conversation. Every time Cassidy tried to bring something up, Willa was able to move the conversation forward first. Cassidy supposed Willa had always been a conversationalist, and it had never been to her detriment before.

"Willa, I..."

Willa smiled tightly. "Let's talk after dinner."

"Oh, yeah. Sure." Cassidy thought to rush through her meal, but Willa asked for an hour before they met up again.

Cassidy paced her room. Her nerves had not only bundled up her stomach, they made her head throb relentlessly. She took a double dose of vita pills and watched the time drip towards an hour as slow as molasses. She met Willa out on the porch when it was time.

The winds had already picked up from the night before, wiping both of their hair into a frenzy over their shoulders. Cassidy had no idea why Willa didn't invite her inside, but it sent her already tense nerves into a frenzy.

"I'm sorry to keep you waiting all day."

"It's alright." Cassidy hoped that came across as convincing. She swiped a hand across her brow to make sure it hadn't grown damp.

"I really wanted to think things through, be honest with myself."

"I appreciate that."

"I think you're so fantastic. I wish we'd met before all of this." She paused. "But I don't think it's fair to either of us to start something right now."

Cassidy sat back in silence. That was exactly what she wanted, wasn't it? The very conversation she'd set out to have. So, why did her heart feel like it had turned to ice?

"I'm kind of still in mourning, aren't I? Or at least, I should be. And I want to give you one hundred percent, but I don't think I can do that. Not to mention, I'm still your boss, and I pay you, and—"

"You're right, I get it." Cassidy cut her off perhaps too quickly, not needing Willa to go on further. "I appreciate your honesty, and I feel the same."

"Oh." Willa's face fell in a clear indication that she hadn't expected Cassidy to want to put a stop to things either. "Great. Then, friends?"

Cassidy smiled. It felt cracked and brittle around the edges. "Definitely."

They chatted for a little while longer, and Cassidy did her best not to check out. She itched to go back to the solitude of her room.

As soon as the door slid open, she let the disappointment and embarrassment wash over her. She cursed herself for making trouble. She wasn't meant to have a future; it shouldn't matter if Willa cared for her or not. But she still swallowed the lump of emotion in her throat that threatened to unravel her composure. She soaked in each new facet of hurt. This was her penance for trying to make something more than what she was able to have. She promised herself to remember this pain the next time she stepped over the lines she'd painstakingly drawn for herself.

CHAPTER 17

CASSIDY WAS ON EDGE all morning. She tried not to be, but her emotions from the previous night stuck to her worse than the dry California dirt. The swelling and stiffness of her joints added to her foul mood. She worked through breakfast, by accident, and because she didn't know how she'd face Willa in the light of day. Her mind hadn't had a chance to rest, and so she hadn't processed what was said.

She wished Sam would hurry up and find a clue. She wished her friends back in Chicago would answer her pings. More than anything, she wished her grandmother were still alive to offer her advice. When she'd died, Cassidy was barely sixteen, still too young and headstrong to appreciate all of her experience. What she wouldn't give to have her tell her what to do after everything.

As she went about the ranch, she was unable to stop

herself from looking for clues about Willa's past. She needed justification—that she hadn't been rejected for the sake of it. She sought out men's work shoes, old notes—any small sign that someone who should have been so saturated into the DNA of the place had been here. But it was as if Willa's husband, whose name Cassidy didn't know, had taken all signs of life with him when he died.

Deep down, Cassidy knew it wouldn't matter anyway. All of Willa's reasons for not wanting to get involved with Cassidy were as valid as her own. But she'd gone into their interaction expecting to *give* a rejection, not receive it. Her pride smarted more than she expected it to. The only positive to her day was it seemed the storm had abated for the time being. The winds slowed back to their usual crawl, and dust settled where it was kicked up instead of traveling along the breeze.

As the day dripped by, Cassidy knew she would either have to face Willa at lunch, or let them both starve. Willa worked across the property, so she decided to start early and minimize any time they'd be at the house together. She put together a salad and quesadillas, cooking like a line chef in the middle of a dinner rush. She ate her portion standing at the counter, and when Willa didn't show, she left her portion on the table with a napkin covering it. It seemed they were both the avoidant type.

Cassidy made a beeline back to the greenhouse and began transferring plants outgrowing their containers. As she worked, her shame built and built until it crested over her in a wave. She'd assured Willa that things would be fine. There was no reason for things not to be fine between them;

nothing had changed. She decided she'd wrap up Willa's meal and go find her out on the property. Damn her nerves and everything else, she couldn't be a coward about this.

She found Willa taking a break under a grand old oak tree. The day was scorching, and the lack of shade between buildings always amplified the drain of the heat. Cassidy held the plate in front of her like a white flag.

"Want some lunch?"

"Please."

Sitting down a respectable distance away, she passed the plate over to Willa, the familiarity between them all but forgotten. She let Willa eat, not sure how to start up a conversation without it being forced. She considered going back to work but figured it would be rude. But the silence between them sat awkward and heavy, making Cassidy's skin tight with the discomfort.

Willa must have sensed something, or felt as awkward as she did, as she cleared her throat and said, "This is good, thanks."

"Yeah. Of course."

Willa set down her plate, clean except for the slight ring of condensation from the warm quesadilla and the tomatoes she'd picked out of her salad. Cassidy was still learning which foods she did and didn't like. "You already ate?"

"A little while ago. Sorry, I thought you'd have been by the house."

"The heat's been making me slow. I kept telling myself I'd finish one last thing, and, well, here we are." She chuckled dryly. Cassidy suspected that wasn't all there was to it, but decided not to push her. It was a partial truth, at least.

She had never lived somewhere with the endless dry heat of California. When she stared out towards the horizon, the heat shimmered up from the ground.

"Thanks for bringing me lunch. And thanks for ... you know."

Cassidy cleared her throat. "Yeah."

"I know things may be weird for a while, so I appreciate you trying."

"I said I would."

"I know. Talk isn't worth much to me though. Not everyone backs it up with action."

Cassidy knew that all too well. Against her instinct not to, she ached to bridge the gap that formed between them.

Cassidy turned towards her. "Let's do something when you're feeling up to it. I promised to show you some stars."

"Okay, sure. Tomorrow? We can take some dinner?"

"Works for me."

Cassidy brushed up on her astronomy on the Net. She remembered most of what her grandmother had showed her growing up, but she wanted to be prepared. She thought back to the nights they'd climb up to the terrace and use a telescope to map out constellations. For a while after Cassidy's mother left, it was the only thing her grandmother could do to cheer her up. Now, whenever she looked up at the stars, she felt as if she were home again, that things were better—or easier, at least.

The following day, she made some fruit sandwiches and a few other sweet things to snack on. She headed around to the main house and knocked, so Willa would hear she'd arrived before she came in.

"All set?" she called out as she walked through the kitchen and towards the living room.

"One sec!" Willa shouted from the bedroom.

Cassidy perched herself on the arm of the couch. She had on an old blue T-shirt and jeans. The autumn air chilled in the evenings, but the whole week, Cassidy had been burning hot like she had a fever she couldn't shake. She hoped it'd pass soon.

Willa emerged from down the hall in a thick lilac sweater and a relaxed pair of dark-wash jeans. "You ready?"

"Yep."

Cassidy realized they weren't off to a great start, but she was hopeful things would turn around. Plus, just spending time together was progress, even if they barely talked the whole time.

Once they made it to the field, Cassidy looked for a place for them to sit. Not finding one, she plopped their stuff down in the middle of the flowers.

Willa winced. "I think California poppies are protected."

"What, by god or something?"

"No, I mean it's the state flower. You're not supposed to trample all over them."

Ouch. Cassidy should have considered it, with Willa of all people. "Shoot, sorry."

Willa shrugged and sat down gently next to her. "What's done is done."

Cassidy couldn't recover the moment, so she busied herself with unpacking the snacks she'd brought. "Hungry?"

"Maybe in a bit."

"Yeah, no problem." Cassidy took a sandwich for herself,

nibbling on one of the corners and wondering if she'd pushed for this too soon. Willa seemed to have an edge to her Cassidy hadn't seen before, and she didn't want to make things worse. But Willa had agreed to come with her, so maybe she wasn't being fair either.

"See any stars you like?"

"Hmm..." Willa craned her neck back. "They all kind of look the same."

Cassidy chuckled. "I get that." She pointed to a bigger and brighter star towards the left of them. "That one? That's Neptune."

"The planet?"

"Yeah, that's why it's brighter than the rest."

"Show me another."

And she did, peeking at Willa's amused expression out of the corner of her eye. As Cassidy pointed out constellations, Willa edged closer—so much so that with each gesture, their arms brushed, and tingles ran down Cassidy's spine. Neither of them tried to move away. She wished they could stay like this for hours.

"Wow, you do like this stuff."

Cassidy chuckled. "Did you think I was lying?"

"No, I'm impressed. I'd never be able to make sense of any of this."

"Yeah, it can be intimidating. There are thousands of stars, and somehow we're supposed to tell them apart."

Willa sighed. "Makes you feel kind of small, huh? All that is out there, and here we are, worried about trampling some flowers."

"Well, yeah, when you put it like that. But I'd like to think it puts all of our problems into perspective. No matter what happens to us down here, the stars are still up there." Cassidy tried to make the words sound light. The last thing she wanted to do was set off an argument between the two of them.

Willa just shook her head. "You're more of an optimist than I am."

Cassidy laughed. "That's never been a word I've used to describe myself, but I guess you're right."

"I wish I could be more like you." Willa shrugged, subdued. "I'm not wired that way, I guess."

"I feel like it can be a choice you make for yourself, too."

"I don't think it's so easy, Cass."

The entire field could have caught on fire for all Cassidy cared, because the only thing she could think about was the way Willa said her name. She savored the warmth spreading down her limbs, unsure if it would last.

"So, what's bothering you?" She asked the question that had been on the tip of her tongue her the entire night. "It's not what happened yesterday, is it?"

"No, we cleared that up. I'm happy to spend the time with you." She paused, looking down at the food she hadn't touched yet. "I think I feel the most awful because I don't miss him as much as I'm supposed to."

Cassidy hesitated. "I don't think you're supposed to feel any certain way."

"But shouldn't I? He was my husband." She picked at the skin lining her thumbnail. "We fought all the time. I kind of have the feeling that if he were still here, we would have separated by now."

"What were you fighting about?"

"Everything. But mostly the ranch. He wanted everything to be synth—even the animals, so we could do other things."

"And you didn't want to?" It was a question, but Cassidy already knew the answer. It was obvious in the way Willa took such pride in her work.

"No. It takes the heart out of it. If everything runs itself, then why should we even be here? He never said it, but I think that's what he was getting at."

"He wanted to move?"

"I'm not sure what he wanted. But he never quite fit being a rancher. I told him he didn't have to do the work with me; he used to work at the bank. But he insisted it was a family business, and we had become a family, so that's what he would do. At the time, I thought it was romantic..." She leaned her head back, letting out a small sigh. "... but I think he grew to resent it."

"That's not fair."

"It's not about fairness, I don't think. We tried too hard to fit together, when I think it was doing more harm than good."

"Maybe you would have worked it out."

Willa let out a dry laugh, shifting ever so slightly closer to Cassidy. "No. He was too stubborn for that. That's what got him killed."

Unease filled Cassidy's gut. "What do you mean?"

"Well..." Willa's sigh was weary. "He meddled when he shouldn't have. He was convinced he'd be the one to solve the bandit problem, make things safer around here."

Cassidy's eyebrows shot up. "How would he have done

that?"

"It started small. Looking the other way when they stole, as long as no one got hurt. Then he started offering them bits of food, medical supplies. It grew more and more, and more gangs got involved. I told him how stupid it was, that they wouldn't stop. But he didn't listen to me."

"And they killed him because of that?"

Willa scoffed. "I've never asked them, but I'd assume so."

"But he was helping them. Why wouldn't they want that?"

"Maybe they didn't want things to be easy, like they wanted to fight and take instead."

Cassidy thought back to what Sam had alluded to. Had they somehow implied that Willa's husband was at fault for his own murder? It certainly seemed like a dangerous game to get involved with bandits.

"There's no good scenario, is there?"

"No, not really." Her voice sounded so small.

Cassidy tamped down her need to express sympathies, since that was what Willa didn't want. It was probably the first time she had been able to speak about all this. But Cassidy wished she could erase all the guilt, how hard she was being on herself.

Willa's throat bobbed as she continued, "The worst part is, I'm just as stubborn. I almost starved the whole town just to prove a point."

Cassidy looked over at her, ignoring the pang in her chest at how beautiful she looked under the milky blue light of the moon. "And do you think you proved him wrong?"

"Most days, no." She smiled at Cassidy. "Lately, it's felt like my luck has turned around."

Cassidy cleared her throat. "You think he's, I don't know, watching over you?"

Willa snorted. "I hope not."

Cassidy looked at her, brows drawn. "Why?"

"If it were me? I don't know. I think I'd be a little shocked if he moved on this fast." Willa's gaze drew down pointedly to where their hands were almost touching, as if they'd been drawn together by an invisible pull.

Cassidy's neck heated at insinuation. There was nothing to do or say to absolve Willa of her guilt. She'd have to get there on her own. But something inside her took flight at the mention that Willa did feel something for her—something real.

"You can't really help how you feel. The whole thing sucks."

Willa burst out laughing, almost on the edge of hysterical. After it faded out, she wiped at the corners of her eyes. "Poetically put. But enough about me. Distract me with more stars."

After Cassidy went on for a little while, Willa was in a much better mood, and Cassidy was too. It was nice for things to start to feel normal between them again. And there was a small, sick part of her that was glad to have learned what Willa shared with her. It was a terrible thing to be happy about, but she felt the perverse joy anyway.

Cassidy tried to hide her wincing and stiffness when she rose from the flowers.

"You alright?" Willa tilted her head in concern.

"Just been sitting for too long." Cassidy pointed out another constellation as they walked back, eager to throw off any questions as to her health. Things were not alright by any measure, but knowing what she did about Willa had made a bit of her heart stitch back together again.

CHAPTER 18

WHEN THEY GOT HOME, they headed to the main house to watch a movie. Cassidy had suggested it on the walk back and was pleased that Willa had said yes. Cassidy's limbs were so heavy from exhaustion that after she sat down, she didn't budge. It was unlike her; she was always fidgeting around or bouncing a leg incessantly. The movie was over in no time, and Cassidy dreaded having to stand back up.

"What did you think?"

"It was fine." Willa drew out the end of the sentence, trying to keep a smile at bay.

"Bullshit. You like these movies."

"Fine! Maybe I do. I haven't watched that many movies though, so I probably don't have good taste."

Cassidy waved her hand dismissively and laughed.

Willa sighed. "I'm so tired, I don't know if I'll even make

it down the hall."

"Tell me about it. At least you don't have to leave the building." Cassidy thought Willa would tease her, but instead, her response was sincere.

"You can crash on the couch if you want. I don't mind. Or take the loft."

"I was being stupid. It's only, like, fifteen feet away."

Willa rose, laying the blanket she had over her legs across the back of the couch. She had changed into plaid red-and-yellow little pajama shorts and a matching red T-shirt. She was so different without her work attire. Cassidy tried not to linger on her legs, how bare they were.

"Well, the offer still stands."

"Thanks, but I'm fine."

"Alright. Good night."

"Night." Cassidy straightened up the mess she'd made of Willa's excessive decorative pillows. She would never admit it, but the short walk back was a struggle. She hoped Willa hadn't noticed the stiffness in her limbs or the faces she made when a flash migraine rolled through her—or if she did, that she chalked it up to plain exhaustion. She didn't want to impose on Willa though, when she had already given her comfortable living arrangements. She also had no idea what she'd do with herself in the morning. Something about seeing someone after they had just woken up was too personal. With the barriers of the relationship redrawn, it was too intimate for Cassidy. She was confident and easygoing with most people, but something about Willa made her second-guess herself. It was new and weird for her, so the sooner she'd grow out of it, the better.

Tom joined her as she returned to her room. She laid down under the covers and tried to fall asleep. Despite how bone tired she was, her rest came in stops and starts. At some point, she succumbed, but to the will of her subconscious.

"You have to be reading it wrong," Cassidy pleaded. She was laid out on the med-bed again. She had lost track of how many times she'd been here this month. Different doctors, different scans, but always the same prognosis ... until this one. The doctor in front of her was someone new, a man in his late fifties with white-blond hair cropped close to his skull and a collection of tattoos across both forearms. Dr. Thorne was stitched onto his pristine coat.

He scratched at his forehead absent-mindedly. "I'm surprised none of my colleagues have come to this conclusion."

"Because it's impossible."

"Those in my profession find that given time, nothing is impossible. You just happen to be patient zero."

She sat up, exasperated. "But what does that mean? How do you treat something you've never seen?"

"We're going to need to run more tests." He put his hand up when she opened her mouth to argue. "I know you've had all these tests before, but not with me. Not for what I'm looking for. Just humor me, and I think I can put together a plan to treat this."

Cassidy reconsidered him then. When he'd introduced himself with a brief handshake, he hadn't seemed different from any of the other doctors she'd seen, but she must have written him off too soon. This was the first time in five years that someone had given her an actual idea of what was wrong with her, and actually wanted to do something about it. The hesitant strings of hope pulled at her for the first time in the entire process.

She sighed. "Okay. When should I come in next?"

"Let's start next week."

All of a sudden, she was back in the waiting room, but the walls went on and on beside her along an endless stretch of chairs. The longer she stared at the pattern on the floor, the more it seemed like it was moving up towards her, ready to swallow her whole. She waited restlessly for her name to be called to go back and see Dr. Thorne.

"Cassidy?" The voice came from behind the closed door. She walked up to it and tried the handle, but it wouldn't budge.

"Cassidy?" came through the door again, but the voice was wrong, deep and distorted. She backed up a few steps, glancing around. She was the only one here. Where were the other patients? There had been other people in the room when she checked in. The lights overhead flickered brighter, the LEDs buzzing with the intensity.

"Cassidy? Dr. Thorne is waiting." The voice was almost imperceptible now, the vowels sounding like echoes, or maybe screams. She kept backing up until her calves

met with the cool metal of a waiting room chair. The hairs on the back of her neck stood straight up, as if a current of electricity ran through her.

A man in all white, not unlike a doctor's coat, came through the door. His wide-brimmed hat occluded his face, except for his dark beard and wicked smile. Teeth too big for a human mouth pointed out as he grinned.

"Cassidy, won't you come in? We just want to help you. You belong to us."

"What?"

The words were saccharine. "I said, you belong with us."

Cassidy started inching to the right, where the lobby door was. The man matched her steps with long strides. His white boots gleamed like bones under the fluorescent lights. She decided there was no other option than to run. As long as she could get out of the lobby and through the front doors, she would lose him on the street. She took off, sneakers pounding noisily against the hungry floors. The click of his boots echoed behind her, but she didn't dare glance back; that would only slow her down. As she ripped open the door and launched through, a gloved hand came down heavily on her shoulder. She screamed.

Cassidy woke up gasping in a shock of air. Her clothes were sticky against her body, and she was all tangled up in her sheets. She held a palm against her chest, waiting for her heart rate to calm. Tom lay curled in a neat little ball near her knees, and he raised his head to glare at her, as if for daring to wake him. She scratched behind his ears until he stretched and laid his head back down.

She sank back into a comfortable position to try to resume resting, but she was apprehensive. If she fell asleep again too soon, she'd get sucked back into the nightmare. It was a bad habit her mind always had for her. It was the first night she'd dreamed of Chicago since she left, but it wouldn't be the last.

She gave up on sleep and pinged Sam, knowing they'd be up at such a late hour. They opened the holo and started up a video feed.

"Hey." Cassidy yawned. "I'm not bothering you, am I?"

"No. Everything alright?"

"Can't sleep. What are you working on? New story?"

Sam gave a dry laugh. "That would be easier. Filling out adoption application forms, believe it or not."

"Sam!" Cassidy shot to sitting up. "That's incredible! I'm so happy for you two."

"Well, nothing to celebrate yet. I've barely started."

"Oh, come on. Don't sound so negative."

Sam gave her an exasperated look. "Come on, Cass. Things aren't exactly in our favor."

"What do you mean?" It was such a naive question, and she fought the twinges of embarrassment.

"Well, no agency under the Corporation is going to send a baby to California. So, that's out of the question. And you know how the abandoned states are. We're not exactly their ideal pairing."

"Someone is bound to see what amazing parents you'd

both make."

Sam sighed. "I'll have to borrow some of your optimism."

"Still, that's exciting. Let me know how it's going?"

They nodded. "Of course. So, what's keeping you up?"

Cassidy sighed. Nothing got past them. "I had a weird nightmare."

"You want to talk about it?"

"No." Cassidy frowned. "You're doing something exciting. Don't let me ruin the mood."

Sam shrugged. "The offer stands, okay? I'm gonna get back to this. Try to get some sleep."

"Yeah. Good night."

Cassidy blinked her comms away and stared into the empty darkness of her room. It felt smaller from her waking up afraid. Her heart ached at the thought of pushing Sam out when they'd been nothing but supportive of her, but she couldn't draw them into any danger. They were trying to build a family, and she would never forgive herself if she did anything to jeopardize that.

She hadn't realized having true friends could be so lonely, the sacrifices she'd have to make. She wouldn't trade any of them for the relief of it, but in the middle of the night, surrounded by darkness, it stung a bit deeper than it normally would.

CHAPTER 19

CASSIDY WAS OUT TAKING photos, despite it being a very, very stupid idea. They were in the midst of a particularly nasty electrical storm, the sky purple from the force with which it had gathered. Every other heartbeat, it seemed that the ground shook from tumultuous thunder or the harsh impact of lightning. A bolt hadn't struck near her—not yet. But the longer she remained outside, the more likely her chances of returning unharmed diminished.

She was unable to reason with herself, despite a tiny voice in the back of her mind trying its best to do so. She'd woken up that morning with the incessant itch to capture, create, leave her mark on something. When she was gone, her photos would be the only thing remaining that could speak for her. It wasn't an unusual sensation for her, but the overwhelming urge was unusually strong that day.

She'd made it as far down the stream outside of town as she could manage before it traveled on its path up the mountain. She hoped that with the right timing, she'd get the reflection of light in the thin rivulets of water the next time a bolt streaked across the sky. Between the rolling thunder and sharp bursts of lightning, she barely heard the boots crunching through the dirt behind her.

A sharp prickling built at the base of her neck, and she slowly turned, already certain of what was causing her unease. Stark against the dark, avenging sky stood the man in all white, as if sent down from the furious heavens to collect her. The hems of Cassidy's pants were caked in dirt from the path through the trees, and her hair was tangled from the relentless winds. Yet there he stood, unflinching and unmarred by the elements. His smile was as sharp as the bolt of lightning that cracked across the sky behind him.

"Hello again, Cassidy."

She didn't have the patience to come up with a retort. These games of his had grown grating. She had no interest in giving him what he wanted, yet she almost wished he would just take it, so this could all be done with.

As if reading her mind, he continued, "No smart remarks today? You wound me. I thought we had something special."

Without a response, she turned back around. What could he do to her? All he'd accomplished so far was using pretty words and her newfound dislike of the color white. She continued along the stream back towards the field as the sky rumbled above her. He didn't even have anything to say to her. She laughed to herself, how she'd lived in fear of this man. He was acting dangerous, but had barely laid a hand on her in all the months they'd been doing their strange dance.

Cassidy cleared past some brush ahead—and all that remained was white. White suit, white hat, white boots. She stumbled back, heel catching on the loose rocks around the bed of the stream. He shouldn't have been so fast, but he had enough tech, from what Cassidy could see. The odds were high that he'd have leg implants too.

He reached out and grasped the collar of her thermal shirt. She tried to wrench out of his hold, but even her synth hand was no match for the strength of his. He lifted her up off the dirt as if she were a child, her feet kicking in the air, trying to find purchase. He hadn't seemed so tall, but it felt like he raised her a full foot in the air before they were level with each other. "No more running, Cassidy." Even like this, she couldn't see under the damned hat, couldn't discern the shape of his nose or the color of his eyes.

She struggled against his grip. "What are you doing here? What do you want?!"

His smile was as bright as the clothes he wore, sinister against the imposing dark of the sky. "Why, I want what you owe us, Cassidy."

"What? Who?"

"You don't own your parts. We want them back." His smile was menacing. "You can keep the rest."

Cassidy stopped struggling, numbed by the shock. He'd been Corporation this whole time? How stupid she was for thinking she'd be able to leave behind her debt and problems, that she was insignificant enough to escape their notice.

She took a deep breath in. "I'm not going back."

"I don't need you to be willing."

She looked down in time to see a thin syringe filled with a dark blue fluid. She tried kicking at his legs, thrashing her neck to get enough leeway to bite one of his arms—anything. But it all stopped mattering once she felt the needle prick the sensitive skin of her wrist.

She came to on the back of a white horse, the even gait sending clouds of dust in their wake. Her wrists and ankles were bound by a thick black cord, and her head ached. She dimly wondered if she'd bumped it at some point. Not that it really mattered, given her present situation. The man whistled as he jostled lightly in the saddle—the saddle she was tied to and slung behind. He hummed faintly and far too brightly for the circumstances.

Cassidy faced the golden sands of the wastes with little room to maneuver, but still she tried to look around. It was barren. Only ruined structures scattered the sparse plains, half buried and rotting, and there was little way to tell what they used to be. Remains of campsites were clustered behind the more upstanding structures, trash and broken supplies serving as markers for bandit groups that had since moved on.

The storm overhead sounded even angrier as they rode farther towards their destination. She couldn't tell if the ground rumbled from the footfalls of the hooves or the heavy storm, but her stomach roiled regardless. Wherever he planned to take her, she knew she wouldn't come back from it. The only way she was getting out alive was by getting off the horse and away from him before they reached their destination.

Before she could even think, a sharp bolt of lightning struck just to the right of the horse, causing it to panic. It tore away from the smoking ground, galloping unsteadily towards the horizon. The second bolt landed much farther away, but that didn't matter to the horse. It reared up, knocking Cassidy, the man, and the saddle off in one smooth downturn. They landed in a heap as the horse bucked and kicked at the ground, kicking the man in the lower leg before galloping farther away.

He groaned into the dirt. Cassidy rolled, taking the saddle with her, and tried to stand. With her limbs bound, it was nearly impossible. The man still hadn't moved, and a fierce desperation fueled her movements. She rocked back and forth in a smooth arc, trying to gain enough momentum to land on her feet. Her arms swung above her like a pendulum, over and over again, until her joints ached with the repetition.

Finally, she was able to get up on her knees and squat backwards into a standing position. The ropes needed to be cut, quickly. She looked back at the man, but he wasn't where he'd been lying on the ground.

A gloved hand covered her mouth, preemptively silencing her scream. She felt a blow to the back of her head and only saw darkness.

The man was limping. Slung over his shoulder, she noticed the way his left leg dragged closer to the ground. She tried kicking and swinging her arms into him, only for him to send some kind of electric shock to the base of her spine. It was like ice through her veins, and it left her skin burning once the pain abated. A small cry of frustration escaped her lips that she muffled quickly in fear of being shocked again. The only silver lining was that he headed back towards town. The familiar skyline had hope swelling in her chest. Her odds of getting back to the ranch were much greater than they had been in the maze of the wastes.

When they'd reached the border of town, she gave one last attempt, swinging her legs down with as much force as possible towards his bad leg. She only made it as far as his kneecap, but it did the job just the same. He buckled, dropping her to the ground. She landed on her knees and was able to push back up to standing, shimmying her legs back and forth to release them from the binding.

This time, adrenaline did not fail her as her legs carried her away from the man. He might have recovered, but she wouldn't dare risk looking back. She didn't hear footsteps, but he had already snuck up on her too many times. The storm above was no help. Thunder echoed around the valley, turning each rumble into a terrifying melody. All Cassidy knew to do was run, and if someone asked her why she'd been running, she'd come up with a good enough excuse. But her body had other plans, and she was starting to feel lightheaded. She wouldn't stop until she collapsed. She couldn't. If he caught up to her, especially after she'd gotten a hit in, he'd probably abandon whatever contract he'd been assigned and end her life once and for all.

The haze across her vision snuck up on her, blacking out the edges like a poorly developed photo. She groaned, trying to push through. She was just reaching the stream and was almost safe. Her legs buckled and met with the muddy bank, smarting at the impact.

She had never seen a more comforting sight than that of the stream, bubbling weakly through the brush. Slowly, she sat up and brushed the mud that had crusted onto her cheek. Cassidy stilled, waiting for a gloved hand to grab her or a white boot to stomp over soggy ground. Her breath evened out when she realized she was truly alone. The sky was so dark that it was hard to tell how much time had passed. She looked around to find herself in the exact same place she was when he had first snuck up on her.

Once the relief ebbed away, she was left with bone-chilling fear. He had never hurt her before, never dared to—or never gotten the chance, maybe. No matter the reason, it was clear that things had escalated too far. If he was desperate enough to kidnap her, he might be desperate enough to try to use her friends against her. She gasped—he knew where she and Willa lived. And although Willa was far from helpless, he now knew it was just the two of them. He could hire more bandits, bring more weapons, an unknowable number of options to endanger them.

Cassidy needed to get Willa and herself away until she

could come up with a plan. She was hesitant to tell anyone what was happening—but she might not have a choice. The sheriff might finally believe her if she could get some kind of proof to identify him with. But she needed time to think, and nothing would come easy under the constant stress of looking over her shoulder.

CHAPTER 20

"We're going on a vacation," she told Willa, first thing in the morning at breakfast the next day. She hoped her nerves showed as excitement rather than genuine fear. She needed Willa and herself as far away from town as possible until she knew the danger had passed.

"Oh, are we?" Willa smiled, amused.

"Yep. This weekend. Only a couple of days. Sam and Finn said they'd get a few people together to keep an eye on the ranch." The fact that they'd been able to find help so quickly, and asked no questions, made Cassidy more grateful than she'd ever admit.

Willa frowned. "I don't know. It's a lot of work, especially if someone's not used to it. And with the animals being organic ... What if something happens while we're not here?"

"Everything will be fine. And we still have our comms if

they need to get a hold of us."

"Are we going far? If we do need to come back?"

"It's just a few hours." Cassidy mustered the most earnest look she was capable of. She needed them to leave Bell Valley—now. Even if she had to force Willa to go with her.

"Right, okay." Willa sighed, then perked up. "Where are we going, then?"

Cassidy's exhale of relief was deep. She wanted to keep an element of surprise, so she told Willa to pack enough layers. The mid-December breeze was bone-chilling. When the sun was out, it was pleasant, warmer than any other winter Cassidy had experienced, but the weather was unpredictable, even when she relied on the net.

Finn's colleagues arrived early, so Willa could show them what needed to be done around the property. She and Cassidy agreed they'd only need to do the essential work of feeding the animals and watering the plants; everything else could wait until their return. But the ranch was Willa's life, so what should have been a quick tutorial turned into a two-hour tour of the property and its history.

Cassidy brought them all coffees once she realized they passed the allotted time and hadn't made it out of the barn yet. It was endearing, seeing Willa talk so passionately about her work. She retreated about halfway through to pack a final few items and clean up the house a bit. She wanted everything to be perfect.

Willa had never been on a vacation, not even for her honeymoon. Their family never had the time to take away from the ranch, and that behavior pattern had continued when she took things over. Not to mention, there was only one destination spot left in California, and it was only open for two months out of the year. It was much cheaper than any vacation Cassidy could have taken in the city, but it still set her back a good chunk of her paychecks.

Cassidy rechecked their bags twice, checked the GPS—though the car would drive itself—and checked her reservation on the Net. She had done all of this the night before, but she couldn't stop herself from doing it again—just to be sure. She took a deep breath and sat on the edge of an armchair. It was so unlike her to be this ... neurotic. But with what had been going on, not to mention the limbo their relationship was in, there was a lot riding on a simple little getaway.

About half an hour later, Willa came in with a sheepish smile. "That took a bit longer than I thought. We're not running late, are we?"

Cassidy laughed. "No, we've got time. Will you be ready to leave at noon?"

"Yes, definitely. I just want to check on my plants one last time." She stopped and looked around. "Did you clean up in here?"

"Yeah, a bit. I hope that's okay?"

"I appreciate it."

Cassidy didn't know what to say, and she couldn't fight the blush that spread across her cheeks and the tops of her ears. Willa was private about her space, and she worried she'd crossed a line somehow. Willa continued out to the porch, whistling.

The strange Californian plants were not bothered by the crisp December air. The crops outside weren't as lucky, but plenty of things were still growing. Cassidy was amused by how California circumvented the traditional seasons and its rules. Of course, some of that came from the general changes since the gold-mining industry had taken off and the Corporation took over. Sea levels had reached an all-time high, before they sank back to lower than before, leaving strange landmasses in their wake. A majority of the coasts had become irradiated with the dumping of material waste and byproducts. With all the tech and implants produced at such a rapid rate, old gear was trashed even faster. Having implants was a choice, but in the next few generations, it might become a necessity to combat the unclean air and harsher conditions of the environment.

Willa finished up with the plants and drew Cassidy from her thoughts. She'd rented an automobile in town, and it drove itself to the edge of the ranch and idled by the gate. She let Willa hop into the back first and followed her in, shutting the door behind them.

"Wow, I've never been in one of these." Willa's gaze bounced all around the interior of the vehicle. The dark leather seats contrasted with the cool LED glow surrounding the doors and ceiling. "Will you tell me where we're going yet?"

"You'll see soon enough." And with that, Cassidy scanned her palm on the biometric reader, starting up the automobile on the predetermined path. Gentle jazz floated from the surrounding speakers.

Willa pressed against the window as they rolled on towards their destination. Cassidy didn't want to speak for fear of drawing her focus away for even a second. They headed west, through the valley. Tall, harsh mountains loomed on either side of them as they took the winding path through. She eagerly awaited the exact moment when Willa would piece together where they were going, when they heard a seagull crying overhead.

She turned to Cassidy, eyes wide and mouth agape. "Are we at the ocean?" Cassidy nodded, but Willa's expression quickly morphed into concern. "I thought you didn't like to swim? And isn't the water still toxic?"

Cassidy smiled. "There's plenty for me to do while you enjoy the water. And no, we're going to a synth-beach. It's supposed to be pretty close to the real thing."

Willa gasped. "Oh my gosh, I've always wondered what the ocean would feel like! And this will be close enough, right? Oh! Do you think they have fish?"

"There might be a synth-dolphin or two—"

Another gasp cut off the end of Cassidy's sentence. "I never thought I'd see a dolphin in my life! This is incredible."

Cassidy was grateful when Willa turned back to the window to watch as the mountains gave way to the coastline. That way, she wouldn't see how red Cassidy had gotten.

The car rolled them right up to the start of the path leading to the resort. "Resort" was a generous word here; it was a duplex made of tan clay and bricks, with intricate mosaic stone steps leading up to the broad front door. Cassidy grabbed their bags and led them inside, where an android was waiting at the check-in terminal. She scanned her chip again for biometric access to their room. Out of the two rooms in the resort, she had booked the double, with a view facing the synth-ocean. The other room, a much larger suite, had already been booked.

She turned to Willa, who had been examining the photos on the walls as she checked them in. "You wanna go check out the sights, or relax in the room for a bit?"

Willa gave her a faux-annoyed look, and that was answer enough for her. They went up to their room to change and set their things down. It was a modest space, about the same size as Willa's living room. A nightstand divided the two twin beds. It was overwhelmingly nautical-themed. Everything was in tones of blue and white, with stripes, anchors, and seashells decorating every possible surface. Upon their arrival, the prisma-screens had been set to shade, so Cassidy turned them off to take in the view.

It was a bit smaller than she expected. The water was so clear and bright, running up against the walls making up the perimeter. It crested in soft, uniform waves against the shoreline. The sand itself was bright white instead of the tan she expected. With only two rooms, even fully booked, she hadn't seen any other guests. It was cold out, but she hoped with it being synth that they would have heating. Cassidy laid their bags on their beds and began rifling through hers for something appropriate to wear. She wasn't going to swim in the water, but she brought a book and a sun shield to lie on the sand. Willa went into the bathroom to change into her swimsuit.

She emerged in a simple blue one-piece, high cut on the sides with a high neck in the front. Her skin contrasted with the color so beautifully, and Cassidy cleared her throat as she turned away. People who were just friends didn't stare at each other like that. Willa slid some loose cotton pants over her suit and grabbed a sun hat, oblivious to Cassidy's inner turmoil.

"Ready to go?"

"Sure!" Cassidy cringed at her overeager response, but followed Willa out to the hall and locked the door behind them with her palm. They took the elevator down, which Cassidy was grateful for. Though they were only on the second floor, she wasn't sure she'd manage the stairs without Willa realizing something was wrong. Her joints—her knees and ankles especially—had been acting up the entire week. They were swollen and sore, making every step a little bit more difficult.

Once they crossed the lobby and turned towards the water, Willa picked up her pace, smiling back at Cassidy. Willa placed her things on one of the beach chairs in the middle of the sand, so Cassidy took the one next to it and laid out her towel. She activated the sun shield, a small device that cast a shield to block UV rays, and opened up her book. It was historical fiction about the war, when different states and companies were all vying for control of the gold mines. In the end, the Corporation had taken over, monopolizing the resources and future tech. In her book though, the Corporation hadn't won, and she was excited to see where the story was headed next.

As enthralled as she was, however, she kept glancing up to see Willa swimming in smooth arcs through the gentle waves. The beach was built in a semicircle, so she swam from end to end in laps through the bright and clear water. Cassidy was impressed, actually, with how they had done everything. The air was salty and fresh, and they had synth seagulls flying back and forth to try to catch the fish that swam up against the barrier. If Cassidy had never seen a real ocean in the movies, she would have never known the difference. She tried to relax and enjoy the serenity, but the throbbing at the base of her skull kept her from immersing in the experience.

She couldn't remember a day by now when she'd felt completely fine, when there wasn't some ache or symptom to plague her. She had learned a long time ago how to live despite it, but that didn't mean she wasn't upset. It was unfair and wrong in a world where someone could buy an entirely new nervous system. Yet nothing could fix her. Most days she was sad, but on a day like this, where she should be swimming with Willa and enjoying this brief respite, all she felt was anger.

Cassidy took a deep breath and decided to take a quick nap to take the edge off. The only thing worse than feeling so lousy would be to take it out on Willa. She laid a towel over her face and dozed off.

When she awoke, Willa was stretched out on the chair next to her, lying on her stomach and reading Cassidy's book. Cassidy's deep green bookmark—one of Willa's handmade gifts after she'd learned her favorite color—stuck out ahead of the section Willa was on. Cassidy made a mental note to try to get Willa a bookmark too. She was a notorious page-folder, and it drove Cassidy crazy.

"How do you like it?" she asked, her voice still a bit hazy from her nap.

"Not bad. Historical can be a bit dry for me though."

"Did you bring anything of your own?"

Willa turned to look at Cassidy. "Who do you think I am? I brought five books." They both laughed, which was interrupted by Cassidy's stomach growling. It didn't escape Willa's notice. "So, where can we eat around here?"

"There's just one restaurant, but the menu seems decent."

Willa pushed herself up into a sitting position, folding the page she'd stopped on. "Sounds great. Let's go."

Cassidy cringed, but followed her lead. As they scanned in at the host kiosk, they finally came across the other guests. A family of four sat by one of the arched synth windows in the back. The restaurant was on the opposite side of the water, so they had holo-screens projecting a scenic view onto the windows. The video feed looped over again as she waited for her bio-scan to authorize. The floor lit up to guide them to their table, and once they sat down, two menu screens projected in front of them.

Cassidy scrolled through the menu, not too sure what would agree with her stomach. She settled on corn soup with bread, and Willa picked the grilled chicken salad. Cassidy transmitted their order and the credits and waited for their food to arrive. The table was more square than rectangular, so they sat much closer to each other than they usually did. The restaurant had soft oceanic sounds playing in the background, and some synth music to keep things from getting too quiet.

The whole restaurant was about as big as Willa's house. Most of the space was dedicated to the entryway and a small lounge. The back half where they were seated had just six tables lined up along the windows. It was odd to have an almost private dining experience, save for the family on the other side of the room.

At the other table, the man's eyes bored into her and Willa as they sat there, so much so that she expected the woman next to him to say something to him at some point. Cassidy shifted in her seat. In the last couple of decades, things had slowly become more tolerant, but California was an abandoned territory. Based on what Sam had told her, and the gaze of the man, she wondered if that made them backwards about a few things. It was obvious what he was assuming about them, and more so that he didn't approve. Or maybe he approved in the unsettling way men sometimes did. Either way, it made Cassidy's skin crawl. She tried to shake it off and focus on how Willa was gushing about her earlier swim.

She was glowing, despite the too-harsh lights of the holo-lamps above them, and she looked so alive. The smile on her face hadn't dimmed since they arrived either, and it made everything else Cassidy was dealing with worth it. Willa might not have another vacation once Cassidy wasn't around, so she wanted to make this one as perfect as possible.

"Do you think you'll join me for a swim later?"

Cassidy had anticipated the question, but she still hadn't figured out how to answer it. Like a coward, she answered, "Sure." She told herself it was to keep Willa's smile intact, but it was more selfish than that. Omissions were a different kind of lie, and she never wanted to be the kind of person who lied regularly. But it had been going on for too long now, since the beginning, so she'd have to make her peace with that.

Their food was decent. Cassidy enjoyed a meal she didn't

have to cook or clean up after, and their conversation never lulled. The man staring at them left before their food had come out, which was a small relief, so they had the restaurant to themselves for the rest of their meal. They headed right back out after their lunch and lay on the sand while they digested. Cassidy drew little doodles around herself while Willa buried her feet in the sand.

It was warm, despite the winter air, and Cassidy wondered if there were underground heaters or a bio-modulator somewhere she couldn't see. The resort, more like a house than anything else, was more impressive than she'd thought it would be. There was an honest simplicity to it that Cassidy enjoyed. Something about the urban maximalism under the Corporation felt stifling. Everywhere you went aways felt the same. California was refreshing in its variety.

After brushing her feet off, Willa stood. "Ready to swim?"

Cassidy gulped. "Sure. I'll go change."

"Great." Willa flopped down on the vacant chair, smiling, and stretched her arms above her head. "I'll be here until you're ready."

CHAPTER 21

Cassidy shuffled up to their room and sat on her bed, head in her hands. She had no way to get out of it, and worse still, she had put herself in this situation. The pain in her skull grew from dull to splitting, so she lay down for a moment. She took deep breaths, willing the pain to abate enough for her to make it through the rest of the day. As her eyes fluttered open, a soft, "Cassidy?" reached her ears, and a gentle hand was laid on her arm.

"Willa? What?"

"I think you fell asleep, silly. That, or you've been hiding from me."

Cassidy eased back up. "No." Her headache had lessened, but still followed her elevation change. She forced out a laugh. "Sorry, I guess I'm too relaxed."

Willa chuckled and withdrew her hand from Cassidy's

arm, but she was sitting on the edge of her tiny bed, so they were almost face to face. Cassidy was breathing slowly, trying to reorient herself, but all she thought about was the way Willa was right in front of her. She wondered if her skin would be saltier from being in the sea.

Willa stared into her eyes, expression unreadable. "So, what do you want to do?" She raked her eyes down Cassidy's body, then laughed. "You haven't even changed yet."

Cassidy was sitting preternaturally still, afraid of what her body would do if she gave it any leeway. But Willa's gaze hadn't returned to her face yet, and she hadn't moved away either.

Cassidy couldn't help herself, and she brushed a strand of Willa's hair behind her ear. It was curly and wild from the synth seawater. "I only need a second, if you still want me to join you."

Willa shivered slightly as Cassidy's fingers accidentally brushed her neck on their way back down to her lap. The air was thick, and a mix of emotions ran through Cassidy. Willa had made herself clear, so she didn't want to assume anything or make the first move when it was unwanted.

She went to slide off the other side of the bed when Willa caught her wrist. "Cassidy, I..."

As Cassidy turned back around to face her, Willa surged forward and pressed their lips together. A small sound of surprise left Cassidy—not that it was unwelcome—as she settled back onto the bed. Willa eased her down and moved to either side of her hips, hovering above her. Her hands were everywhere—in Cassidy's hair, down the seam of her shirt, and up the outside of her thigh. Cassidy's head was spinning, and for once she didn't care how ill she was. Instead, she was consumed by a tremendous need growing in her core with each of Willa's movements.

Cassidy shifted and put her hands on the back of Willa's neck, drawing her in closer. A heady rush of pleasure bolted through her every time a soft sigh escaped Willa's lips. Cassidy's organic hand ran from Willa's neck down her back and toyed with the hem of her shirt. When she received no protest from Willa, she skimmed it underneath. Her hand trailed up her side until her fingertips met with the top of her swimsuit. Her skin was so soft and warm as Cassidy edged along the fabric. She got to the front and inched her fingers up until they lightly grazed Willa's nipple through the fabric.

Willa moaned. It was the first time Cassidy heard a sound like that from her, and she was done for. She repeated the motion with different levels of pressure to get the best re-action from Willa. It was somewhat of a challenge she cre-ated for herself: how to bring her the most pleasure. Willa followed suit, cold hands brushing up Cassidy's sides and making her arch in surprise. She didn't normally wear a bra, and certainly not on a beach vacation, so nothing blocked Willa's path as she continued exploring the contours of her body.

They were both breathing heavily, the air growing hot around them. Cassidy slid Willa's shirt off her body and leaned up to leave kisses on the crest of her shoulder and the valley of her collarbone. Willa drew Cassidy's shirt over her head next, getting it tangled up at the collar in her haste. Willa pivoted them with her hips to lay Cassidy down, but the movement twinged something in her spine. Cassidy's sharp intake of breath was not one of pleasure.

Willa froze. "Hey, did I hurt you?"

Cassidy rolled her shirt back onto herself and looked up at Willa. Her pupils were blown so wide that she could hardly see the amber of her eyes, and a light blush spread across her cheeks and the center of her chest. She was so beautiful, and Cassidy's heart broke a bit looking at her.

"I'm fine, just sore. Come here." She moved in, but Willa moved back, concern drawing her brows together.

"Sore? Are you okay?"

"Yeah, it's nothing."

But Willa was too perceptive. She backed off Cassidy's lap and curled her legs in at the foot of the bed, throwing her shirt on. "Be honest, Cass. Do you think I haven't noticed how you've been acting these last few weeks? How you wince whenever you stand up, how late you stay up at night? Tell me what's going on."

Cassidy sighed and leaned against the headboard. The few embers still smoldering between them would be extinguished by what she'd have to say next. Cassidy preemptively mourned what they could have been like together if she hadn't done this to them. "I wasn't honest about why I came here. Not completely."

Willa stared at her, waiting for her to continue. She wasn't going to ease Cassidy through their discussion, then.

"I've been ... sick, for a while. But every doctor I've seen can't find anything wrong with me."

"What has that got to do with California?"

"There was supposed to be a doctor out here to help me, but I don't know. We think it's a dead end."

"'We'?"

"Uh, Sam and Finn. They've been helping me out."

Willa's eyes filled with hurt. "Am I the only person who didn't know about this?"

"It's not like that, Will."

Willa recoiled at the nickname. "What's it like, then?"

"I'm desperate. Whatever this is, it's killing me."

"Jesus, Cassidy."

"But I'm still able to work. No reason why I can't."

Willa glared at her. "That's not the issue here. I asked you—multiple times, in fact—what was wrong. And you lied to my face."

"What was I supposed to say?"

Willa's voice was rising. "This! This conversation we're having. We should have had it on your first day!"

"It didn't matter."

"It did! What if you got hurt while you were working? Some of the things I asked you to do... It would've been my fault. And do you think it doesn't matter now? With whatever this is?" She gestured between them. "Did you think you could keep this a secret forever?"

Cassidy's cheeks burned. "I didn't think I'd be around long enough for it to be a problem." At the hurt in Willa's expression, she continued, "I didn't expect to like it here. To make friends. To meet you, and..."

Willa sighed, running a hand down her face. "I'm not going to pretend like I don't understand where you're coming from. But you had every opportunity to tell me. If not as your boss, then as your friend. And whatever else..."

"Fuck, I know. I messed things up, and I'm so sorry. I

never wanted to lie to you, honest. The longer I was here, the harder it was to bring it up again."

"Even when I asked how you were? It was easier to lie then?"

"No, I just—"

"I've never lied to *you*, Cassidy."

"I know. You didn't deserve that. I'm sorry."

"I know you are. But I need to think about things. How this will work, if it even can."

Cassidy swallowed down the tears threatening to form. "What are you saying?"

"Take the week off. Let me think about everything."

"Are you firing me?"

"No. I have no idea what I'm doing. And you need to give me time to think it all out."

"Okay, I get it. That's fair."

Willa sighed, long and heavy. "You only booked two nights, right?"

"Right..."

"Then we'll leave tomorrow."

"Willa, no, I wanted you to enjoy this. I didn't want—"

"It's too late. And I can't be here with all of this hanging over us. Let's go home."

Cassidy just nodded; she had no moral standing to disagree. Willa went back out to the beach and stood at the edge of the water, letting the waves wash over her ankles before receding over and over again.

Cassidy had made a lot of dumb mistakes in her life, but this was something else. She had thought she'd broken the pattern a while ago, but she would consider it self-sabotage, even. She paced around the room, thinking of a way to fix things, until the pounding in her skull returned, rendering her immobile.

She couldn't enjoy the moment she'd had with Willa, the intimacy she hadn't let herself feel with someone else in a very long time. There would be no one else after Willa, she was certain. She couldn't put someone else through this pain if she wanted to. She wished she was able to sleep, so she could at least dream of how Willa felt under her hands, the sounds she made. But even that seemed out of her grasp. She supposed that was the least she deserved. And when Willa did finally return to the room, she didn't speak to Cassidy. She sat on her bed and read one of her books, the only sound in the room her flipping pages.

Neither of them went down to have dinner, and they didn't have breakfast either. Cassidy called a car and went to check them out early; it was barely seven in the morning. She wouldn't get any credits back for their early departure, but she supposed that was some of the karma due to her.

They got into the car wordlessly. Willa looked out the window the entire drive back, but her expression was clouded. There was no sense of wonder or curiosity at the surrounding landscape, and that was the part that settled in the pit of Cassidy's stomach like acid; she had stolen that from her. She had ruined their trip, and maybe even their relationship. She'd sit in her feelings for the drive home, at least, before she'd start to figure out what to do about it.

She was anxious for a variety of reasons. Besides the fight, they were leaving two days too soon. Cassidy hadn't formulated a plan for what to do about her *problem*. She wasn't exactly hard to find in a town as small as Bell Valley, but she wanted to come up with some kind of measure to ensure her and her friends' safety. The last encounter with the man had escalated so greatly, she didn't know if she'd survive meeting him again.

She pinged Finn to let his friends know they wouldn't have to tend to the ranch after all. He, of course, wanted to know if they were alright—and the gossip, Cassidy suspected—but she brushed him off for the time being. She was disappointed in herself enough already; she didn't need anyone else to be witness to it as well.

When they got back, Willa wordlessly took her bag and retreated into the house. Cassidy dropped her things off and immediately headed back out. There wasn't a chance she'd be able to stay cooped up on the ranch, a handful of feet away from Willa, stewing in her mistakes.

She walked out to the poppy field, following the horizon of the mountains as her guide. As she went, she replayed every moment Willa asked about her, or the nights they'd spent talking about each other and their lives. She'd had more than a handful of chances to tell Willa; it would be a lie to pretend otherwise.

By the time she made it to the field, her head and shoulders were throbbing, as if physically bearing the weight of all her worries. She stood at the border of the flowers, unwilling to trample them again, and looked out to the distant mountains. They were fuzzier than they looked upon her last visit, and a surge of panic rushed through her. Her ocular implants were supposed to maintain her vision at twenty-twenty, and it seemed like even they were failing too. Would her chip go next? Would she lose all access to the Net, tech, and the modern world?

For the first time in all of this mess, Cassidy screamed, the sound echoing through the valley. The end of it broke off into sobs before she realized what was happening. She curled inwards, shoulders shaking as her body was wracked with emotions. Her life and body seemed to be in a race to see which could fall apart faster. She wasn't sure which one was pulling ahead at this point. Her sobs slowly faded to hiccups and sniffles, each jerk of her body pulled a sharp twinge from somewhere in her side. She wasn't even afforded the chance to cry without being in some sort of pain.

Without checking her chip, there was no way to know how much time passed. It could have been hours or minutes before she straightened herself up. She had never been one to dwell—never gave herself the time to—but it felt like she had to before she could move on. She needed a solution, and she wouldn't take no for an answer anymore. She couldn't. She pinged Sam and Finn, needing to think aloud and get their input.

Their feeds came up in her oculars, and the backs of her eyes burned with tears again. They were both too polite to comment on her puffy eyes and red nose. She swallowed thickly, not wanting to beat around the bush any further. "Willa found out."

Finn, at least, didn't look surprised. "Aww, Cassidy. What happened?"

She explained it to them quickly, leaving out both the more intimate and humiliating moments.

After a beat of consideration, Sam cut in, "Where are you

now?"

"We came back home, but I've been out walking. I ... can't be there right now."

"You can't stay outside forever." Finn frowned. "Why don't you stay at my place? My workshop has a daybed, and we can figure the rest out."

"I don't want to impose."

He rolled his eyes. "Cassidy, please. We're both worried about you. Let us take care of you."

She sighed. It only solved one of her problems, but she would have to take what she could get. "Okay. I appreciate it, Finn."

"Get packed, and ping me when you're on the way. Sam and I will meet you at the creek."

Cassidy nodded and logged off, leaving them to discuss further without her. She was grateful to have somewhere to go, but it made everything feel that much more real. And what if she and Willa never worked things out?

She shook those thoughts away. She had enough on her plate without worrying about things that hadn't happened yet.

When she returned to the ranch, she saw no sign of Willa, so she gathered her things into her backpack as quickly as she could. She had accrued so much more than she arrived with, so plenty of things had to be left behind. She was hoping to return soon anyway, so she prioritized the essentials. Her camera, photos, and new clothes would all have to stay. She did gather the little bookmarks and small gifts Willa had given her; the thought of leaving them for Willa to see seemed like a statement Cassidy wasn't trying to make.

She slung her bag over her shoulder as the door hissed closed behind her, and she ran straight into Tom. She knelt and gave him some extra scratches behind his ears, not sure how often she would be seeing him for a while.

"I'm not kicking you out. I wouldn't do that to you."

Cassidy hadn't heard Willa walk up. Her stomach roiled with nerves; this was the only thing she hadn't wanted to happen.

"I know. I figured it'd be easier if I wasn't around right now. For both of us."

Willa nodded, not disagreeing. "I'll ping you when I'm ready to talk."

Cassidy smiled sadly and headed for the gate. There was nothing to be said at that moment.

CHAPTER 22

The walk to Finn's place was like a trance. He and Sam did their best to distract Cassidy and lift her spirits, but she couldn't muster more than a one-word response to most of their conversation. She hadn't been to Finn's house yet, and she hated the pallor that had been cast on visiting for the first time. He lived in a spacious apartment above the carpenter's shop. It was no wonder he'd been so quick to arrive during the fire.

He had plants everywhere, rivaling Willa. The thought sent a fresh pang of sadness through Cassidy. He had so much interesting furniture around the room, some of it unfinished or half painted. Most of his furniture had been built by hand, and the walls were filled to the brim with family photos, posters, and art. He nudged her down the hall and opened the last door on the left.

"I hope you don't mind that I've still got some stuff in here. You can always have my room, if that'd make you more comfortable."

"No, it's great. Thanks, Finn." And it was. Aside from the daybed in the corner was a huge drafting desk and easel along the wall, framed by an arched window. He had moved as much out of the way as possible, not that Cassidy needed a lot of space. It was twice the size of her room on the ranch, and it suited her fine. She walked over and ran her fingers over the canvas on the easel.

"You paint?" she asked.

"Here and there. It's just for fun."

"You're really talented." He was working on a landscape of the mountains behind the church building, before the fire. She wondered if he found the scenery fascinating, or if it was an excuse. "Are you gonna give this to her?"

Finn's laugh was stilted. "No. She wouldn't want a random painting."

Cassidy arched her brow. "I think you'd be surprised."

Finn didn't argue and set her bag down at the foot of the daybed. "Why don't you get settled in, and then we can grab something to eat for lunch?"

"Sure, sounds good."

Finn patted the doorway as he left Cassidy to it. She unpacked her clothes in the trunk he'd cleared out for her, and she made a small pile of toiletries to leave in the bathroom. She settled down to catch her breath, the pain in her temples returning twofold. Before she realized it, she was drifting off, waking up to a much darker room. Her chip read five, which meant she'd slept through lunch and most of the day. She hoped Finn hadn't waited for her to eat.

She padded out to the living room to find him playing a holo-game. The level projected around him as he walked through an imaginary jungle, fake holo-gun in hand. He turned at the sound of her arrival, hands drawn. "Oh, hey, you're up." He paused the game, and the projection flickered around him. "You feeling okay?"

"Yeah, didn't sleep much last night."

He seemed ready to say something, but changed his mind. "Right. Are you hungry? I was going to start on dinner soon."

"Can I help?"

"Just relax, play the game if you want. You're my guest."

She pouted. "Finn..."

"Cassidy..."

She gave him the saddest eyes she could muster until he sighed and threw his hands in the air. "Fine. You're even more stubborn than Mara."

She laughed and followed him into the kitchen. It was much smaller than the one on the ranch, but it had an adorable pass-through window with some bar stools on the other side. Finn started setting out ingredients, sliding over onions and peppers and other things for her to chop. They set up Cassidy's portable projector—one of her most treasured belongings—and played an old sitcom in the background as they worked.

After about forty-five minutes, they cobbled together a spicy pasta dish. Cassidy had seconds. Her appetite had been fluctuating over the past month, so when she was capable of eating, she tried to take advantage of it. She insisted on washing the dishes, which bothered Finn, but she did it anyway. The thought of doing nothing—not working or helping out around the apartment—and taking advantage of Finn's generosity made her skin crawl.

They wound down the evening watching more episodes of the show they'd started in the kitchen, until Finn yawned and decided to head to bed. Cassidy headed back to the spare room, but of course, sleep would not find her. She leafed through the drafts Finn had left on the table in the corner. It was littered with a variety of personal and professional projects, ranging from furniture pieces to entire buildings. Cassidy was impressed with all of it, especially the math component, as it barely made sense to her looking at it.

She wondered what she could have become if she hadn't gotten sick and spent the better part of the last decade in waiting rooms, searching for a cure. Would she have developed a skill like that? The sad part was that she'd never know, and based on the symptoms that were progressing, she didn't have too much time left ahead of her to find out.

What was she doing? Making friends, settling in, imagining a life she wasn't able to have. It was selfish to insert herself into these people's lives when she would soon leave a gaping hole in them. It was for the best that she and Willa would probably be parting ways. She was already mourning a lost love; Cassidy had no intention of putting her through that again. Before Cassidy spiraled further into her thoughts, she crept into the kitchen for some water.

She grabbed a glass from the cupboard above the sink and held it under the purifier connected to the tap. Turning the water off, she turned and headed back through the space. Her steps were even and measured until she saw that the door was wide open; there hadn't even been a creak to alert her. The door had a bio lock; there was no way for it to have opened of its own accord. She glanced around the room, too dark for her failing oculars to pick up any extra detail.

But white always shone in the darkness. How he'd found her, she had no idea. She whispered for fear of waking Finn, "How did you get in here?" She looked behind herself for a kitchen knife, a big spoon, anything to put between them. She wouldn't make the mistake of underestimating him again. But if she backed up any farther, he'd be able to corner her in the narrow kitchen, and she couldn't risk that.

"I'll admit, you have more fight in you than I guessed, Cassidy." His grin looked feral. "I won't be making that mistake again."

Cassidy's synth hand flexed instinctively, the gold of it the only part of her visible in the dark. She was still clutching the glass, wondering if she could use it as a diversion. "You need to leave. My friends have nothing to do with this."

He cocked his head to the side. "Are they your friends? Really? Do they know you've been lying to them?"

Cassidy fought the instinctual urge to back up a step, his presence so intimidating that some animal part of her urged her to flee. "I don't know what you're talking about."

"I know the lies come easily, but there's no point in lying to me. This is just a transaction." He put his hands up in front of himself, a small sliver of skin and gold visible where his sleeve gave way to gravity. "Just come with me, and then this can all be done with."

She almost wanted to give in to him. She was dying, out of options, and it seemed like soon she'd be out of time.

Wouldn't it be easier, and keep her friends safer, if he was gone for good?

He must have sensed her hesitation, because he took one slow, long step forward. Cassidy flinched. He was directly in front of her, blocking the narrow path from the kitchen out to the living room. But if she distracted him and got past him, she could lead him away. He hadn't come for Finn, but she didn't know what his limits were, or if Finn would be left alone.

That thought alone snapped her out of the manipulations he'd been working on her. She wanted to scream at herself, how easily she'd almost given in. She needed to fight.

This was also her only chance to get something on him. DNA under her nails, a strand of hair—any kind of proof of who he was. She hoped the sheriff had the basic evidence-processing equipment to do something with whatever she could grab off him. Him working on behalf of the Corporation would not go over well in Bell Valley. As long as she could prove that was who'd sent him, then the town would do the rest for her.

She surged forward, aiming for his stupid beard, the small flash of skin under his sleeve, whatever she could get her hands on. He smoothly held an arm out from his side, as if he were stretching. Cassidy didn't expect him to aim that way, and she tried to duck under, but lost her balance. She fell, and the glass shattered across the hardwood floor.

Suddenly, the lights flicked on, and a bleary-eyed Finn was standing in the living room in front of her with a small handgun drawn. It was strange to see someone so friendly and gentle so comfortable with a weapon. No steps sounded, but when she looked around, she was sure she was alone. She tried to clear the fear from her face before Finn got a good look at her.

"Cassidy? What happened?"

She chanced a quick look at the door to find it shut again. "I didn't mean to wake you. I was just getting some water."

He looked around and sighed, disengaging the charge on his gun. "Are you okay?"

"Yeah... I slipped. I'll clean it up."

"No, I've got it. You can go back to bed."

"Finn, it was my fault. And I woke you. Let me clean it up." Her tone was sharper than she'd intended it to be.

"It's fine, Cassidy." He sighed. "I'll bring you water after I pick up all the glass."

"I'm not a child. I can do it myself."

"I don't think you're a child. But you're my guest, and—"

"And?"

Finn broke eye contact before he continued, "And you're ... unwell."

She crossed her arms over herself. "This wasn't because of that."

He put his hands up, placating her, but it only made her angrier. "Okay, maybe not. But you don't need to exert yourself."

He didn't believe her. And now she was a lousy guest, waking him up and making messes. He was trying to be a friend to her, but he hadn't signed up to be a babysitter. Embarrassment burned across her cheeks, and she realized she was still on the floor. She stood up slowly. "I'm not going to collapse from using a holo-vac. I'm sorry for waking you.

Please just let me do this."

"Fine. See you in the morning."

Words that should have been tense were still far kinder than she deserved. She waited for the click of his bedroom door before she started crying, silent, ugly sobs that she couldn't slow. She knew she was taking things out on Finn, one of the only few people she had left. He had no idea of the danger she'd placed him in by taking advantage of his kindness. She couldn't stop the anger; it was coming out of her every pore. She had no idea what was happening to her, but she didn't like the person it was making her become.

Once she could see through her tears again, she grabbed the vac from the broom closet and cleaned up her mess. Then, once she was sure Finn was asleep, she crept to the door and opened it slowly, not wanting to make a sound. The hall was dark and quiet, empty. She made sure the door was locked before she crossed back into the kitchen. Then she got herself a new glass of water and returned to her room.

It was all too much for her to reconcile on the heels of her argument with Willa. Who did she think she was? That she would be able to run from the Corporation, so looming and final? Finn was one of the best people she'd ever known, and she was nothing but a liar. It was all too much.

She rifled through her bag until she found the last of her Chroma. Only a few emerald crystals remained in the tiny bag. In a town as small as this, she wasn't sure she'd find more, or be able to afford it, but her state of mind was not one of temperance. She crushed it into a fine powder and waited to be sent into oblivion.

She came to late the next morning, almost in the afternoon. Lying in the daybed, she stared out the large window at the overcast sky. She'd have to apologize to Finn, but she was reluctant to have that kind of conversation on so little sleep and the ebbing high she still felt. She sat up, her body waking and letting back in the pain and shame from the night before. The room felt smaller than it had when she arrived yesterday, the overcast sky somehow still too bright.

Cassidy stretched as much as her limbs would allow and crept out into the hall to wash up in the bathroom. The fluorescent lights above the mirror pulsed erratically, getting stronger and stronger until they made the backs of Cassidy's eyes ache. That was mostly due to the Chroma, its name coming from the colors and visions it produced. It was a popular nightlife drug for techno clubs and synth raves, but Cassidy had been using it on and off for so long that all it did was send her into uninterrupted sleep.

She stared at herself in the mirror, barely recognizing who stared back. Her skin was so pale, despite her spending so much of her time out in the California sun. Her face was a collection of severe angles from the weight she'd lost, her eyes dark and without their usual spark. She leaned in closer, not sure about the odd gleam in the corners of her eyes. She blinked as a molten silver tear slid down the side of her nose. She wiped at it quickly, her chest growing tight. Implant fluid, shiny as a crystal, webbed between her middle and index fingers.

She splashed cold water on her face and brushed her teeth twice. Implant fluid coming out of anywhere was a bad sign, but coming from her eyes was worse. Her panic and ebbing high warred for dominance within her body. The aftermath was wretched. The worst part of Chroma—besides coming back down—was the sour tang it left all over the mouth. The whole process only left her feeling marginally better, but she didn't want to hog the bathroom when it was the only one in the apartment.

There hadn't been any sound of activity since she'd been awake, and she wasn't sure if Finn was home after all. She hurried back to the spare room, ignoring the pang her stomach gave as she turned away from the kitchen. She didn't want to help herself to Finn's things, so she'd have to go to the grocer when she regained her strength.

As she was heading back to the room, Finn's bedroom door creaked behind her.

"Cassidy." She stiffened, but turned around. Finn padded down the hall, not looking much better than she did. "Have you been awake long?"

"A little while."

"I'm glad you got some rest."

She cringed internally, but didn't correct his mistake. Passing out on Chroma was about the same as staying up the entire night. "Did you sleep okay? You look..."

He laughed tonelessly. "Tired. I've been thinking about everything. I'm sorry if I embarrassed you last night."

"No, I should be apologizing to you. You were being a good friend, and I was awful."

"I can't pretend to understand how you've been feeling with everything. But I don't blame you for being angry."

She fought past the lump in her throat. "Still. I shouldn't have reacted like that. But I appreciate you trying to understand..."

"And?" He tilted his head to the left.

She sighed. "I don't want every conversation to be about my ... condition. I can still have normal conversations, and do normal things, and break glasses normally."

"I can respect that. But if you ever do want to talk about it, I can listen."

She grabbed both of his hands in hers, the heat of them radiating through her organic hand. "Thank you. You're the best."

He crinkled his nose dismissively, but there was warmth in his smile. "You wanna go eat? You slept through breakfast."

Cassidy released his hands. "Sure. Let me get ready. Have a place in mind?"

"Yeah, it'll be my treat."

They had just gotten over a fight, so Cassidy was in no position to argue, but being pampered by Finn was starting to feel like a debt she wouldn't be able to repay.

She'd just started to dress when Sam pinged her.

"Sam? You okay?"

"Yeah, I think I may have found a lead."

Cassidy stared at them, wondering if she'd heard correctly. "Are you serious?"

"It's not perfect, but it's a start. Can we talk?"

"Yeah. Finn and I were about to go eat. Join us?"

"Sure, I'll meet you outside."

They both logged off, and Cassidy filled in Finn. She couldn't help but think of the last time she'd had this feeling—when Dr. Thorne had first made all of his promises, then vanished into thin air.

They sat down at the local diner, the only real restaurant

in town, with their meals. Cassidy's hamburger and fries sat steaming in front of her, but she made no move to start eating. She gave her full attention to Sam.

"I think I know where that doctor is," Sam began as they pulled out the lettuce on their tuna sandwich before putting it back together. "But it's not going to be easy to get an appointment."

"Why?" Finn asked through a mouthful of his lunch.

"He operates by invite only. He doesn't work at either of the official clinics. You have to apply, and hope he's interested enough to take your case. And it won't be cheap."

"And you're sure it's him?" Cassidy asked.

Sam nodded.

"How much?"

"It depends. But the initial appeal is three thousand cred-its."

"Three *thousand*?" Cassidy echoed in shock. It would take her six weeks to earn that much. "What if he doesn't take the case?"

Sam grimaced. "The fee is nonrefundable, for his *consid-eration*." With their emphasis on the last word, there was no mistaking how they felt about the whole thing.

"I don't know, Cass." Finn set down his fork. "This sounds like some kind of scam."

"What other options do I have? He's the only one left who might be able to help me. I know him; he's not a bad person."

"What about if he takes you on? How will you pay for treatments?"

Cassidy scowled. "I don't know, Finn. But my credits won't be any good to me if I'm dead."

Neither of them said anything. They knew Cassidy was sick, and they knew she was getting worse. But this was the first time death had crept its way into their conversation. It had a sobering effect on the table.

"You're right, I'm sorry. I just don't like the thought of this guy taking advantage of you."

Finn was sitting next to her in the booth, so she put a hand on his arm. "I know. Thank you. But if he is the man I remember, then I really think he'll help me." She turned to Sam. "And thank you for this. I searched all over the Net and didn't come up with anything. You're amazing."

They blushed and nodded, not expecting the praise. It was new for Cassidy too—having support and feeling grateful for it. She wanted to make sure they knew what it meant to her if things didn't end well.

CHAPTER 23

Now that Cassidy had a plan, she needed to earn credits. She hoped she would be able to do so on the ranch, but she was prepared to find the means elsewhere if Willa needed more time. Time was the only thing Cassidy could not afford to give her. While she gave Willa space over the next few weeks, Sam supplied her with photography jobs for the paper, and Finn gave her busywork for his upcoming projects. She picked up supplies and ran errands for him, and he and Sam were kind enough to pay her the same rate she would have earned on the ranch, despite the work being much less arduous.

They had asked at their fateful lunch if they could donate a portion of the required fee, but Cassidy wouldn't have any of that. So, this was their less-than-subtle way of still contributing to her. She didn't see the point in refusing their generosity a second time. And at least this way, she gave them something in return, as trivial as it might have been.

When three weeks were almost up, and Cassidy had earned about half of the needed amount, Willa pinged her to meet. She'd taken more time than she'd asked for, and Cassidy assumed that meant their meeting would be a goodbye.

The next morning, she made her way to the ranch after breakfast. She'd been having an uncharacteristically normal week health-wise, but on the walk over, her stomach was in knots as bad as when she was having an episode. She opened the gate and was hit with homesickness she didn't expect. The calls of all the animals, the smell of hay, and even the mountain range drove a bolt of joy through her. Returning soothed something in her she hadn't realized was restless. But she had to push those feelings away; they'd only make things more painful once they said goodbye.

She circled to the front porch of the main house and found Tom curled up on the top step. He lifted his head when she approached and meowed in recognition.

"Hey, buddy," she cooed as she scratched under his chin. He stretched his front legs, limbs shaking with the effort, before circling her repeatedly. She laughed and pet him each time he came back around.

The door hissed open, and Willa walked through. "He's been an absolute menace these past few weeks. I think he missed you."

Cassidy's throat was almost too thick to speak. "I missed him too." She looked up at Willa then, expression clouded. They both knew what she meant.

"Do you want to come in?"

"Sure." Cassidy gave Tom one last scratch and then followed Willa inside.

Whatever she'd made for breakfast still filled the space with fragrant notes of rosemary and honey. Willa led them into the living room and sat on the couch, gesturing for Cassidy to take the armchair. Ever the hostess, she had already laid out two cups of coffee. Cassidy cupped hers, enjoying the warmth seeping into her hand and sensors. She waited for Willa to speak.

"I appreciate you coming. And I'm sorry it took me so long to reach out."

Cassidy rubbed at the back of her neck. "It's alright."

"How have you been doing?"

"Fine. Finn is a great roommate. I've been doing odd jobs for him and Sam. Sam thinks... Well, we think we found the doctor who can help me."

Surprise and something else flashed across Willa's face. "Wow. That's amazing! I'm happy for you."

Cassidy filled her in on everything Sam told her—the money, application, all of it. "I've still got a while to go, but I think I'll have a shot."

"Now I feel terrible for asking you not to work this whole time."

"Willa, you had no way of knowing."

"But I do now. And I've been thinking about a few things."

"Go on."

"I understand why you didn't tell me any of this, honestly. But I can't say I wasn't hurt by it. Or that I'm not still hurt. But I feel like I can move past it and work together again ... as friends."

Cassidy was shocked, although the last part made her heart sink. But it was much better than she was expecting. "I understand. And I'm grateful that you're giving me a second chance."

"There are going to be a few changes. We're not going to split the workload. I'll be doing the more labor-intensive tasks. And if you're having a bad day, you need to tell me. I don't want you working through an ... episode."

"Okay, I can do that."

Willa's tone turned sharper. "And no more lies. You keep me up to date with this doctor and whatever else is happening. I can't give you a third chance if you keep lying to me."

Cassidy nodded. She had no intention of repeating her mistakes. But she didn't want to make long, heartfelt promises. She'd have to show her she meant it. "Thank you, Willa. So, should I move back into my room?"

"If you want. Tom will be happy to have you back. But if you're more comfortable living elsewhere, I understand." Willa was still looking down at her hands, and Cassidy wished she'd meet her eyes.

"I think it'll be easier to live here."

"Okay. I'll give you the day to move back and settle in, then you'll start again tomorrow."

"Alright." Cassidy tried not to let any emotion show on her face. Reconciliation was what she had been hoping for, but this Willa was even more distant than the one she'd met on her first day. So closed off, so cold. Cassidy hoped things between them might thaw, and she hoped she had enough time to earn it.

She headed back to Finn's to find he was out working, so

she decided to clean up a bit. It took her twice as long, with her hip giving her pain whenever she crouched down or put too much weight on it. But after a few hours, the place looked spotless. Once she was done and starting to pack her bag, the front door opened.

"Cass? You home?"

She went out into the living room to greet him. "Hey, how was work?"

"Oh, good, thanks. Did you and Willa talk?"

"Yeah. It was ... okay. I'm gonna move back to the ranch tomorrow."

Finn's face lit up. "That's great! I kind of thought you being here meant it didn't go too well."

"What, did you think I'd leave without saying goodbye?"

"No." He laughed and glanced around. "Or without cleaning the entire apartment."

Cassidy's grin was uncertain. "It was the least I could do."

"For the last time, I was happy to help. You don't owe me anything."

"Well, you know me. But thanks for everything. I know I haven't been the easiest person to live with."

"It's nothing. My door is always open if you need it."

She crossed the room and hugged him, shaking with the force of his laughter. "I guess I've turned you into a hugger too."

"Don't tell anyone." She smiled into his chest. She would miss living with Finn; she'd never shared a space with someone she got along with so well. But the ranch was where she belonged. "Want to make dinner and watch the last episode of Cyber Cops?"

"Is that even a question?" he scoffed, setting his work bag down next to the entryway table. "Nachos, or spaghetti and meatballs?"

"Dealer's choice," Cassidy replied as she followed him into the kitchen.

They cooked their last meal together full of jokes and laughter, then watched the last few episodes of their sitcom with their meal. It wasn't a goodbye, but the evening still had a finality to it. They stayed up well into the night.

When Cassidy returned to her room, she finished packing under the holo-light above her bed. Her oculars were not displaying night vision like they should have been, so she had to rely on lights, as if she didn't have the tech at all. It made her anxious to think her implants would slowly stop working, but it was something she had been suspecting for a long time.

By the time she finished packing, it was almost dawn, so she made no attempt to rest. She studied the sunrise from the beautiful window of Finn's workroom, trying to commit as much to memory as possible. The rising glow dissipated so quickly—and she took that as her cue to leave.

To her surprise, Finn was already up and cradling a cup of coffee in a travel mug. He smiled, lopsided. "Ready to go?"

"Um, yeah. I didn't expect you to be up."

"Well, I'd have to be to walk you there." He linked his arm with hers, passing over the coffee. It had cream and no sugar, the way Finn liked it. It wasn't Cassidy's usual order, but she'd grown fonder of the taste in the past couple of weeks.

"Awww," she teased between sips, "you big softy."

They passed the church, now almost complete. "Hey,

that's looking great." Cassidy nodded towards the building. "How much longer do you think it'll be?"

"We projected March, but I think we'll have it done next month."

"Wow, you shaved off an entire month? That's impressive!"

Finn gave a sheepish smile. "Well, the crew does it all. I just design and manage."

"I'm sure Annabelle is excited to move back in. Do you see her very often?"

"You're not very subtle." Finn pouted, but they both laughed. "I see her every few days to update her on the progress. And of course, I see her around town, but we don't talk."

"That's a shame, Finn. You should ask her out."

He frowned, but didn't respond, draining the last of their shared coffee instead.

When they reached the ranch, Cassidy propped open the gate. "Do you want to come in?"

Finn, for his part, looked conflicted. "I'd like to, but I need to be on site at eight. And I think I'll need another coffee, since you hogged most of the first one."

Cassidy laughed. "Fine, that's fair. Ping me though, next time you're free."

Finn pulled her into an enveloping hug. "I will. Don't worry, you can't get rid of me." He pulled away and closed the gate behind him. "Give Willa my best."

Cassidy nodded and waved before taking her things back into her room. She unpacked, mostly clothes and toiletries, before heading out to see what Willa wanted done first. She was back in the horses' pen, cleaning out their hay, and

Cassidy wasn't eager to join her. They hadn't outlined their new division of labor, so Cassidy figured she'd take care of the chickens while she waited, since it was something she had always done.

She opened up the first pen and let them stream past her in a chorus of clucking. But when she wandered inside, she couldn't remember what had to be done. Had it been so long that she'd forgotten? She stared blankly at the rows and rows of roosts and boxes in front of her, hoping something would jog her memory.

Eggs! She needed to get the eggs. She scooped them up, but forgot to grab a basket, so she doubled back and dropped them in one outside the pen.

A flash of anxiety rushed through her as she tried to remember what else she was supposed to do, so she just let out the birds and collected the eggs from the other pen as well. Something was clawing at the edge of her mind, a feeling that her task wasn't complete, but despite all of her efforts, she couldn't remember what.

Willa finished what she was doing with the horses and joined Cassidy in front of the coops. "Hey, you already took care of the chickens?"

"Yeah." Cassidy shifted, sweat beading at the nape of her neck.

Willa's eyes roamed across the pens, sticking in a few places that made Cassidy's chest tense, before returning her gaze. "That's great, thanks. Why don't you work in the greenhouse until lunch?"

Cassidy was happy to do so. With winter almost over, she would be able to start the new rounds of seeds she had been holding off on. She doubled back around to grab some of her supplies from the shed and saw Willa poking around in the chicken coops, refilling the feed. Cassidy cursed herself for messing up such a vital part of the task. Who'd forget to feed the animals?

Was everyone in her life just humoring her? How long would things go on until she was a burden to all of her friends?

She activated her chip and logged into her bank account. She didn't have close to enough credits to apply for a consultation, and it would take almost another month of full-time work to earn it. Would it all even be worth it in the end? She'd wring her friends dry of their empathy and their credits for nothing in return.

She ended the day early, claiming a headache. It was partly true; something in her always ached. But she needed to get herself together. She had hoped for a smooth transition back into her routine, but it was clear that things would not be that easy. Cassidy always had a bad habit of beating herself up for not getting something right away. She was spiraling, and she had to snap out of it before she took it out on Willa and ruined their tenuous new beginning.

Even Tom steered clear of her self-loathing for the evening, and her chest ached with loneliness. She already missed Finn's comfortable apartment and the routine of her friends. The homecoming she longed for seemed to still be a ways away.

CHAPTER 24

THE NEXT FEW WEEKS were easier than Cassidy expected, given the way she had catastrophized about her return. She and Willa fell into a routine not too far off from the way things used to be between them. It wasn't perfect, but it was much more than Cassidy deserved.

By the time two weeks had passed, Cassidy was so near to her goal. She'd have enough saved by the end of the following week, and then she could submit her case for review.

It was also February, and true to Finn's estimations, the church was finished. He planned a small ceremony in town to unveil it and celebrate all the work done to repair it so fast. Finn invited Cassidy and Willa, the latter being non-committal in her response. Cassidy got ready to head out around sunset, unsure if she should wait for Willa or not. Willa still wasn't going into town all that often or hanging out in crowds of people, so Cassidy understood if she wasn't comfortable attending an event. She pinged her and got no response, so just to be safe, she headed to the house to check on her before she left.

"Willa? I'm leaving for Finn's thing. Are you coming?" she called out to the silent house. The only light on was in the bedroom down the hall, but the door was closed, and Cassidy didn't dare open it. She was disappointed, but it was Finn's night, and she didn't want to be late.

She made it there as the last few stripes of orange disappeared from the sky and gave way to an uncharacteristically clear blue. The weather, while still cold, was also much more bearable, so Cassidy didn't mind that they'd be outdoors the entire evening. She was scanning the crowd for Finn or Sam when a hand brushed her shoulder.

"Cassidy, I'm so glad you could make it!"

She turned to find Annabelle smiling, cheeks rosy from the cold and nose red under her smattering of freckles. Her deep purple dress contrasted with the pale olive of her skin.

"Hey, Annabelle. This must be an exciting night for you, huh?"

"It's more for the crew. They must have done this in record time. I'm glad to see so many people here celebrating." She glanced over Cassidy's shoulder before returning eye contact. "Did Willa come with you?"

"Something came up with the ranch. I'm sure she'll be by soon." She wasn't sure why she felt the protective urge to lie on Willa's behalf, but Annabelle didn't question it.

Annabelle clapped her hands together. "Marvelous! I'll look out for you two later, then." She squeezed Cassidy's arm before making her way farther into the crowd. She barely made it ten feet before she got pulled into another conversation.

Cassidy continued to edge toward the back of the field, keeping an eye out for anyone else she recognized. Holo-lights started to float up around the space, bathing everything in a soft blue glow. It wasn't dark enough for the stars to be out, but it was as if the stars had come to them. She was admiring the view as she saw Sam and Alex out of the corner of her eye and waved them over.

"Hey, you two." She pulled each of them into a hug.

"I haven't seen you around much," Alex said as he returned her embrace. "I hope you're still taking photos."

She smiled. Not sure if Sam had shared anything with him, she settled on "I've been a bit busy. How about you two?" She turned to Sam. "Are you covering this for the paper?"

"Of course. And if anyone deserves the press, it's Finn and his crew."

"Is Willa here somewhere?" Alex must have noticed she'd been standing alone.

Cassidy frowned. "She couldn't make it tonight."

"That's a shame. I know Finn was hoping she'd be here."

"Yeah, me too." She glanced at Sam, hoping they could move the conversation forward, but then the sound of a microphone cut through the crowd. They all turned towards the church. It had a massive red bow strung across the door. Finn, some of his crew whom Cassidy remembered from their time on the ranch, and a handful of other people stood in front of the steps. Finn was standing with the micro-phone, looking as if he wanted to be anywhere else. His emerald-green suit looked dashing against his dark skin. He and Annabelle made quite the pair, standing there together.

"Evening, everyone! Thanks for coming out tonight to celebrate the completion of the church rebuilding. We don't usually do this sort of thing, but the church and school being destroyed has deeply affected our community, so it felt right to commemorate its completion and return. I promise I'll keep it short..." He paused as scattered chuckles rang throughout the crowd. "I wanted to recognize the amazing crew who completed all of this work in just five months. That may sound like a long time to some of you, but it's not. So, here's to them!"

The crowd erupted into a chorus of cheers as Finn stepped back and gestured for Annabelle to take his place. Cassidy and Alex cheered loud enough for the entire town, and Finn smiled knowingly in their general direction. He seemed to be relieved to have the spotlight off him, but he was a natural.

"Thank you all for coming to celebrate with us," Annabelle began. "And thanks to Finn and his incredible team—Mark, Lin, Jane, and Todd—who made this building even better than it was before." She looked out at the crowd. "I hope most of you are eager to resume our normal activities, although some of you have enjoyed an extra-long winter break. We'll resume the spring semester on Monday, so enjoy your last weekend off." She winked as a few children groaned at the news. "I also want to thank everyone who lent their support in helping put the fire out and in finding me a place to live. This is not the kind of thing you ever expect to happen, so I certainly wasn't prepared. I'm grateful to live in a community that looks out for one another. So, thank you, and enjoy the rest of the evening."

Cheers filled the little valley as Annabelle cut the red ribbon across the front door. Soft music floated through the air as people went back to their conversations or waited in line for the refreshments. A hand met Cassidy's elbow, and she turned, expecting to find Annabelle or Finn, but found Willa standing sheepishly behind her.

"Hey, you came!"

"Yeah, sorry for not answering. I hadn't decided if I was up for it or not."

"That's okay. Finn will be really happy you're here. Did you catch the speeches?"

"Some. I..."

Before she could elaborate, Sam and Alex turned back from a conversation with someone next to them.

"Willa, hi! It's so nice to see you," Alex gushed.

Willa pulled each of them into a hug, a genuine smile now on her face. "How have you been?"

As the two of them caught up, Cassidy let the words wash over her. An itch from behind her ear turned into a full-on tension headache that made her head feel like it'd been stuffed with cotton. She yawned in an attempt to relieve the pressure, unsuccessfully. Her mind was fuzzy, until she heard her name.

"—think so, Cassidy?"

She turned to Willa, who had her eyes trained on Cassidy. "Hmm?"

"Don't you think we should all have a dinner party when the first spring crops come in?"

"Oh, yeah. Definitely! We've been doing a lot of planting,

and it should be a good year."

Alex nodded enthusiastically and continued speaking with Willa, but Sam kept their gaze on Cassidy, their expression concerned. They creased their brows subtly, and Cassidy shook her head. She knew what they were asking, but this wasn't the right place to discuss it.

"Thank you all for coming out." Finn approached their group, his eyes widening at Willa's presence.

"Of course, this is awesome for you."

"Thanks, Cass." He pulled her into his side. "Have you all eaten yet?" Everyone shook their heads no. "Well, grab some plates, then. The food wasn't cheap." Finn laughed. His joy was infectious, and Cassidy couldn't help but laugh too, squished up against all the people dearest to her. She forgot about her headache, her pains, her fears as Alex passed her a plate, and Willa loaded it up with ridiculous servings before she could protest.

They found seats off to the side near the back of the church and dug into their food. It was a modest sampling compared to what Cassidy was used to; they were still recovering from the food shortage that had plagued the town prior to her arrival. Mara found them all and looked between the filled chairs, so Cassidy grabbed one from a neighboring table and scooted over to make some room. She'd received so much forgiveness in her time in California, it was only fair that she extend that to someone else.

People filtered by throughout their conversations to congratulate Finn, but he remained with them for the rest of the night. Close to an hour later, Annabelle fluttered back over and took a seat between Willa and Finn, much to Finn's chagrin. Annabelle didn't seem to notice the blush that spread across his face, or the way Cassidy kept wiggling her eyebrows at him, as she intently listened to a story Alex had been telling. Sam sat to Cassidy's left, quietly adoring Alex as he spoke.

Eventually, though, it was so late that even the holo-lights floating above them did little to light the area, and a deeper chill set in with the breeze. Everyone drifted apart, saying their goodbyes, until only Cassidy, Willa, Sam, and Alex were left. Mara and Finn walked back to town together, laughing about something, and Annabelle slipped away to say her goodbyes to people still scattered around the field. Alex and Willa were discussing something and paid no mind when Sam and Cassidy stepped a bit away to have their conversation.

"You're doing okay?"

"I'm alright. Been worse, I guess. I should have enough by next week to submit."

"That's fantastic!" Sam paused. "And you're sure we can't help at all?"

"Are you kidding? This is all because of you. You've already helped so much."

"Yeah, I just..."

"Listen, Sam, I appreciate it. But things aren't so dire that I can't afford to wait a week, I promise."

They sighed, but smiled, as if they had expected her refusal. "Okay. But you'll tell us when you do submit it?"

"Yeah, of course. Now, come on, we don't want them to think we're gossiping." She patted Sam on the arm, and they rejoined their group, who were none the wiser. After a little bit more light conversation, they said good night and went their separate ways. The crowd they were leaving behind had considerably thinned. Only the androids cleaned up, and a few stragglers remained against the sounds of crickets and owls in the distance.

"I'm glad you decided to come, Will." Cassidy forced the old nickname out, hoping that it still fit.

"Me too. I would have regretted missing it, so thank you for pushing me."

Cassidy arched a brow. "Did I?"

Willa laughed dryly. "I think everything I've done lately has been because of you."

"I can't tell if that's a good thing or a bad thing."

"A bit of both. But the good always comes with the bad. I don't mind."

"I've missed this, you know. Spending time together."

Willa rolled her eyes. "I see you every day, Cass."

She swatted her arm gently. "Don't be dense. You know what I mean."

"I'm just giving you a hard time." Willa's smile dissolved as she sighed. "I'm sorry I've taken so long to come around. I didn't mean to punish you."

"You're not. If anything, I'm punishing myself. But I never expected anything from you." She grabbed Willa's hand and squeezed. "This is enough."

"I'm glad. And I don't scare easily. You can always talk to me."

"I do."

"You say that, but you're still being gentle with me. About your condition."

"Yeah," Cassidy sighed, "I am. But I hope you of all people understand why."

"What do you mean?"

"I want to be able to forget about it sometimes, if that's even possible. I don't want to be the sick person, any more than you want to be the widow."

"Oh." She stared back at Cassidy for a moment before continuing, "Of course I understand. I'm sorry I didn't see things that way 'til now."

"I'm grateful that you care, truly. But with you, Sam, and Finn always asking how I'm feeling, it gets to be a bit overwhelming."

"Right. Well then, you won't get that from me anymore." She straightened up. "What did you think about Finn and Annabelle?"

"Oh my god, have you noticed it too? They'd be perfect together!"

"I know! They need to get out of their own way."

By the time they got back to the ranch, it was finally like no time had passed, like nothing had driven them apart in the first place. Cassidy said good night to Willa and scooped Tom up on the way to her room, eager for the company. In some ways, she still had a roommate in Willa, but she'd grown fond of the closeness she'd had in sharing the apartment with Finn. Tom didn't snore like Finn, but he did take up all her legroom, so she was trading one inconvenience for another.

CHAPTER 25

By March, Cassidy had finally scraped enough together to submit her case to Dr. Thorne. It was in just enough time as well. Not only was she contending with the physical aches and pains, but her mind had started to elude her as well. It was taking her twice as long to finish the books Willa lent her, and she was constantly messing up simple math, like cooking measurements or feed amounts—things she should be able to do without thinking at all. She'd taken to leaving herself notes for simple tasks to complete, so she'd know she'd done them. She'd never come to terms with the degradation of her body, but that had been something she understood. Her body was sick, and thus it began to break down. But watching her cognition slip away was a different kind of injustice.

She pinged Sam the day prior, and they sent her the Net

link to the doctor's page, and the instructions to unlock it. She needed three different passcodes to enter the real site behind the prop one being used to dissuade unwanted visitors. She was surprised by the paranoia of it all.

The application, along with the ridiculous amount of credits, required a full-body scan, a written testimonial of what problems she was facing, and a list of her implants. Cassidy had never attended a higher-level school, but it was like an entrance application to a rigorous institution rather than for a medical professional's consultation.

It took her two days to gather her data on breaks, during meals, and after work to put it all together. She and Willa sat in the living room on comms with Sam and Finn when Cassidy was ready to submit. It was underwhelming—uploading and hitting send, then transferring her credits over to the encrypted account. It stung, but she still believed what she had said: it wouldn't matter what credits she had if she wasn't alive to spend them. The only proof that she'd submitted her case was her being booted from the site and the emptiness in her bank account.

"I guess that's a good sign?" Willa winced. They'd all gathered to celebrate something a bit more concrete.

Finn shrugged. "Well, progress is progress. When do you hear back?"

"No idea. The application didn't say. Sam, did you find anything when you were researching?" They shook their head, and Cassidy sighed. "I guess now I wait."

"Well..." Finn glanced at Willa, eyebrows raised. "It'll be your birthday in a few weeks, Cassidy. Why don't we throw something at the ranch?"

Cassidy groaned. "I don't know. I've never been much of a birthday person."

"This is kind of a special birthday, Cass," Willa prodded, "and it's never too late to become a birthday person."

She looked between the three of them. Willa and Finn had such ridiculous grins on their faces, it was obvious they were up to something. Sam was more nonplussed, but they always had a solid poker face.

Cassidy groaned again. "You three already planned something, didn't you?"

"Maybe...?" Finn scrunched his face up, bracing for Cassidy's response. "Would that be so terrible?"

She took a beat, weighing her options. At best, this would be the start of a long line of birthdays she celebrated with them. At worst, well, she'd at least have left them with one last memory of everyone together. "Fine. I guess." She crossed her arms, not willing to concede to their excitement. She'd always loved a party, but something about being the focal point of one sucked out some of the enjoyment for her.

"Such a sourpuss," Willa teased. "It's supposed to be fun!"

They chatted aimlessly until Sam had to go, and Finn decided to log off as well. Cassidy was already smiling again by then, no longer fixated on her fears about the doctor or her condition.

Willa squeezed Cassidy's hand. "I've missed them this past year. I'm glad they're back in my life. Thank you."

"I'm not sure how much I had to do with it."

"Don't be like that. You know how much you've helped me." Cassidy smiled, not arguing for once. Willa continued, "Are you nervous?"

"Yes. It'd be hard not to be. But there's not much else I can do."

"I have a good feeling about it."

Cassidy did her best to return Willa's smile, not nearly as optimistic. But she appreciated her faith. She let Willa believe for both of them.

Cassidy gave her one last look. "I'm gonna turn in. See you tomorrow."

"Night." Willa picked up her latest knitting project as Cassidy left. The familiar sound of clacking needles followed her out the door.

It was another two weeks until she heard back about her application. The directions were cryptic, but guided her to an alleyway in the only other inhabited California town, Mariposa. It was farther inland, about three hours each way in an automobile.

Everyone offered to travel with her, but Cassidy declined. She didn't want to take on the reactions of another person if it all went badly. Yes, she promised to fill them in when she got back, but she was used to it all—unlike her friends. Sometimes, someone thought they were helping by getting angry on her behalf, but it would only weigh on her. This was her last chance too, and she came to terms with it. So, she didn't want anyone to talk her into or out of something she didn't want to do.

She said her goodbyes to Willa and waited for the automobile to pull up at the gate. Finn and Sam had insisted on renting the deluxe model for her, so she could travel in comfort. After paying the initial fee, she was so low on credits that she couldn't refuse their offer, even though it plucked at something in her pride. It was similar to the one she'd rented to go to the resort, but a bit higher off the ground, and in a sleek chrome instead of black. The inside was larger than it appeared. Plush couch-like seating wrapped around the entire interior, softer than her bed at the ranch. Besides the usual refreshments, fruit and sandwiches had been prepared for her.

The first hour, she was content to watch the landscape as they hovered through the mountains. She'd done a bit of research on the town they were heading to before taking the job with Willa. She'd only ended up picking Bell Valley because Willa's job offer came with free lodging. It was ironic that she'd ended up in the wrong town, even though she was very happy with how things had shaken out for her.

She spent the remainder of her trip drifting in and out of sleep. She'd brought a novel along, but the brain fog she'd been experiencing made concentration too difficult for her. Her nerves increased as she got closer and closer as well, so she tried to bypass the growing anxiety by sleeping through it. She hadn't had an entire REM cycle in weeks. Any time she was close to sleep, she'd be drawn out of it in a panic. The sensation was like being dropped off a cliff, but it was as if her brain were preventing her from reaching unconsciousness. She didn't want to think about the implications of that.

Time seemed like an abstract concept more than a reality, until the arrival chime sounded and the automobile slowed to a halt. It dropped her off at a five-minute walk from the town, per her request. There was no reason for anyone to see that she'd come in a luxury transport vehicle; they might try to rob her, or worse. She pulled up her map and the directions from her messages. Despite being so near to each other in location, the two towns were nothing alike. Where Bell Valley was sleepy and romantic, a memory of times before, Mariposa was a miniature of any tech city she'd been to.

The buildings were tall and shiny, not a piece of wood or brick in sight. Hoverbikes and automobiles traversed the crowded streets that made up the heart of the city. The shops and streets were bustling, and the lack of wanted and missing persons posters didn't escape Cassidy's notice. The population was double, maybe even triple that of Bell Valley, which was a relief. She'd blend in more easily, so no one would notice or question her comings and goings. She was surprised the tech was so advanced and that they seemed to have some semblance of order. For a town abandoned by the Corporation, they sure didn't seem to be hurting for it.

Cassidy followed the path projected from her chip, which led her down several winding streets until she came upon a narrow alleyway. She walked halfway down and noted a subterranean staircase with no markings or signage. The coordinates were correct, so she tried the door. Locked. She examined the area again and turned her gaze onto a small camera to the top right of the door. It whirred to life and scanned her briefly, before there was a faint click, and she tried the door again.

The steps were steep and led her at least a story or two underground. She followed a long, dimly lit hallway. Two rows of holo-lamps stretched along the length of it. Her steps echoed choppily along the space, repeating themselves. Cassidy was grateful that there was only one door at the end of the hall; she didn't want to have to keep trying doors to find the right one.

This door had a biometric reader, the data for which must have been pulled from the full-body scans she'd submitted. It tingled until the door hissed open for her. The room she entered was massive, an open-plan space with no dividing walls or interruptions. It was dark, lit with the neon of screens that hung on the walls or were projected around the space. On the right, two desks were crowded with seven monitors clustered on top of or next to each other. In the middle lay a massive Arachnae machine, unlike the ones Cassidy had seen in Corporation hospitals. It was twice the size, with more instruments and protrusions than she was used to. There was no telling what extra capabilities a machine like that had. In the back was a row of cabinets, the screens shielded in a tinted material that hid their contents from view.

The doctor was sitting in the far left of the room, fiddling with some sort of holo-schematics projected in front of him. His hands hovered on either side of the projection, fingers tweaking the changes made to the design. His blond hair was close-cropped, and a long scar ran parallel to the neural implant chip behind his temple. His arms were entirely cybernetic, though Cassidy didn't recognize the model. Could Sam have been incorrect about him being Dr. Thorne after all?

She cleared her throat, unsure whether he hadn't heard her come in, or didn't care to greet her. He fiddled with his work for a moment longer before setting his gaze on her.

Cassidy inhaled a quick gasp. The doctor's eyes had been replaced with tech that looked organic around the edges, but where the irises should have been resembled a camera lens, even protruding like one. They whirred slightly as they focused on her in the doorway. It was unsettling to look at, and she couldn't understand the benefit of tech that appeared so inorganic and off-putting. But it must have some medical benefit for him to have done that to both of his eyes willingly.

She didn't recognize him with all the new implants, but his voice sounded exactly the same.

"Miss Frisk. You're early."

CHAPTER 26

SHE WAS SURPRISED BY the coldness of his tone; he had never spoken to her like that before. Cassidy checked her chip for the time, taken aback. She was only four minutes early.

"Would you like me to wait in the hall?" Her question had an edge to it that the doctor didn't seem to pick up on.

"No, no. You're here now. Might as well get it over with."

Cassidy bristled, but stepped farther into the space. He nodded his head towards the med-bed under the Arachnae, which she settled on and connected into.

He just stood next to the machine, tilting his head as if he were listening to an interesting conversation. He hadn't even looked at her data yet. Cassidy shifted in the bed, confused by his strange behavior. After a few more minutes, she broke the silence. "Do you not remember me?"

"As if I could forget you, patient zero."

Something in his tone was erratic, bitter. It made Cassidy uncomfortable, and she itched to move the conversation forward. "Then tell me what's wrong with me."

He waggled his finger back and forth, right in front of Cassidy's face. "First, we'll discuss what I require. And then you can ask your questions." Cassidy swallowed her irritation, waiting for him to go on. "I'll need to start over. I'm sure you've ... progressed, so I need a new baseline."

"How much would everything cost me?"

"I'll get to that." He began to pace. "I'll need you to sign a nondisclosure agreement before we begin. I'll hold all rights to your data, results, and treatment plan. You will not share any of what we do here with another soul."

Cassidy huffed out a laugh. "Isn't that a little extreme?"

"The Corporation has eyes everywhere. And I won't risk myself to help you." He muttered something else under his breath that Cassidy chose to ignore.

"What else?"

"You'll let me conduct follow-up testing for as long as I see fit. I take it you're not staying in town?" Cassidy shook her head. "Unfortunate. That would have made things less difficult."

"So, let's say I agree to everything. What can I expect?"

"We'll need to run tests for two to three weeks, then once I'm confident in the cause, I can perform the operation." He repeated the end of the sentence, seemingly unaware he'd done so.

Cassidy paused. "How can you be sure I need surgery if you don't know what's wrong with me?"

His posture stiffened. "I know what's wrong with you. I

intend to find out why."

"What is it, then?"

"Telling you now will accomplish nothing."

Cassidy let out a breath of frustration. Throughout this entire process, not one doctor, nurse, or even android had considered that they were talking about her body, her life. She was tired of being treated like she was some prop.

The doctor continued on, oblivious to her rising anger, "The fees will be consequential. That's the nature of operating outside the system. I can work up a payment plan if you think it will be an ... issue." The last word dripped with condescension.

"How much?"

His eye began to twitch, the movement mimicking the zoom of a camera lens. "I'd estimate eighty thousand credits."

Cassidy jolted, wondering if she'd heard him right. "You can't be serious."

"You want a cure, no? And I think you've surmised that you don't have the luxury of time."

"There's no way I'd make that kind of money before I drop dead."

The doctor blinked at her, considering. "Your implants are fifth gen still, yes?" Cassidy nodded. "Good. Being in this hellhole, I've seen less and less of the new tech. An implant for my personal use should be an adequate down payment."

Cassidy couldn't help the way she reared back. "You want to *harvest* my implants?"

"Please, you make it sound so crass. Consider it a trade."

"You mean a downgrade."

"Your tech won't matter if you aren't alive to use it."

Cassidy had said much the same. But she couldn't ignore the slimy feeling it gave her to think about trading parts of her body—cybernetic or not—for credits. Like she was a collection of goods.

She had to think. He was interested in her for a reason she couldn't figure out, and she also didn't understand what had happened to change him so drastically. She tried to stall. "Why did you leave the Corporation? Why did you tell me not to look for you?"

"We're not going to be discussing this." His words took on a higher pitch—was it fear?

"Why not?" Cassidy pressed.

"This is not an interview, Miss Frisk. You can take my offer, or prepare your last wishes. It matters very little to me, but I am your last chance at surviving."

This was another game. Him, the Corporation—they all wanted something from her and were willing to discard the rest.

"How am I supposed to trust you?"

He laughed—and laughed, and laughed. Cassidy glanced at the door, wondering if she should just leave. He sighed eventually, the last bit of crazed laughter falling from his lips. "Why, Cassidy, you should know better. You can't trust anyone."

"What happened to you?" she whispered.

"I've already said that is not something we'll discuss!" he screamed, and Cassidy jerked back. Then, more quietly, he snapped, "If you bring it up again, I'll be dropping your case."

"I've spent over a year looking for you. You promised to help me. I'm entitled to an explanation."

"You're entitled to nothing!" he bellowed. "Everyone thinks they're owed something. What about what *I* was owed?" He began to pace. "My career, my family... My life's work..." He turned towards her again, eye implants roaming over her feverishly. "My organic body. Do you think I wanted this, Cassidy? Did I deserve this? For *you*?" He enunciated each word venomously: "What. You're. *Owed?*" He started to advance on her, and Cassidy felt the strongest tendrils of fear curling in her gut since she'd walked down the stairs.

She needed to leave. He wasn't the same man she had known, and whatever had happened since he left had cost him too much. He might have even succumbed to the sickness. With all the implants, it would be no wonder. He sparkled in the light, more man than machine, and Cassidy bolted towards the door.

"Don't lose my IP, Cassidy!" he shouted after her. "You'll feel differently as the clock ticks down." His unsettling cackle followed her down the hall.

Cassidy climbed back up the stairs, sweat building at the base of her neck. The light pouring out through the door burned her oculars as they adjusted. She let out a scream of frustration and kicked a garbage bin near her, sending it rolling down the alleyway. She sank down to sit on her heels, head in her hands. He had been her last opportunity, the person who was supposed to save her. She worked for weeks, and her friends had done so much to help her. She willed the tears not to come and fought the shame burning in her gut at the idea of having to tell them how it all went. She wished she'd followed his advice in the beginning and never tried to find him.

She was just a sick person who wanted to live. Never in her life had she wanted to live so much—and now her hope was ripped away again.

The automobile was not programmed to start the return journey for another hour and a half. She was too despondent to explore the vibrant town. A symphony of sounds and smells floated around her, but she felt as if she were in a glass box, removed from it all. She made it out to the prearranged location outside Mariposa and waited on the ground for the automobile to pull up. Her mind was so numb that the hour-long wait felt as if it were only minutes.

She sank into the plush seat and rested her head back, sighing. Now that she had nothing left to distract her, the reality of her situation crept back in. How much time did she have left? Cassidy wanted to curse at the unfairness of it all. She was lost to her thoughts for the rest of the ride, until the automobile was idling in front of the ranch gate.

Willa knew when she expected to be home, so Cassidy didn't have much time until she'd have to face her. Still, she sat inside for longer than necessary, choosing to be a coward. These were the last moments where there was still hope in the air. After she told them all about what happened, they would have to face the grim reality.

By then, Willa left the main house and briskly reached the front gate as Cassidy stepped out of the vehicle, Tom trailing behind her feet. Cassidy bent down to scratch under his chin as his purrs kicked into gear.

She rose back up, knees and hips protesting the stress, and

pulled Willa into a hug. "Hey."

"Hi." Willa laughed. "Let me get your stuff." She let out a slight huff as she slung Cassidy's bag over her shoulder. "Come on, let's get you in the house, and you can tell us all about it."

Cassidy swallowed down the lump in her throat. "Us?"

"Sam and Finn are here. You didn't think they'd miss the news, did you?"

Cassidy laid her hand on Willa's arm, halting her. "Will, it's, uh ... not good news..."

Willa's face flashed with the briefest flicker of shock, but she pulled herself together faster than Cassidy expected. "What do you mean?"

"I'd rather only have to explain it once, if that's okay. I just want you to be prepared."

Willa nodded, but didn't say anything else. By the rigidity in her shoulders and the quicker pace she set, Cassidy knew how she took the news.

Sam and Finn were in the living room, waiting on the couch. They both glanced up when she and Willa came around the corner. Finn shot up, wrapping Cassidy in an enveloping hug, while Sam loomed behind him. Finn was beaming, already asking questions that filtered out of Cassidy's ears. Sam saw her expression though, the tears she was fighting.

"Why don't we sit down?" Willa cut in, bringing over an armful of synth-sodas. They used to be Cassidy's favorite, but the carbonation had started to give her a headache over the last few weeks. Willa circled back and brought Cassidy a glass of iced tea instead. She was grateful and mourned the fact that the other woman knew her so well. It made things that much harder.

Cassidy squeezed between Sam and Finn on the couch, so she wouldn't have to look them in the eyes while she delivered the news.

"How'd it go?" Finn was bouncing the couch cushions with the incessant shaking of his leg, a nervous habit Cassidy picked up on when she stayed with him.

She sighed. "Dead end."

Sam leaned towards her, speaking softly. "He couldn't do it?"

"Not exactly..." She relayed everything to them with increasing chagrin.

Sam was the first to break the silence. "I'm sorry, Cass. I had no idea he'd act like that."

She affectionately patted their knee. "You had no way of knowing. I'm still grateful you tried." She looked between the three of them. "I'm grateful for all of you."

"We're not cutting our losses yet." Finn leaned forward, forearms resting on his knees. "There must be something else."

Cassidy sighed. "I don't know what else to do, Finn."

"We can't just give up," Willa cut in.

"It's not giving up. I have to play the cards I'm dealt. We don't know how much time I have—maybe years."

Willa's voice was quieter, her earlier resolve shaken. "Years of what though, Cass? What if you get worse?"

"We'll have to see if it gets to that point. Maybe it never will."

Willa shot up. "So, that's your solution? Wait and see how

bad it gets? Until it kills you?!"

"Listen, I've been fighting this for years. I've tried everything."

"You can't know that."

Cassidy tried to speak gently. "I do. This is it."

Willa scoffed, but made no response.

Sam rose, approaching slowly. "Willa—"

"I'm gonna get some air." She stormed off into the kitchen. Cassidy felt like she hadn't taken a breath for the entire conversation. She'd never seen Willa so angry. Even after their fight at the beach, she hadn't been so livid.

Finn sighed, balancing his head on his hands. "That could've gone better."

"I hope she didn't upset you." Sam stopped, looking like they wanted to say more.

"I'm fine. I just don't understand. We all knew it could've gone poorly." Although none of them could have guessed they'd find the doctor so *unstable*.

Sam nodded in agreement. "I hope you know where she's coming from, though. Let her cool down a bit. This is all your choice, and we support however you want to handle it."

She ran her organic hand through her hair. "The way he spoke to me... I seriously would rather die than let a psycho like that cut me open."

Finn winced. "Don't talk like that. You don't know if..."

She turned to face him. "I think we do know, Finn. And now I just want to enjoy whatever time I have left."

CHAPTER 27

THE REST OF MARCH dragged on. Some days held no reprieve. In her better moods, she savored the slowness of it all—letting the sun soak into her cheeks as she had lunch on the porch with Willa, laughing at Finn's jokes as they walked through town, basking in pride at creating art with Sam. But each day passing left her a little more certain she wouldn't reach the end of the year. She hadn't found any peace in that—she never would—but it allowed her to accept each day for what it was. A bad day was still another day, so in a way, she welcomed them too.

Her birthday was approaching rapidly, and more often than not, Willa was shoving something into a closet, or speaking quietly on comms until Cassidy came into the room. She was terrible at hiding what she was up to—not that Cassidy minded. Her birthday, even if it most likely was her last one, wasn't a day she placed much importance on. But she was happy to let her friends do whatever they needed to do to feel like they'd done something nice for her. They'd all been picking up the slack for her much more often than she was comfortable with. Her pride hung around as stubbornly as her illness.

Willa made all of their meals, did most of the animal care, and prepared for harvesting all by herself. Whatever Cassidy did took three times the effort, and she only remembered half the steps anyway. Some of Finn's construction friends started to stop by once a week to take care of odd jobs now that the church was renovated. It did ease Cassidy's worries a bit about how things would be once she was gone. It was a morbid thought, to imagine the world without oneself in it, but it was something she couldn't help but do.

Annabelle stopped by too to bring Cassidy little things to try to ease her pain. Some days, Mara would join and help Willa with chores around the house. Cassidy and Annabelle would sip on bitter teas as Cassidy schooled her disgust with each sip, and they'd talk about their lives. She appreciated how Annabelle never once asked how she was feeling. Instead, she wanted to talk about her travels, her photography, jobs she used to have. Cassidy talked about being raised by her grandmother, on the days when the pain didn't sharpen all her words into barbs.

Those days became far too frequent for Cassidy's liking. She spent half her time asleep, and the other half, she was apologizing for her sharpness or tone. She didn't want to deal with herself, so she had no idea how anyone else could stand it. It was a vicious cycle of lashing out, then feeling shame for doing so, on and on. She was trying. Her friends were trying. There was just nothing anyone could do to have an effect.

She and Sam were sitting in the darkroom developing Cassidy's latest batch of photos one night. She'd been snapping anything and everything that caught her eye, desperate to memorialize it all. She no longer cared about composition or framing, but took whatever was right for her. Photos were one of the only ways to express her thoughts when the brain fog and exhaustion halted her words.

They'd been quiet for the better part of the hour, remarking on her work and talking about small-town gossip. The red emanating from the ceiling used to put her on edge, but now it dulled her headaches and soothed her eye strain. She loved it: still having a purpose. Sam set up a stool for her to complete the drawn-out steps without losing all of her stamina. The walls were a battle between her photos and theirs. There was hardly any blank space left. She liked seeing a small way in which she'd left her mark.

Sam broke the silence. "What are you going to do with all of these?"

Cassidy shrugged. "The better question is, what are *you* going to do with all of these? I'm not going to need them."

They sighed, a small smile playing on their lips. "I'll never get used to how morbid you've become."

"Dying will do that to you." Cassidy laughed.

Sam was silent for a while. "Are you scared?"

"Of course. But I've been scared of this for years, doing whatever I could to avoid it. It's almost, I don't know … relaxing to give in."

They frowned. "It's not fair."

"No, maybe not. But what is?" She stood up, leaving her latest print to soak in the tray. "Can you promise me something?"

"What?"

"Look out for Willa and Finn. You have Alex. Don't let them drift apart again, okay?"

"Of course not." They shifted, wrestling with their thoughts. "Can I ask, are you and Willa...?"

Cassidy sighed. "No, I burned that bridge. But we're good, in a different way than I hoped."

"Just taking what you can get, right?"

Cassidy's smile was framed with sadness. "Right."

They continued for a little longer until Cassidy's head was bothering her too much. Sam insisted on walking her home, and Alex gave her a fierce hug. They grew more intense every time he said goodbye to her. She cherished it. Her left leg had been dragging, and she walked slower than usual, but Sam never minded. They told her about the stories they were working on for the paper, and the ways Ranger had gotten into trouble that week. Cassidy would miss their conversations.

She started to get lightheaded as they passed through town and made their way towards the field. She ignored it, used to the unease. But by the time she reached the bridge, she was having trouble walking. Sam glanced at her sideways. "Cass?"

"Sorry, I need a second..." Her words came out sloppy as she leaned against the railing of the bridge for support.

Sam crouched down to her level, their gaze boring into

hers. "What is it?"

"Just ... dizzy..." But now Cassidy's breaths were coming harder too, until she was wheezing like she'd been running the whole way. She started to teeter past the railing.

"Shit." Sam wrapped a hand around her arm to steady her. "What do you need? Can you sit down?"

She nodded, finding words too difficult, and let Sam guide her to the ground. The edges of her vision darkened in a vignette, and the crickets around them all sounded so far away.

"Cass? Stay awake, okay? I'm going to find Finn. I'll be back in five minutes. Please don't move."

As if that was possible. She tried to laugh, but only a hiss of air escaped her lips. Their footsteps retreated as she tried to focus her vision. She let her head loll against the side of the bridge, forehead tilted up towards the stars. She picked out her favorite constellations until her vision went black.

She came to again between Sam and Finn's arms. They were already past the clearing and almost to the ranch. Finn was muttering something too low for Cassidy's ears to register. He stiffened as she started to move her limbs on her own. "Hey, Cass. You with us?" She grunted, but no words came out. Everything hurt, deeper and sharper than she was used to. Her mind was in a million places and nowhere all at once, but in the back of it all, she wondered if this was it. She would have liked more time, but she couldn't fight it as much as she wanted to.

She blacked out again, and this time she had no idea how long. She woke up in a bed twice as large as her own and covered in a deep purple comforter. The room was unfamiliar, but made perfect sense. If she were well, she would've taken greater care to look around in this room she had always wondered about. The door was closed, but voices filtered through from the other side. At times, it sounded like they weren't speaking English at all, but some strange gibberish. She only picked out bits and pieces.

"—much longer is this supposed to go on—"

"—getting worse—"

"—don't care what the doctor—"

"—have to respect her wishes—"

Her whole body was heavy, like she'd sink through the mattress with the force of it. It was a bizarre sensation, but altogether preferable to the pain she had been in. She couldn't tell who had been speaking—Willa and Sam, or Willa and Finn—but she thought she heard heavy steps and the slamming of a door. Hadn't they all known this was coming? She wanted to rest for a bit. She closed her eyes and drifted off as Willa's bedroom door creaked open.

It was light the next time she opened her eyes. There was a glass of water on the nightstand that she reached for and gulped it down, cradling the glass between both of her hands. She swung her legs off the bed, using her hands along with her body's limited strength, and gingerly stood up. She padded down the hall, seeing everything from that angle for the first time. Willa was asleep on the couch, pillows strewn everywhere to make space for her. She was curled inwards, facing the back cushions and snoring.

Cassidy didn't want to wake her, guilty for having slept in her massive bed while she was curled up on the couch. She wasn't sure why they'd brought her into Willa's house; her own room was much closer to the gate. If her chip was to be believed, then it was half past seven, so Cassidy decided to start on breakfast. She pulled a chair up to the counter and began chopping peppers and onions to make a scramble. The one thing the ranch always had plenty of was eggs, and it required the least amount of work to put together.

Cassidy stirred as the eggs went from runny to solid, and the kitchen filled with the scent of peppers and onions. She seasoned it with salt and pepper. She would add hot sauce to her portion, but found Willa had no taste for anything past mildly spicy. She was about to get up and grab the plates when Willa came through the doorway. Her hair was pulled up in a messy bun, and the half-moons under her eyes were darker than usual, but her smile was brighter than Cassidy expected.

"Hey, what are you doing up? You could've woken me if you wanted breakfast."

"I know, but you seemed like you needed the rest." Willa raised an eyebrow at the irony of that statement, but let Cassidy continue. "Why was I in your room?"

Willa looked down, crossing her arms in front of her. "I wanted to keep an eye on you. In case..."

"Right." Cassidy gulped. "Well, I'm okay. It was a little touch-and-go. I'm glad Sam and Finn were here."

Willa exhaled sharply, not responding for a moment.

"Cass, you looked half dead. I thought... I didn't know if I'd wake up and find you gone."

"I'm sorry, Willa. It was just a bad episode, though, okay?"

"Come on, Cassidy. We're watching you die! Why are you letting it happen?" Then she said more quietly, "Why are you doing this to all of us?"

"You didn't see what Dr. Thorne has become. He couldn't have helped me."

Willa threw her hands up in frustration. "You didn't even let him try!"

Cassidy shook her head. "What's the point? It was my decision. It's done. We don't even know if the doctor could've helped me. And there was no way I could pay for those appointments. So, I don't know why you're picking a fight about it."

"You really think that's all this is? Me picking a fight?"

"Well, what is it then?"

"I *love* you, you idiot." Willa's voice cracked on the last syllable, and she turned away. "I love you ... and you're making me watch you die."

"Willa, I—"

"I wanted you to fight because *you* wanted to. Not because of anything I felt. You're right: it is your decision. But do you think no one will care when you're gone?"

Cassidy stood and turned to face her. "Hell, Willa, don't you think we should've had this conversation before I went to see the doctor?"

"So, you're saying you would've done things differently if you knew how I felt?"

Cassidy shifted her feet, but didn't respond.

"That's what I thought." Willa sighed. "I'm not hungry. Just put my breakfast in the fridge." She walked out as soon as the words were in the air.

Cassidy sat back down, stunned. How had she missed this?

She had always lived on her own, on her terms. It hadn't occurred to her to think about anyone else's feelings, as terrible as that sounded. She hadn't had someone care for her since her grandma died. What a terrible irony to know she'd had something she longed for so desperately, and it couldn't matter anymore. She could admit that she was being selfish. But what else could she do? Life had forced her to be that way for too long.

Cassidy slammed the pot she'd used into the sink and regretted how it dinged up the rim. It didn't calm the torrent of emotions raging through her. She caught movement out of the corner of her eye from the window above the sink. She thought it might be Willa going out to work, but a figure dressed in all white stood out under the morning sun. She blinked, and it was gone.

She shot up, intent on following. Who else could it be but him? She'd had enough of being threatened and stalked. If he had the audacity to show up after the last time, then she'd make him regret it. Cassidy unlocked the safe under the loft stairs and took out the lightest plasma gun, hearing it hum to life as she charged out the door.

CHAPTER 28

SHE LOOKED LEFT AND right, but didn't find him anywhere. Her gun rocked against her shoulder as she took off towards the fence, ignoring the way her hip ached with the pace she set for herself. Once she rounded the storage shed, she caught him again, near the vegetable gardens.

"Hey!" she shouted as she advanced. Her vision tunneled; all she was focused on was making him leave her alone. Hadn't the Corporation taken enough from her? She couldn't even die in an abandoned corner of the world without being reminded of them and their destruction.

She neared him as he leaned against the fence, hat down and obscuring most of his face. One hand was in his front pocket, and the other toyed with the ends of his beard. He was whistling, the tone low and rich. Gone were his pristine white gloves, the state-of-the-art model of his hand implant glinting gold under the harsh sun. The sharp hum of her ammunition button activating was the only sound she greeted him with.

He sighed and reached up, taking his gilded synth hand and slowly removing the hat from his head, holding it to his chest. His hair matched the color of his beard, dark curls sticking out from being under the hat. A strong brow framed bright blue eyes, which were clearer than Cassidy expected them to be. Her gaze tracked the gold implant that ran down the column of his throat and disappeared under the neckline of his white button-down shirt. She had never seen him before, not truly. He looked like the few pictures she'd seen of her father before her grandma had hidden all the frames.

She leveled the gun at his chest. Thanks to Willa's training, she knew her aim was true. "You have some nerve coming here."

His sparkling blue eyes met hers. "You look a little worse for wear, Cassidy."

"I'm *dying*, asshole. So, I guess you'll get what you came here for."

His usually sharp smile was subdued, just barely bringing out the dimple in his left cheek. "But where's the fun in that?"

"You know me. I live to please."

His chuckle reverberated in the space between them. "I will miss our conversations."

"Yeah, they're really something." She swallowed the lump in her throat. Seeing Willa being fearless was nothing like having to be fearless herself. "You know I can't let you leave."

"That's supposed to be my line."

She let out a dry, mirthless laugh. "I can't have you threatening my friends. And I'm not scared of you anymore."

"Cassidy, Cassidy... You know I'm not a threat to anyone. Not even you."

She scoffed. This from the man who had been stalking and threatening her for the better part of a year? His denial was almost insulting. "Can't take the chance."

"I know." He kneeled down slowly, clean white pants meeting the dirty ground. How easily he acquiesced to her. She didn't want to question why.

A deep breath in. Could she end a life? Even his? There was a small comfort in knowing she wouldn't carry the burden of it for very long. And she could leave knowing her friends were safe from the Corporation's ever-reaching grasp.

She met his eyes—she owed him that much—and squeezed the trigger. Every bone in her body felt the weight of that choice. Her weakened muscles shook with the recoil, and the bullet sailed ahead. It went straight through the empty expanse where the man had been kneeling and evaporated when it made no contact.

He wasn't there. He never was. She wouldn't see the man in white again—because he was waiting for her on the other side.

She laughed at the absurdity of it all, the trick she'd played on herself. It was a relief that the Corporation hadn't found her after all, but her laugh took on a choking intensity when she realized what her mind had done to her.

Willa came running from the house, her own weapon in hand. "I heard a shot! Is everything okay?" She neared Cassidy like she would a startled horse. "Cass, what happened?"

Nothing was okay, but in this small way, she would be okay. The deep fears that burrowed into the recesses of her mind had evaporated when she pulled the trigger. A bolt of exhilaration took hold over her. If she could conquer him, she had a bit more bravery than she gave herself credit for.

Cassidy turned to Willa, abandoning the gun at her side. She had enough extra bravery to let out a truth between them that she'd been keeping out of reach since the day at the waterfall. "I love you too."

Willa cupped her face reverently and kissed her like a goodbye. They didn't speak on the walk back to the house, hand in hand. They lay together like lovers who had all the time in the world. Willa ran her fingers through Cassidy's hair with one hand, the other intertwined with her organic one. Calloused fingertips brushed against Cassidy's swollen knuckles. Willa hummed quietly, the sound vibrating through the place where Cassidy's ear lay on her chest. Cassidy drifted off, and when she woke up, Willa was still next to her, reading a book.

She stretched, feeling lighter than she had in months. Willa glanced over, noticing the shift in the bed.

"Feel any better?"

"Somewhat." Cassidy eased herself up into a sitting position, sipping on the water Willa had left on her nightstand.

"Do you want to tell me what that was about?"

Cassidy winced. "It's not going to make sense."

"Try me."

Something about their fight cleared the air between them, almost to the way things were before everything went wrong at the beach. She didn't want to talk about the man in white; that was one thing she'd always keep to herself. But she did want to clear the air between them.

"So, where are we at? I understand if you don't want anything to change, since I'm..."

Willa put her book down, shifting to face Cassidy. "I don't want to waste time being mad at you. I want to enjoy whatever we have left."

Cassidy grasped her hands. "I'm grateful."

The next two weeks, they spent all of their time together, watching movies and taking things easy. Willa hired two temporary hands to do most of the ranch work, one of them being Mara. She popped out often to check on things, unable to leave everything in someone else's hands, but she spent a considerable amount of her time taking care of Cassidy.

Sam popped in about every other day, sometimes bringing Alex or Ranger with them. The nights they brought Ranger were Cassidy's favorite. Tom didn't know what to make of him, so he'd stand around with a puffed tail and arched back until they left. Finn would stop by every day after work, taking walks with Willa as Cassidy napped, and cooking them both dinner.

Cassidy was the most at peace she had been in a very long time. She was always in pain and declining in different ways each day, but she had friends, love, and a home. She couldn't enjoy it for as long as she wanted to, but it would have to be enough.

By then, Cassidy was a week away from being thirty-one, and she was walking with a cane. It wasn't anything fancy, like she would've gotten under the Corporation, but it was solid and did the job well enough. Willa even knitted an emerald-green cover for the handle. It seemed the birthday party was still happening, and there was nothing Cassidy could do to stop it, apart from ... well, the inevitable.

Cassidy said no presents; what use would she have for them? She was already giving her things away, what little she had; there was no need to add to the balance of it.

The day of the party arrived and Cassidy had barely slept the night before. It was a strange perversion of the night before Christmas with her grandmother. She'd be up half the night, listening for the sound of her presents being delivered. Then she'd spend until daybreak squirming in anticipation, high on the thought that her presents were down the hall, and all she had to do was walk over and open them. She had once, when she was eight. She opened up a paint-by-number kit she'd begged for, with only the fading stars to judge her. She felt so guilty that she taped the wrapping paper back together and cried until her grandmother came to wake her up.

That sour memory didn't stop her from missing Christmas though, or the holidays in general. No one in California celebrated, past going to church or having a small meal with family. She wanted to decorate the town, give out presents, and celebrate like she was used to. But California was a hard place that bred hard people, and she knew it would take a lot of time and resources to do something so frivolous.

When she did make it out of bed in the early afternoon, Willa had already set up the bulk of the decorations. Green and blue streamers crisscrossed the ceiling of the house. Outside, holo-lights led out to the barn over benches, tables, chairs, and anything she could find so their guests could gather under them. The party wasn't supposed to start for another five hours, and Cassidy couldn't imagine what else Willa had left to do.

A friend of Finn's was spreading new hay out for the horses in their corral.

"Jack, have you seen Willa around?"

He turned, arms bundled around a small lump of Timothy hay. "Oh, hey, Cassidy. I think she's still out. She left about an hour ago with Finn and Mara."

Cassidy frowned, but nodded her thanks. Willa watched her like a hawk, only willing to let Cassidy out of her sight when she had to sleep or use the restroom. It was odd that she'd leave her alone with only an acquaintance nearby.

In the meantime, she made herself as presentable as possible. After a shower, she did her best to do something nice with her hair. It was still too straight and yellowish for her liking, but she put it in a half ponytail and tied an old ribbon around it to be festive. The weather was perfect, mid-seventies with a late spring breeze, so she put on jeans and a cardigan Annabelle had loaned her.

The task took about an hour and a half, much longer than it used to. Willa still hadn't checked in on her. She ventured back out to poke around the greenhouse and check how her seeds were doing. They would bloom in the next few months. Cassidy wondered if she'd get to see them. She spent as much time there as she was able, relishing the dirt under her fingernails and the sun on her back. She thought about all of the things she took for granted, being alive, being present. It made her feel better in a way, thinking about dying. It made all the positives in her life that much brighter as all the negatives drifted away. What could be worse than the end?

She carried her new mindset with her as she waited for her birthday party.

CHAPTER 29

CASSIDY WAS OUT IN the open area where Willa had set up all the tables and chairs when the first guests started to arrive. Sam and Alex came a bit early to help with some finishing touches. To Cassidy's relief, they didn't bring her a present, but Sam did have all of her developed photos in an envelope for her. The walk was too far to visit very often, so she hadn't been back since the last disastrous time.

Annabelle was next, right on time, bearing fresh flowers and homemade bread. When Cassidy raised an eyebrow, she insisted it was a hostess gift, not a birthday gift. She sat with Annabelle, sipping on fancy flavored waters Willa bought in town. Willa and Mara had returned about twenty minutes prior with catering that Mara's mother, the owner of the diner, had graciously prepared. There was still no sign of Finn, though.

Cassidy motioned for Willa to join them, but she smiled and indicated she would later. She was still fluttering around, hands full of different baskets of things. Cassidy frowned to herself. She was supposed to enjoy the evening too.

The sun was starting to set, and the glow of the holo-lights contrasted the deep blue and red settling on the horizon. Willa had speakers set up, so a jazz record played in the background. It wasn't Cassidy's favorite, but she admitted it made more suitable background music than her usual synth-pop. Willa finally joined all of them outside, looking a bit haggard, but smiling so wide that her dimples popped out.

"How y'all doing? Need anything?"

Cassidy rolled her eyes and patted Willa's arm. "Enjoy the party. We can all take care of ourselves."

"Everything looks amazing," Annabelle joined in. "You did a great job, Willa."

Willa blushed, but didn't find the words to respond.

Alex steered the conversation for them. "Annabelle, you must be happy to be back at home."

"These last few months have been so refreshing. I'm glad to get back to normal."

They talked about everything except how Cassidy was doing, for which she was grateful. Willa had only been sitting down for about thirty minutes when she and Sam wandered off into the house.

Annabelle's face brightened. "Oh, I didn't think you were coming!"

Cassidy craned her neck around to see Finn walking towards their little group, with a sheepish smile and flowers in hand. He'd come from the direction of the back gate instead of the main one. "Hey, y'all. Sorry I'm late."

Cassidy shot up and wrapped him in as tight of a hug as she was capable of. He took a seat between Alex and Annabelle, angling his body towards the schoolteacher. Cassidy was certain he didn't realize he was doing it. Before he could get too settled, Willa bustled out with giant dishes of steaming hot food. Sam followed behind her, balancing three trays towards the tables lined up along the edge of the party area.

"I hope everyone's hungry!" Willa announced, placing the final dish at the end of the row. Despite them being outdoors, it filled the air with incredible aromas of cilantro, onion, pepper, and all kinds of meats. It was way more food than was necessary for their small gathering, but Cassidy wouldn't complain. It looked like a mix of food from the diner and some of Cassidy's favorite dishes of Willa's.

Everyone got in line to help themselves and fill their plates as Willa stood back watching. Cassidy joined her, smiling. "Guess you got what you wanted."

Willa turned to her, as if somewhat in a daze. "Hmm? What do you mean?"

"Wanting to cook for people. This is like a one-night restaurant experience."

Willa's smile was small, personal. "I guess you could look at it that way."

"Thank you for this, Will. You didn't have to go to so much trouble." Willa fixed her with a hard stare that dared her to continue the thought. Cassidy laughed and relented, "I mean, I appreciate it. This is perfect."

Willa wordlessly squeezed her hand before drifting back into the house to grab the millionth thing she was certain was required at the party, or else it would be a complete failure. Cassidy smiled to herself and joined the line for food. She was determined to try a little bit of everything, so when she told Willa how amazing it was, she would mean it.

They all sat down, each claiming a piece of mismatched furniture, and enjoyed the food. It was silent from how intent everyone was on enjoying what was on their plates. Willa had a decent sampling, but just picked at it absent-mindedly while she scanned the crowd to make sure everyone was enjoying themselves.

As they ate, they told Cassidy stories of themselves growing up. Finn, Annabelle, Mara, and Willa had all gone to school together since age five. It was before the church was built, so they'd alternate between different people's houses, or meet out in the empty field on a good day. Beth, now retired, used to be the teacher before Annabelle filled the position. They all talked about her so fondly that Cassidy wished she'd been a little less self-absorbed and had gone to meet her.

Cassidy was a bit jealous of how long they'd all been friends; she'd never had that. But she enjoyed hearing the stories. She loved hearing how Annabelle would chase frogs in the field instead of listening to lessons, or how Finn used to let Mara put his hair into puffy pigtails during their lunch hour. They told each anecdote so vividly, it was like she had grown up along with them. She, Sam, and Alex didn't have a way to relate to their upbringings, all being from different places, but they weren't outsiders either. The conversation never dwindled as they ate, until the plates were stacked and taken into the house to be washed later. Finn set up a small bonfire they all huddled around, fending off the breeze that settled in. Everyone was bathed in a stark orange light that stuck on their cheekbones and the tips of their noses.

Tom came around to wind around people's legs and croak for attention. He was hamming it up, and their guests played right into it, cooing about how cute he was and scratching him behind the ears until he'd flop down onto the dirt. When he got tired of the attention, he settled down in Cassidy's lap and fell asleep, snores mingling with the soft jazz.

Willa slipped away at some point and returned bearing a beautiful baby-green-and-purple cake with giant sparkler holo-candles with the number thirty-one on them. To Cassidy's chagrin, they sang her "Happy Birthday" as the sparklers crackled off the top, lighting up Willa's exuberant smile. Willa and Alex passed out the slices, a delicious lemon-and-blueberry cake with a vanilla filling. The last person to have made Cassidy a cake for anything was her grandmother, and it meant something that Willa had gone to the trouble for her.

"How did you get an entire cake?" Cassidy asked between mouthfuls, eyes wide.

Willa laughed. "Finn and I each baked a layer, and we decorated it at his place."

That explained his tardiness, then. Her heart hummed with appreciation, and she was surprised to find she enjoyed being cherished. She'd spent so many years being forgotten and ignored by her parents before she went to live with her grandma that some small part of her had come to expect the worst on days that were supposed to be special. It was fitting that her last birthday was her best.

Things wound down at their own pace. No one was in much of a hurry to leave. For the first time in a while, Cassidy had been able to get out of her head for the entire evening, and she hardly paid her symptoms any mind. Everything was more tolerable because of how loved she felt, how she mattered to these people who mattered to her.

Annabelle was the first to leave, blaming the following school day for her early departure. Cassidy didn't envy how early she'd have to be up as she hugged her goodbye. Over her shoulder, she made a face at Finn he was pretending to ignore. She decided there was no point in being subtle. "Thank you so much for coming, Annabelle. It's so dark, why doesn't Finn walk you home?"

"Oh, that's alright. I'm not going far. I don't want to be any trouble."

"It isn't," Cassidy quickly answered for him, shooing them both towards the gate.

Willa snickered behind her hand. Once they were far enough away, Mara gave her a high five. Things had been brewing between those two long before Cassidy was in the picture, and she was determined to bring them together before she was gone.

Mara drifted off soon after. Not one for goodbyes, she thanked them for hosting, wished Cassidy a final happy birthday, and saluted the group as she sauntered towards the gate. That left the four of them, until Finn was due to return, assuming he wasn't mad at the stunt she'd pulled and didn't return at all.

Sam and Alex shared an oversized armchair close to the fire. Alex absent-mindedly played with a lock of Sam's dark hair curling behind their ear as Sam and Willa chatted about a band they both liked. Cassidy marveled at the quiet intimacy of it and wondered when that sort of thing would happen naturally, if she and Willa would get the time.

Eventually, it was too late for them, even being night owls themselves, and they started on their goodbyes. Willa offered them the loft or the twin unit to Cassidy's dwelling, which had sat unused this entire time, but they politely declined. As long of a walk as it was, they were apprehensive to leave Ranger by himself to get into whatever trouble he'd find.

Cassidy gave them both long, pressing hugs, unwilling to let go. Sam had almost as much to do with the party as Willa, and she was so grateful for all of their effort. The night had been something she would have planned for herself if she'd had the care to. It was humbling to have someone who understood her. They eventually set off hand in hand with packed containers of leftover food toward the sapphire-stained horizon. Willa followed them to the gate, finishing a conversation she and Alex had started while Cassidy said her goodbyes.

Finn returned as Cassidy picked at the last slice of cake, running her fork through the ribbons of frosting. He sat down next to her, and she grinned. "So, how was the walk with Annabelle?"

He cracked half a smile. "You're relentless, you know that?" She didn't respond, forcing him to continue. He sighed, "It was nice. We talked."

"And?"

"And that's it." He gave her a pointed look, and they both

laughed.

Cassidy sighed. "I'm not giving up on you two."

"Yeah, yeah." He put on an annoyed expression, but Cassidy knew his mannerisms too well. She decided that would be her final gift to him, however she could make it happen.

Finn helped gather all the trash and decorations, so critters wouldn't get into them overnight. Willa kept shooing him off, but he smiled and helped despite her insistence that he relax. Cassidy knew it was because she couldn't afford to do more than one thing at a time, and without his help, it'd take them all night. She fought down the guilt that emerged. Willa offered to let Finn crash with them, since he'd gone to the trouble of coming back, but he declined. They did make plans for lunch later in the week, which lightened the unease in Cassidy's chest. She was suddenly adrift in thoughts of a future she'd have no part in, the fathomless depths of despair growing within her.

Then it was just Willa and Cassidy. The place was still a mess. Furniture was strewn all over the area they'd set up, lights flickered above them, and containers of forgotten food were lined up along the perimeter. Willa brought the rest of the food into the house, while Cassidy attempted to start organizing the furniture for where it needed to be put away. She hadn't made much progress before Willa softly grasped her hand and pulled her back into the house. They passed through the living room with missing furniture and the kitchen stacked high with dirty dishes and headed directly to Willa's room—though as of late, it had more so become *their* room. Cassidy's things littered half the room; she was much messier than Willa and constantly tried to pick up after herself, to no avail.

They had mostly kept to their sides, sometimes waking up involuntarily in each other's arms. It wasn't something they spoke about. They changed into their sleepwear quietly, neither breaking the unspoken rule to keep their backs to each other. It was a continuation of the strange dance they did, away from their deeper truths. It was too raw, too painful, too close to the end. Finally, well past their usual bedtimes, they ended the night reading under the covers. They'd recently swapped books, and Willa had been enjoying the one Cassidy picked out for her—so much so that she almost didn't hear the quiet confession from Cassidy.

"Thank you for putting everything together. It was one of the best birthdays I've ever had."

Willa smiled behind the pages of her book. "Yeah. You deserved it."

Cassidy couldn't agree, but for once she couldn't quite argue either, so she just closed her book and willed herself to fall asleep in spite of her racing mind. Socializing always recharged her battery, so to speak, rather than drained it, and she always had a hard time with the comedown. On really high nights, she'd indulge in Chroma just to quiet her mind, but she'd used the last of her stash after seeing the man in white again. And she was dying, so there was no reason to accelerate the time she had left with such a nasty substance.

But that meant she was stuck in her head, left to dwell on everything she'd been blissfully free of the whole night. She finally had something to lose, and she was guaranteed to lose it. Had she not done enough? Given up too easily? Her chest started to ache with the burden of the what-ifs. To have come so far and survived so many deadlines, only to now stop short at a question mark was a lot like giving up. Maybe Willa was right. But she feared it was too late to heed her warning now.

She tossed and turned for the better part of an hour until even Willa turned off her bedside light and slid fully under the covers.

"Will?" she breathed, hoping she wasn't too late. The woman fell asleep faster than should be possible.

"Yeah?"

"Do you think you could do something for me?"

CHAPTER 30

IT TOOK ANOTHER WEEK until Cassidy and Willa had the free time to fulfill her request, and they were able to do so with an unexpected gift from Finn. In the week that passed, Cassidy's joints were hurting too much and her dexterity was abandoning her too fast for her to walk without the use of aids. Her cane was no longer enough, so Finn stopped by one cloudy morning to bring by a project he had been working on for her.

It was like a wheelchair found in every Corporation hospital, but it was rounded at the bottom and hovered almost a foot in the air. Finn showed her the controls. "I was thinking this would help with getting around, since the ground is so uneven." Cassidy leaned on his and Willa's arms as they guided her into the chair. Her stomach preemptively dropped in anticipation of her weighing it down to the ground, but it didn't so much as falter as she sank into it.

"I don't know what to say, Finn. This is incredible." She and Willa hadn't been on a hike since their trip to the poppy fields well over half a year ago. She longed to take one last trip and had almost given up on the idea. She winked at Finn as he left out the front gate, ready to act on her final wishes. Dr. Thorne's last words came back to her like a sick joke, but he wouldn't be right. Not entirely. She would never give in and crawl back to his horrendous basement.

They set out after lunch, back to the waterfall. That was where she had first realized Willa was a person she couldn't live without, when she felt like California could be home.

With the hover chair, she could do laps around Willa, but she refrained and kept an even pace at her side as they traversed the mountain. This time, she knew all the plants by heart, even the blooms that had been out of season the last time they'd crossed these paths. She still let Willa explain each one, listening as if they were secrets of the universe. She picked the flowers Willa approved of as they went, creating a wild bouquet of pinks, oranges, and yellows, her little handful of a sunset.

Cassidy slowed their pace towards the top, taking it all in—the way the storm clouds cleared for them as they made their ascent, giving way to crystal-blue skies kissed with fluffy white clouds. She had thought a storm would roll in by the looks of things that morning, so she was grateful the weather had done her a favor.

Once they broke into the clearing, they were surrounded by the chorus of wildlife and water and soft conversation ahead.

Willa frowned. "I didn't think anyone else knew about this place."

Cassidy moved ahead, intent on her goal. She tapped at the back of her chair to make sure her bag was still strapped over it. Just ahead in the clearing, Sam and Finn had set up a small picnic on a puffy green blanket. Willa looked at her, stunned, and then a bit suspicious.

"Cass...?"

Cassidy grabbed her hand and pulled her towards their friends. It was a bit awkward at her height in the chair, but Willa followed her anyway. Sam and Finn had a spread of fruits, sandwiches, and sides that Finn had made the night before, per Cassidy's instructions on what Willa liked best. They had also brought Willa's favorite strawberry soda and some sparkling water. It wasn't the grandest gesture, but it suited them. Willa had never been one for flashy declarations or overly nice things. Sam and Finn hugged both of them once they reached the blanket's edge. Willa just stood there, looking like she was about to be the butt of a joke.

"What's going on?"

"I wanted us all to get together. I have some things I want to say." Cassidy leaned on Finn as he lowered her onto the blanket to sit with them.

Willa still looked a bit apprehensive, but joined them and sat to Cassidy's left. "When did you plan all this?"

"After my birthday."

Willa gave a sly smile. "Very sneaky."

Finn passed out food as Sam filled little plastic cups with their drinks of choice. Cassidy set up the flowers she'd picked in an empty cup. It had turned into a warm day once the weather cleared, but the mist from the waterfall cooled their little alcove. The food was great; Cassidy didn't have room for much, but she nibbled at a bit of everything. They talked aimlessly until it was time to get to the point of why she'd gathered them all here.

"I thought this would be as good a time as any for this conversation, while my brain is still cooperating." She laughed to try to cut through the somber air that settled over the group. "I wanted to thank you all, for everything you've done for me. I didn't think I'd meet such amazing people out here. I can't tell you how grateful I am."

"Of course, Cass." Finn smiled. "You don't have to thank us."

"I don't know if I'll get another chance to. I have something for each of you." She leaned back to the chair and untangled her bag from where it was slung. She pulled out her camera first and set it in Sam's lap. "I want you to have my photos and my camera. There's no one better to take care of it and create more memories with it."

Sam, for the first time she'd met them, blinked away a heavy tear. "I'll treasure it always. Thank you."

She dug around for her projector, which held all of her old movies, and handed it to Finn. "You love these movies more than I do. I should have given this to you sooner."

Finn laughed and sniffled, throat thick with held-back tears. "I'll watch every single one of them."

Finally, Cassidy pulled out a small box and handed it to Willa. "You've changed my life. Whether I have ten or a hundred days left, I will love you through all of them. I'm sorry for constantly screwing things up. Thank you for not quitting on me." Willa was sobbing by that point, tears running down her face. She made no effort to wipe them away as she opened the small box. There were developed photos of all the portraits Cassidy had taken of her, as well as photos of the two of them she had taken when Willa hadn't noticed.

"Oh my god." Willa gingerly picked the stack up and started to shuffle through them, when her breath caught at what was in the bottom of the box.

"It was my grandmother's. I hope it's sized right."

Willa, almost in a daze, pulled out a dainty gold ring with an amethyst set into the center of the band. It would have made a huge dent in Cassidy's medical debt, or Dr. Thorne's fee. By sheer luck up to that point, she had never sold it off; maybe something in her knew it was always meant to belong to Willa.

"If we'd had more time, I'd ask you for real, to make it official. But I won't make you go through that again. This is so you can always remember how much I love you. You don't even have to wear it if you don't want to."

Wordlessly, Willa slid it onto her ring finger, which had been bare as long as Cassidy knew her. She stared at it for a beat before turning and kissing Cassidy. She tasted like strawberries and tears, bittersweet. "I love you too. It's beautiful, I'll never take it off." She glanced down again, then said in a small voice, "I would have said yes."

All four of them were crying at that point, but Cassidy wasn't embarrassed. It was almost cathartic to share this with them. She hated that she was causing this, through her own actions or not, but at the same time, a small part of her was glad. She mattered. When it was her time, she wouldn't be lost to the world. She'd linger in them, in some small way. It was finally enough for her.

No one spoke for a while. Cassidy's head rested on Willa's shoulder, and her hand clasped Finn's. Willa was rubbing Sam's arm as she hummed an old folk song. Between the scattered sniffles and the rush of water behind them, they listened to her voice fill the air. Cassidy hoped if there was a place afterwards, it would feel like this—loved and warm and whole.

She hadn't expected to grow so fond of California. But now, knowing it was the place she'd die, she found it was the only place she wanted to be. Such a harsh, dangerous land, but full of the most genuine and caring people she'd ever met. The edge of the world wasn't such a bad place after all.

The following weeks moved like years. Each day was a different kind of trial for Cassidy, some new obstacle she had to learn to cope with. Some days, her mind wasn't with her at all, and she couldn't remember basic tasks, like how to get around the ranch or use the bathroom. Those days, she did her best not to lash out at Willa, who she feared would only remember her in those moments—where she was more a patient than a lover, a burden than a friend. Her friends all drifted through her consciousness, visiting on good and bad days alike. Tom took to living in the house and sleeping in their bed. When Willa tried to shoo him away, he would hunker down, using all his body mass to become immovable.

On the days Cassidy had the strength to, she would sit upright and brush his fur for hours. Most days, though, she couldn't do much more than toss and turn in bed. Her body hurt from whatever was wrong with it, and it hurt even more from being bedridden. Willa tried to walk with her in her chair as much as possible. The fresh air was nice for Cassidy. The end of spring was making way for summer, and there was a sweetness in the air. Cassidy wished she'd see another fall; it had turned out to be her favorite season in California.

It was midsummer when she was no longer able to leave her bed at all. She wasted away as a harsh sandstorm raged outside. Particles of rock and debris battered the windows relentlessly. Finn and Sam stopped by together every day, despite the conditions. They'd have long conversations with Willa outside the bedroom door that went in and out of Cassidy's ears. Sometimes their speech was low, but sometimes someone was louder than the others. Time didn't mean very much to Cassidy during those weeks. Willa brought her meal trays several times a day, or small snacks and water. But she didn't eat.

There was finally a day when she was well enough to get out of that room. The room she had always wondered about had now become too familiar. She wanted to look at a different color of wall and see the sun beam in from a different direction. She used her arms to swing to the side of the bed, elbows shaking with the effort. Her head was throbbing, but that was nothing new, so she did her best to ignore it. Her chair was just past the nightstand, and she motioned for it to glide to the edge of the bed. Even parked right alongside her, it was a monumental distance. She steadied herself, taking in a few deep breaths, then lifted herself up and over. By a few inches, she missed the seat of the chair and pitched forward, meeting with the floor. Her hands couldn't move fast enough to break the fall, and her whole body smarted. More than pain though, she felt a jolt of panic as she tried to right herself. Adrenaline worked to get her limbs moving, but it wasn't enough. Frustrated tears collected in the corners of her eyes. Willa would have heard the thud and would come to check on her in moments.

But she was tired. Tired of hurting like this, having Willa see her like this, being reduced to this. She wished whatever was taking over her body would get on with it and save her from the relentless torment.

Willa shoved the door open. "Oh, Cass! What happened?" She lifted her under her arms and got her settled back into bed. When she could no longer hold her tears back, they poured down her face, and Willa brushed away each one. "I've got you. Relax. Try and rest."

Cassidy wondered if the next time she rested would be the time she didn't wake up.

That was the last time Cassidy tried to get up, or had any longing to. She'd resigned herself to these four walls, content with the fact that she at least saw flashes of Willa's face.

That was the way her life dragged on, until one night she woke up suddenly, gasping for air. Her throat burned, and she tried to grasp at it, but her arms wouldn't work. The entire right side of her body was numb. The pain in her head and abdomen was excruciating. She'd hoped her end would be slow; maybe she'd be unaware. But this? This was agony.

Willa woke up from her screams and was asking Cassidy questions she couldn't make out. Her brows were drawn together as she tried to get her to lie back down. Cassidy thrashed in her grip, left arm and leg flailing out of her grasp. The glass of water on the nightstand crashed down to the floor. Willa shot up and activated her comms, pacing at the foot of the bed. Cassidy's vision was going in and out, black and fuzzy around the edges. In her ears was an incessant ringing. It drowned out whatever Willa was saying to whomever she'd pinged. The pain wouldn't stop as it rolled violently through her body. She gave up before it did, succumbing to nothingness.

CHAPTER 31

SHE KNEW SHE'D SEE him again, but she didn't expect for it to be so soon. Wearing all white, he blended into the blinding abyss she found herself in. When she neared him, he removed his hat and met her eyes. Something in them shone like regret.

"I didn't think you'd be here so quickly, Cassidy."

She laughed. "That makes two of us."

"Do you have any questions?"

She considered. Was this a small gift to her, or was everyone given this? She started with the first thing she thought of: "Will it hurt?"

"No." He shook his head. "That part is already over."

Cassidy nodded. "Okay." She took a beat, wondering if there was a limit to the questions she could ask.

"There isn't." He smiled.

She scowled. "Keep out of my head." Then she swallowed past the lump in her throat. "Will my friends be okay?"

"You know loss, Cassidy. What it does. But this will not break them."

She wondered how Willa would go through it all again, but it was a comfort to know she had the others with her this time.

He tilted his head slightly, his neck implant fluid with the movement. "Don't you have another question for me?"

Her last question was not one she was sure she wanted the answer to. She would find out soon enough, but she didn't know if she should hear it from his lips or not. But he wouldn't lie to her—she could feel it—so it was better to be prepared. "Is my grandma there?" She wasn't sure where *there* was—good or bad, before or after.

His smile was genuine for the first time since she'd seen him on that train just over a year ago. "Yes. She's missed you very much."

Cassidy's laugh might have been a sob. Whatever it was crawled its way out of her on nothing but the pure joy at the thought of seeing her again. They had so much to catch up on. All the little arguments they'd had, the lessons she'd tried to impart to Cassidy, the love she gave her unconditionally. She needed her to know what it had all meant to her as the years went by, as she grew out of her stubbornness and selfishness.

Why had she been so afraid, if this had been waiting for her the entire time? She mourned Willa, Finn, Sam, all of her friends. But she wouldn't fight against fate. If she wasn't supposed to live, then she was tired of raging against it. She was grateful for the last year, that she'd found the people she loved so dearly. It had changed her, and that was worth a lifetime of suffering. But now it was time to rest

He held out his hand for her, as he'd tried to do the whole time. "Are you ready?"

She started to reach for him, but hesitated, looking down. The gold dripped from her palm like it was molten and evaporated into the ether. She stared at the two organic hands in front of her, moving them as if they were brand new. The shock made her think. These were hands that would never pet Tom again, never run through Willa's dark hair, even as it streaked through with silver over the years.

Was she ready? She'd never see Sam and Alex build the family they deserved, or watch Finn fall in love, like she'd gotten to with Willa. And Willa... Was she willing to put her through the pain of losing a loved one again? So soon? Cassidy flexed her hands one last time, and the decision was clear.

CHAPTER 32

There was another blinding light. She was detached from her body, floating as if she were at sea. Maybe she had crossed over into the pool under the waterfall, like she'd hoped for. She tried to open her eyes, as if fighting off years of sleep. Her vision was so fuzzy, she only made out shapes and colors. But wherever she was, it was much darker than the waterfall. Her senses started to overload, and she groaned.

A voice, distant and bloated, floated past as if she were caught under a current. Her focus sharpened a bit as she realized she wasn't in any pain. No part of her body felt like anything, and it was the sweetest relief. She almost didn't want to move for fear of ending her bliss. She blinked to try to refocus her vision, but it was still as if a film were draped over both her eyes.

A voice again, louder this time, floated through her being.

Was someone trying to bring her back? She was so weightless and comfortable; she didn't know if she had it in herself to keep fighting day in and day out, just for another day of suffering. She tried to peer down at herself, but it was all white. She closed her eyes again, wondering what place she'd find herself in next.

She had no idea how long it'd been since she last opened her eyes. When they fought back open again, her vision was still blurry, but she gathered more of her surroundings, and her head was clearer. As soon as she got her bearings, a bolt of fear sliced through her. Her riotous heartbeat rocked in her chest. She knew exactly where she was, and what she was lying on. Cassidy never thought she'd be back, never wanted to be, but she was back in the clinic in the alley.

She tried to sit up, but a heavy weight strained across her legs and abdomen.

"Whoa," came a voice from somewhere around her, hard to make out. "... were thrashing ... had to restrain..." But it faded out.

Her eyes were still heavy and sluggish as they rolled around the room, but she was getting used to them. Someone sat in a chair an arm's reach away from her. She tried to speak, although her tongue moved wrong. She couldn't muster more than a few grunts. The person sleeping in the chair woke up and shot toward Cassidy, laying a hand on her arm.

Then, a commotion. Steps, shuffling, clattering, some beeping. More people surrounded her. Water met her mouth, and she fought to swallow before it spilled down her chin. It was too cold, and her body was still too light.

"Where...?"

"You're okay, Cass. We're with the doctor."

Willa's voice was the sweetest sound. She hadn't been sure she'd ever hear it again. But she wasn't okay, or saved. Dr. Thorne loomed behind Willa, a smug smile stretching his face.

"What the hell did you do to me?" she spat towards him, but her words slurred and ran together. She closed her eyes and took a breath. She didn't understand. "I thought I was dead." Her voice was little more than a whisper, and her body was so unfamiliar.

"Damn near." Finn. He hovered beside Willa, looking equally worse for wear.

"What happened?"

"You seized, and then your heart stopped. I called Sam and Finn and brought you here. Sam got the coordinates from your chip."

Cassidy wanted to scream. They'd done all this because of her, and for what? So she would live a few more months? She was still headed for the same destination, whether now or in the future.

The doctor stepped closer. "You're lucky your friends have more sense than you do, or we might not be having this conversation."

Cassidy's words came out like steel: "What. Did. You. Do?"

"I saved your life. I could have done a better job if you'd gotten over yourself and started the treatments when I wanted to, but you'll live."

"I'm cured?" she gasped. "You actually did it?"

He nodded, eyes roaming all around the room. He was

looking around as if he'd never been there before.

Her head was swimming, but she needed answers. "I can't feel my left hand. And my eyes—"

The doctor frowned. "Yes, I expected that. The surgery was ... unconventional, and I expect you'll have side effects."

"Side effects?"

"I had to remove your ocular implants and replace your hand with a traditional prosthetic. I'm afraid cybernetics won't be an option anymore."

"What? Why not?"

"Because they have nothing to interface with. I've removed your chip."

Cassidy's blood ran cold. "That's not possible."

"Not until now. Your case was special. I'm afraid your chip was malfunctioning. I've never seen anything like it."

"They're not supposed to do that."

"Should we keep stating the obvious?"

"You're saying my *chip* was making me sick?"

"Evidently." He paused for an uncomfortable amount of time. "I've kept it as a donation of sorts, for further testing."

Cassidy fought to keep the tremble from her voice. "What does this mean, then?"

"You're no longer Connected, so you won't be able to access the Net, earn credits, or use any biotechnology. And your oculars did too much damage before I removed them, so you'll most likely experience a steady loss of vision." He rolled his eyes at her slow expression of terror. "Oh, cheer up. Things could be worse. You would have died." He laughed erratically, and everyone else in the room did their best to ignore his odd behavior.

"So, I'm Unconnected, without tech or implants—and I'm going blind? That's the best you could do for me?"

"So ungrateful. It was all you could afford, at any rate. I cut you a generous deal."

Cassidy glanced at her friends, none of whom would meet her eyes.

She asked again, but softer, "What did you do?"

Willa grasped her hand, as if steadying herself. "I sold the ranch."

Cassidy's stomach sank. "No! Willa, that's your family's ranch! Your life!"

Willa started to tear up. "It's only land and buildings. That can always be replaced."

"You can't have done that for me."

Willa smiled. "But I did. And I don't regret it, so don't be upset. Please."

Cassidy couldn't help the tears leaking from her eyes, burning on their way down. The doctor cleared his throat and went to fiddle with something in another corner of the room, not wanting to be a part of the moment. Finn and Sam knelt at her med-bed, both still looking unsure.

"How long has it been?" Her voice still sounded strange to her ears.

"Five days." Sam swallowed. "You've been out of it for four, then around yesterday, you started coming around."

She turned back to Willa. "I don't know how to thank you—any of you." She laughed. "You three literally saved my life."

"We're just happy you're still here," Finn replied, looking like he'd lived two lives since she'd last seen him. This whole thing must have been awful to go through.

"What do we do now?" Cassidy wanted to be unrestrained; she wanted to test out this new-and-old body of hers.

Willa read her mind and began unstrapping her. "We rented rooms at the inn. We'll stay the night and go home tomorrow."

Cassidy didn't want to think about what "home" meant, what that wouldn't be—all because of her. She sat up slowly, noticing the stark white med clothes she'd been changed into. True to the doctor's word, where her implant used to line her palm and fingers was now a plain metal prosthesis. The fingers stuttered under her command, but they still worked. She'd make do with the rest.

It was strange though, not to have the presence of a chip in her skull. The world was more still, somehow. She couldn't tell the time or the date, and she had no idea how she'd manage without credit or the net. But something was thrilling about knowing she'd be able to figure it all out.

She tested the rest of her limbs, unused to the push and pull of her joints without the presence of pain. She smiled at the relief, then at her friends, who hadn't given up on her so that she could have this. When she had given up on herself, they did this for her. She wrapped the three of them in an unsteady hug, listing back towards the bed and dragging the three of them with her.

"Let's get out of here. Just give me a second."

They nodded and went to wait out in the hall. Willa glanced back, but Cassidy only smiled and waited for the door to hiss shut behind her. She got up and turned to the doctor, still in another corner of the room, pretending not to have been listening to their conversation.

"I don't care what you do with my chip or what you find from it. I don't want anything to do with it from this point forward. No one can know we did this."

He stared at her for a moment, and it was the most human he had seemed to her since she'd found him in that alley. Something haunted lined his expression. "I agree." They'd both lived under the Corporation; they both knew what a discovery like this would bring.

She smiled, despite herself. "You kept your word."

"I promised I would fix you."

He reached out his hand, and she shook it. She would never like him, and she hoped to never see his face again. But he had done what he promised to do, and she was grateful.

She joined her friends in the hall to start her new life.

It had been three weeks since she was brought back from the dead, and it was their last day on the ranch. Most of the furniture was staying as part of the sale, so they only packed up their personal belongings. The Mariposa rancher who bought the place insisted they'd keep organic animals, so they got to stay as well. Tom, however, was not a part of the negotiations. He howled in his carrier as Cassidy tucked him in under a blanket.

"Oh, hush. You're going to love living with Finn." She'd miss seeing him every day, but it wouldn't be for forever.

Willa was in their room, doing a final clean of the space.

She couldn't stand the idea of giving the place away with it being messy. As she waited, Cassidy did a final sweep of their boxes. They were all labeled and ready to go to a shed at Sam and Alex's place, where they'd stay until Cassidy and Willa settled into their new home. The two of them had stopped by the previous day to help pack and share one last meal at the ranch together.

Finn's crew were due to pick everything up within the hour, so Cassidy wanted to make sure they weren't forgetting anything. There was an entire box of Willa's records that she found too hard to trim down, but outside that, they didn't have too many things. Both of them traveled light, it seemed.

Cassidy's unwieldy set of keys sat on the entryway table, ready for their new owner. Her pocket was empty without them. Willa eventually emerged, wiping the sweat from her brow. "Everything set?"

"Ready when you are."

They took the boxes out to the front gate and locked up the main house. Cassidy stood and looked it over one last time. This was the first place that had felt like home in a long time, but now she was taking home with her. She glanced at Willa, wiping away silent tears, and kissed the corner of her brow.

"You need a minute?"

Willa sniffled. "No, I'm okay. I've had the whole month to prepare for this, but it feels strange now."

She couldn't imagine how deep it was for Willa. She had been born here and promised to look after things for her mom. And now she was saying goodbye. Cassidy left the last box at the gate and picked up Tom's carrier, the weight strange under her prosthetic. She'd gotten a lot of practice with it, but it would never feel like her tech.

The walk to Finn's was slower than necessary, both of them trying to absorb every detail for the last time. The sun coming through the trees, the scuff of their boots across the dirt, the bright white of the church across the clearing. Cassidy tried to imprint all of it in her memory.

Cassidy used her old key once they got to Finn's apartment.

"Hey," she called loud enough so he could hear them.

He emerged from his office, closing the door behind him. "Hey, you two." His face lit up as his eyes landed on the cat carrier. He crouched down and wiggled his fingers in the air holes. "Hey, buddy. Welcome to your new home." Cassidy set the carrier down and opened the door for Tom to explore.

Finn rose back up, and she pulled him into a hug. "Thank you for taking him."

"Of course. I'm gonna spoil him rotten."

Cassidy laughed. "He pretends to be tough, but he's secretly a cuddle bug." Tom, given the outdoor cat he had been, was poking around every corner of the apartment as if they'd taken him to another planet.

Finn smiled. "Promise you'll check in?"

Willa laughed. "Of course. You'll be sick of hearing from us."

Finn shook his head. "Nah. I will miss you though. But you two deserve it."

All three of them hugged, so tight that the pressure pinched Cassidy's ribs. The sharp panic it brought was an instinct, a gross reflex she'd have to break. She repeated to herself until her heart calmed; she was fine. She was healthy.

She was alive.

They said their goodbyes to Finn and Tom and headed back out to the street. They walked hand in hand until they reached the train station out of town. Cassidy turned to Willa, her eyes bright with excitement. "You ready?"

Willa kissed her in response.

EPILOGUE

"Hurry up and get into frame," Willa teased. Her skin was glowing, offset by the bright blue of her swimsuit. It was Cassidy's favorite color on her. She'd spent hours under the sun that day, and she was radiant. It took everything in Cassidy's willpower to keep her hands off her. They'd been in New Hawaii for two weeks and had a week left before they started back to California. They'd been swimming, eating, and exploring nonstop, only relaxing when they returned to their hotel room at the end of each day.

Cassidy pushed her wire-framed glasses up the bridge of her nose for the umpteenth time, worried that they were sitting crooked on her face. Willa grabbed her wrist, bringing it back down to her lap. "They suit you, Cass, don't worry."

As a parting gift—or an apology, maybe—Dr. Thorne had made them custom for her. With cybernetics and Corporation medicine, hardly anyone needed glasses anymore. Cassidy was certain she'd never seen an optical store before. She was grateful for the pair, despite how strange they were to wear. She was also grateful for the lump sum the doctor had wired to Willa as payment for Cassidy's "contribution" to his research, even though he'd been adamant on doing no such thing. Perhaps he did have a conscience after all. With that nice little sum, they'd been able to extend a week-long trip by another two.

Cassidy settled in next to Willa as the comms rang, smelling the salt and musk of her hair. They'd grown so much closer during their time away, and a lot of the guilt Cassidy carried had started to ebb away. Willa gave so much to her, so Cassidy was glad she could give her something she'd always wanted in return. Some days she still buckled under the weight of all Willa had given up for her, but she was there to banish those fears.

Sam and Alex appeared on the comms, breaking her from her thoughts. Sam's hair was longer than the last time she'd seen them, but they looked so well rested. It was beautiful to see.

"Wow, look at you two! How's NH?"

"It's amazing!" Willa gushed. "Everything I'd hoped it'd be. But I am excited to head home soon."

"Well, no complaints from us, we both miss you," Alex cut in. "I love the glasses, Cass. How are you feeling?"

She blushed, grateful for the compliment. Willa had been telling her so since she'd started wearing them, but she was her partner, so of course she would think so. "Thanks. It's still a bit weird with ... everything, but honestly, I'm almost back to normal."

"That's amazing." Sam paused. "Hey, have you heard from Finn lately?"

"He pings me photos of Tom almost every day." Willa laughed. "But he's been too busy for comms. I'm sure it's taking up a lot of his time."

"That's an understatement." Alex chuckled. "I've been helping him on-site this last week, and it's going well."

"Is it?" Cassidy cut in. "He won't tell us anything about it."

Alex gave a wry smile. "I'm sure he wants it to be a surprise. But it's going to be everything you two asked for and more. Even Tom will be pleased. The backyard will be great for him to explore. And..." He drew out the word. "... Annabelle brings him his lunch almost every day."

Willa squealed. "You're kidding! So, it's official?"

"Yeah," Sam sighed. "If you thought *we* were obnoxious, they put us to shame."

"I can't wait to rub it in his face. I just wish I could take credit for it."

"I think it's safe to say you pushed things along, Cass." Willa pecked her on the cheek. "I'm happy for them."

"That makes four of us." Alex laughed.

Cassidy edged farther into the frame. "And what about you two?"

"The application is still pending, but things are looking good. Ranger is as rambunctious as ever, so he's been great practice."

"That baby is going to be so spoiled."

"With so many godparents, they won't be lacking for attention." Sam smiled.

Cassidy was out of her body with joy. Her friends were all thriving, and she had the things she never thought she'd be able to have. The bumps in the road were inevitable—it was only a matter of time—but for once, it was something worth weathering. If she'd asked herself a year ago where she thought she'd be now, the answer would have been dead, or something so far from the truth.

"Absolutely." Cassidy wrapped an arm around Willa. "Thanks for taking our comms. I know we'll be back in a week, but we wanted to catch up sooner. I'm sorry it's been so long."

"You two have been busy enjoying your vacation, we don't mind. I hope you've been taking photos for us."

"Of course." Cassidy had purchased a new camera model the week before they left for the trip. She would never ask for her gift to Sam back; it was much better off with them. But she couldn't resist the idea of capturing everything they saw on their travels. "See you soon?" They'd taken a train up to Oregon and then a boat out to New Hawaii, since no one ever went directly to California; it wasn't the most convenient to travel from.

"Yeah, we'll pick you up at the station. Your train gets in around seven?"

"Yes, thank you so much. See you both soon." Willa blew them kisses as they all waved goodbye and then hung up the feed. She turned to Cassidy. "I can't wait for the house."

"Me either, and I miss Tom."

"I know. It's so strange. I always wanted to travel, but I didn't expect to be so homesick the whole time."

Cassidy kissed her hand and up her wrist. "You're lucky,

then, to have a place to miss."

Willa sighed when Cassidy reached a sensitive spot on the inside of her arm. "Well, now you do too."

"You're right, I do."

Acknowledgements

This is the last page I've written for *Golden Ruin*, and it feels like the hardest. This book was a labor of love from not just myself, but the fantastic people that helped shape this story into something I'm immensely proud of.

Thank you to Louise, Kal, and Robin for your expertise and work on this story. This story is richer for having each of you touch it.

Thank you to Theresa and Charlie for bringing this world to life. I'm so grateful you each created such beautiful art for this story.

Thank you to Max and Riley, who read a very early (very rough) draft, endured countless texts, and just shared in my joy as I created this book. Writing can be a very lonely experience, but the two of you made it feel a lot more whole.

Thank you, dear reader, for taking a chance on a debut, indie author. I will cherish the fact that you chose to spend your time here in the pages of *Golden Ruin*.

And lastly, thank you to my parents who have always encouraged my creativity. I can do this because of your love and support.